RIVALS TO LOVERS

Also available by Elise Wayland

Writing as Rachel Mans McKenny

The Butterfly Effect

RIVALS TO LOVERS

A Novel

ELISE WAYLAND

alcove
press

Books should be disposed of and recycled according to local requirements. All paper materials used are FSC compliant.

This is a work of fiction. All of the names, characters, organizations, places, and events portrayed in this novel are either products of the author's imagination or are used fictitiously. Any resemblance to real or actual events, locales, or persons, living or dead, is entirely coincidental.

Copyright © 2025 by Rachel Mans McKenny

All rights reserved.

Published in the United States by Alcove Press, an imprint of The Quick Brown Fox & Company LLC.

Alcove Press and its logo are trademarks of The Quick Brown Fox & Company LLC.

Library of Congress Catalog-in-Publication data available upon request.

ISBN (hardcover): 979-8-89242-275-8
ISBN (paperback): 979-8-89242-173-7
ISBN (ebook): 979-8-89242-174-4

Cover design by Ana Hard

Printed in the United States.

www.alcovepress.com

Alcove Press
34 West 27th St., 10th Floor
New York, NY 10001

First Edition: August 2025

The authorized representative in the EU for product safety and compliance is eucomply OÜPärnu mnt 139b-14, 11317 Tallinn, Estonia, hello@eucompliancepartner.com, +33757690241

10 9 8 7 6 5 4 3 2 1

To the English teachers who taught me to love books,
and to the romance authors who taught me
to love books about love.

PART ONE
The Proud

Eliza never knew from where it came—the pangs for something bigger, something brighter. She only knew it came with increasing regularity.
—E. J. Morgan, *The Proud and the Lost*

At The Hill, you could look into the valley and see nearly everything that counted in this damn world: the trees and the flowers. The city? Why, a speck in the distance. I could not write in the city. At The Hill, I wrote and lived and gardened contentedly.
—from the collected letters of E. J. Morgan, edited by Estelle Morgan-Perry

CHAPTER ONE

Mo

Maureen Denton flicked a half-eaten tortilla chip out of her hair, then looked accusingly at her roommates. "Which one of you threw this?"

"Listen, you're lucky there was no queso on that one, Mo. Next time, no promises." Sloan handed her a napkin and narrowed her brown eyes. It was almost six on the first warmish day in April, and the patio was full of New Yorkers out enjoying the lingering daylight.

Mo was trying to enjoy, and trying to listen to, her friends, but it was hard while waiting for the most important phone call of her life. "I'm sorry. She said she would call by five and it's seven and—"

"It's barely six," Sloan corrected. "I was giving my ratport, and you were a million miles away."

"And the weekly ratport is a sacred roommate tradition and you need to take it seriously." Mackenzie rapped her spoon on the table lightly. Mackenzie had been Mo's first and closest friend since she moved to the city. Today she wore a bright-orange-and-red dress that accentuated her ample bust and hips, a good example of what she declared "fat Ms. Frizzle flair." Mackenzie had majored in theater before getting her master's in library science and now put her talents into reading stories for the eager repeats at her morning story hours. As a librarian, she was very good at reading books and too good at reading people. "You're worried it's bad news."

Mo scoffed unconvincingly. "I'm just worried we settled too fast on the name *ratport*. We should have called it a rodent roundup."

"*Rodent roundup* sounds like a cowboy kids' TV show from the 1950s," Mackenzie said. "Ratports are serious rat journalism. Tom Brokaw levels of rat investigation."

Sloan nodded. "Exactly. So, to *repeat* my Emmy-worthy report: When I was leaving work today, there was a group of people in Times Square all circling this rat, who was standing up on its hind legs staring at the billboards. Little-rat-in-the-big-city vibes. Honestly, reminded me of your ex-boyfriend, Aaron."

Maureen threw the chip back at Sloan. Sloan ducked. It was unfair, really. Sloan's reflexes were impeccable from years of playing lacrosse.

Mackenzie shook her head. "Doesn't beat my rats-holding-hands entry from last week."

"Paws," Mo said, finally reentering the conversation. She kept getting phantom vibrations in her pocket. Her roommates were angels for trying to distract her, but they failed.

That wasn't a phantom vibration this time. Mo pointed at her phone.

"Go! We'll pay and see you back at the apartment," Sloan said.

Rivals to Lovers

"Good luck!" Mackenzie called after her.

* * *

The phone vibrated in Maureen's hand, a detonation device. It might as well have been one. All her dreams could go up in smoke. She took a deep breath before accepting the call.

"Hi, Yuri." Maureen tried to keep her voice level. Her agent had received the manuscript a month ago. Email was the most emotionally undermining invention. A letter was something you could kiss and send off or clutch to your chest before you opened it. An email? Nothing so glamorous. Her email, and the attached project, sat somewhere in the (digitally) towering stack of manuscripts for Yuri to examine, and she hoped it would succeed where her last one had failed.

A sigh across the line and a single word. "Mo."

That one word from Yuri's mouth chilled Maureen's spine. Holding the phone between her ear and shoulder freed Mo's hands to tie her long, blonde hair back with the omnipresent hair band on her wrist. "Oh no," she said, "What's wrong?"

Yuri Eikura was a senior partner at Eikura, Schier & Gurnett Literary, famous for having an eye for literary fiction. Four years ago, Mo had snagged Yuri's interest with her first project, a novel about a waitress slowly dissociating from reality while she worked at her local barbecue restaurant. Unfortunately, though it hooked her fantastic agent, the book never found a publisher. *The quiet novel*, editors kept saying in their rejections. Why was quiet bad? Anyway, it was, and she had written something else. But second projects, ones written after you had already secured an agent, felt tenuous. What would happen if Yuri hated it? It felt like Yuri telling Mo she hated her literary DNA. Even though Mo's first novel had been barely obscured autofiction, this novel, the one that had been sitting in Yuri's inbox for a month, was the book she had wanted to write since she was thirteen years old.

"You hate it," Mo said.

Yuri exhaled so loud that Mo could swear she felt the air move against her cheek. "Oh, I love it, that's not the problem."

The first half of the sentence didn't compensate for the second. "What problem?"

"Can I tell you for one little second about how good the book is before I dive into the bad news, or do you want me to thwomp you right now?"

Mo bit her lip. "Praise first." She took a few steps farther down the street and leaned against a building for support.

"It's genius. Honestly, one of the best things I've read in years. Eliza's character is so fresh, so funny, so real. I bought every second of the dialogue, and the reinvention of the Westerly estate as an early-aughts McMansion? The ending? My God, the ending, Maureen. It's a beautiful adaptation of Morgan. Wharton meets Fitzgerald swirled around with Occupy Wall Street. I'm making that little pinched gesture right now with my finger and thumb. Can you picture me making that gesture? I'm doing a chef's kiss right now, so picture that."

Mo did. "But."

"But—and honestly this is a big but—the copyright hasn't expired yet on *The Proud and the Lost*. You know that, don't you?"

Mo stared at her shoes, the ghosts of a dozen passersby's shoes crossing in and out of her peripheral. "I saw that some other books from around that era had splashy contemporary adaptations recently. I assumed it would be okay."

"E. J. Morgan's estate has kept up the copyright past its usual expiration. The original novel was written in 1929, which typically would have put us in a safe position, but the estate has been maintained by Morgan's daughter, Estelle. She hasn't allowed for any derivative works. None. Not even a new film adaptation, and you know people have been angling for that since the eighties."

Mo, like every other high schooler in America, had been treated to the 1950s movie version of *The Proud and the Lost* after completing the book. It was grainy and overacted, and several students slept through it.

Mo had a movie poster of it on her wall. "So it's a no?"

"It's tricky."

"Tricky impossible or tricky possible?" Yuri could work miracles—not miracles that had involved Mo's first book selling, however. Mo didn't want to press her. She was lucky to have an agent at all, let alone one who had sold several critical darlings and even more best-selling novels. Yuri was in her late fifties—middle aged, middle height, and with the most intense eye contact of anyone Mo had ever met. She had been the daughter of two lawyers and originally had gone into contract law before swerving to start a boutique literary agency with her first husband at age twenty-six. She'd dumped the husband but had kept, and grown, the career.

"I'll tell you what," Yuri said after a short pause. "I know the agent who represents Morgan's estate. We can get in contact with him, but he might not be inclined to do favors."

Mo wished she had time for industry gossip. Once a year Yuri took her out for drinks, and she luxuriated in it. Feeling like an insider when Mo had started as a nothing—still was a nothing—made her feel powerful. What else was writing except imagining other people's secrets? And the writing world often held some good ones of its own.

Mo knew she should have emailed Yuri the idea while drafting it. She'd contemplated it, but there was something so big and all-consuming about reimagining a book that had meant so much to you. The process was like the *Lord of the Rings* fanfic Mo had written in high school. She'd put those stories up on the internet, enjoying the simple act of sharing her work with the world. Could she publish her *Proud and the Lost* manuscript on some site anonymously as Morgan fanfic and avoid getting sued? Probably, but that wasn't how she pictured this book existing in the world. The fact that its original source was a novel published more than ninety years ago made Mo want to scream. She could do this project justice, and if she had a chance to talk to someone at the Morgan estate about it, she was positive she could prove that. "Could you make that connection? I don't want to give up without having tried."

An incoming text dinged, interrupting her thoughts. Keyed so deeply into the conversation, she had almost wandered all the way back to her apartment without realizing, weaving through the evening commuters. Her favorite flower stand on the corner had closed for the day. She paused near it as she listened to Yuri's closing words. "Long shot" was the most frequent phrase, but all of publishing was that. Mo had to at least try. Yuri said she'd contact the estate's agent and let Mo know the next steps.

After hanging up, Mo checked her missed text. It was from her boss, Amy, checking in for an event they were doing tomorrow. Complete cliché that she was, Mo had moved to New York from Iowa to pursue her writing career. Working in catering allowed her to live with two roommates in a place with no bedbugs. Good enough. She had a place to live, her health, a job, and a foot in the door—it was just that that door wasn't likely to ever open for her, at least not for this book.

She wished the flower stand were still open. She'd buy herself a bouquet of cheer-up daisies, something her dad used to do for her when she was a grumpy teenager. There was something, though, on the sidewalk.

A single-stemmed red rose. It peeked out between a trash can and an old box holding leaflets. She hadn't gotten roses since she'd broken up with Aaron a year ago. The sight made her mouth quirk at the edges. The city was giving her a gift at the end of a long day. As she leaned over to pick up the rose from the sidewalk, she noticed something else between the trash can and the newspaper box.

A rat held the long green stem, chewing tentatively on the end of it.

All her life she'd trained herself to be one thing, and that was unflappable. Don't let them see you're shaken and you win, even if you look like you lost. Don't scream. Don't freak out.

She lifted herself back to standing, stepped back, and ran directly into an elderly man carrying an armful of groceries.

An hour later, after buying a fresh dozen eggs for Barry Studebaker, who happened to live two floors below her, she finally made it back to her apartment. Mackenzie and Sloan were thrilled to hear Mo's ratport.

They didn't ask about the phone call, as if they sensed she couldn't handle rehashing it yet.

She didn't expect a big break. She didn't expect to become a literary darling, but she had needed to write this book. And now, book written, was it too much to hope that it would get read?

CHAPTER TWO

Wes

Wesley Spencer considered lighting his entire laptop on fire. While that wouldn't solve the problem of his inbox in a concrete sense, it would feel *so* good. He loved making decisions that felt good in the moment. Unfortunately, there were moments after those moments. Moments in which he'd have to explain the fire alarm blaring to the neighbors and the destruction of company property to his bosses. Worst of all, the thousands of unread emails would not somehow disappear in this process. The number, four digits, stared at Wes from the anchored bar on the bottom of his screen. The eyes of that number bore through him while he was trying to work on Things. *Things* sounded abstract and amorphous, and sometimes it was. Client feedback, contract drafts, invitations to editor lunches and drinks sessions that he couldn't turn down for fear of offense that would compromise some later deal. Wes loved his job, he really did, but if he could have done that job in the middle of a forest with no Wi-Fi, he probably would have been a kinder and better person.

As it was, he was not kinder or better.

There were few great writers. There were even fewer great agents, at least those known outside the highly specialized literary circles Wes trod. He didn't know why he needed to be great, but what *were* you if you weren't great? *Fucking email*, though. He'd spent two hours sorting and prioritizing tiny icons this morning: red stars and blue stars and exclamation points and why didn't Outlook offer a tiny little bomb icon? Even after those two hours of sorting and snoozing, he felt overwhelmed.

Wes's phone rang. It rang a lot—a necessary part of the job. He was almost grateful for a different piece of technology to feel overwhelmed with.

"Hello, Novel Literary. This is Wes Spencer." This dialogue was one he'd learned from his internship, substituting another agent's name.

"Wesley. Hi."

He didn't know if it was him conjuring her, but the voice rang familiar from those intern days at Eikura, Schier & Gurnett. He shivered. "Yuri?"

"Yes, hi, new number. Glad you picked up." She said it in a rush—busy woman, things to do—but had she feared he wouldn't pick up? Because really, if he'd known it was Yuri Eikura, he wouldn't have. He would have let it go to voicemail, and if the first words out of her mouth weren't *I'm sorry for how things ended*, he would have deleted that voicemail. But here he was, on a phone call with the woman who had fired him and generally made his life harder by doing so.

"I'm going to hang up now," he said, though he didn't know if he had the nerve. Even though she couldn't—shouldn't—be able to overturn his career at this point after signing the NDA. Still, it was nerve-racking to know she remembered he was out there.

Yuri seemed to be waiting to see if Wes followed through on his threat, and when he didn't, she said, "Okay, so I know you represent the Morgan estate."

"I do." It had been pure luck that he got the position, but he was grateful for it now more than ever.

"I have a client who wants to adapt P&L."

"Profit and loss?" he asked. His heart skipped a beat, then two.

"Ha ha," she said, not actually laughing at his not actual joke. "She's finished this incredible adaptation of *The Proud and the Lost*, and we'd like to pitch it to the estate. Truly, Wes, it's one of the best manuscripts I've read in years. I think it would make us all a lot of money."

He could not be hearing what he was hearing, because he also had been writing an adaptation of *The Proud and the Lost*. It was almost finished. It was almost perfect, in fact. "You actually read it?"

"Of course I actually read it. Mo Denton is my client, after all."

Mo Denton. Mo— "Oh, Maureen Denton?" Wesley coughed, the name ringing a bell. It was worse than that—Wes had put a Google alert on that name. Looked like he needed to change, or add to, that Google alert to include *Mo* alongside *Maureen*. It wasn't a stalking kind of thing; he did this for all his clients, and even though Maureen *wasn't* his client, he had a certain stake in her career. When he worked at Yuri's agency, he'd been assigned to read slush. If he ever thought he got too many queries a week now, that was dwarfed by Yuri's daily intake. She typically had two interns at any given time reading queries and skimming the first few pages. If anything caught their attention, the interns would forward it to Yuri. It had been a grueling job, and at the beginning, Wes had passed along the first thing that really caught his eye, only to have Yuri leave her desk, walk to the pod he shared with the other intern, and read a sliver of the paragraph in an ironic voice. "This is a total, *total* rip-off of Franzen. Do you read?" she had asked.

"I read *that*."

"Read more. Read better. And don't send me this." And she'd turned and left.

It had been a full week before Wes found anything else promising, and then he only forwarded it to her with a demure "Good premise." He hadn't gotten scolded for that one. He sent a few more—but nothing stopped Wes's heart like Maureen Denton's query and first pages had. Vulnerable—that was the only word for it. The yolk of the words was smeared all over the manuscript, raw and sweet and bright. When Yuri ended up signing her as a client, Wes felt victorious, and not only because he had found a client in the slush pile before his fellow intern. Mainly, he felt Maureen's book was something beautiful that would touch people someday.

And then Wes left—was fired—before he found out how that story ended. And so, the Google alert, one that hadn't ever pinged his inbox with a deal announcement from Publishers Marketplace or a prepublication interview with *The New Yorker*. Nothing. He had honestly forgotten about that alert, but like a seventeen-year cicada, it wouldn't be forgotten now. Here was the fruit of that interest.

Wes's stomach twisted. He remembered how *good* Maureen's—Mo's—first project had been. Quiet, maybe, but the prose was lush. He tried not to be curious what she could do with the themes and characters of *The Proud and the Lost*, especially since he had written his own book reworking those characters and themes. Maybe hers would be horrible. Maybe he didn't have anything to worry about. There is nothing vainer than hope. There is nothing more hopeful than vanity.

Wes had been silent for at least thirty seconds, practically ten years in phone time. Maybe Yuri thought he'd grown the balls to hang up on her. More likely she thought he couldn't string a sentence together.

Accurate.

"I don't know what you want me to do," Wes finally said. "The Morgan estate has been extremely litigious in pursuing cases which even suggest a connection to *P&L*."

"I'll be honest, Wes. If this manuscript wasn't good, I wouldn't have made the phone call. I know the right way to do this, and I'd like to go through you rather than finding work-arounds."

"Is that a threat?"

Yuri gave the verbal equivalent of a shrug. "Oh, Wes," she said.

"Oh, Yuri," Wes said, as if he hadn't called her Ms. Eikura every single day of his internship. The familiarity that came with using her first name should make him feel like they were equals, but it did not. He could see Yuri going to his boss, or writing to Estelle directly, and he did not like that idea. Estelle read her mail, every piece of it. Every piece of fan mail that came in through the years passed through her careful fingers. She even wrote back.

Maureen had written a new novel. Maureen's novel was an adaptation of *P&L*. And he didn't want to talk to Estelle about it. "I'll try to bring it up with her, but no promises."

"You'd get a cut, you know. Just keep that in mind."

He wouldn't get a cut, though. He didn't want a cut from someone else's book. The first step of showing his book to Estelle was resigning from his place representing the trust, but he'd been putting that off until his book was absolutely perfect. Mostly perfect might have to do. Wes hung up and stared at his half-written letter, knowing that instead of introducing the one book, the book of his heart, he might have to introduce two.

He could pour a glass of whiskey, à la Hemingway, and write a missive full of braggadocio, but if he was already thinking in ten-cent words, alcohol wouldn't help. Estelle Morgan-Perry was a plainspoken woman in every interaction Wes had with her. He'd also changed his mind, knowing that a letter was the surest way to reach her. Email was faster but less likely to be opened. For this, Wes would break out the seventh-grade calligraphy-camp skills. It was time to tell her about his adaptation.

* * *

Two weeks later, he was in Greenwich with an iPad full of cookbooks.

On Wes's manuscript wish list, he called for "Literary and upmarket fiction, fantasy with a twist, nonfiction books about lesser-known events, and cookbooks," which made for a wonderful collection of persistently excellent prose, dragons, long-form-podcast-worthy histories he knew nothing about, and cookbooks. Wes did cook, but it was lonely cooking for one.

Often, he took the best bets to his mother's house to try out some of the most appealing recipes.

Wes's mother had a name that people associated with home and gardening. Her name was the kind that people looked for, one that paired well with the phrase *stamp of approval*. Over the past thirty years, she had, both literally and figuratively, remade herself as Ulla, with a self-titled magazine and lifestyle brand. *Ulla*, it turned out, meant *determination* in Old Norse, but really it was a shortening of her given name, Ursula. She didn't want to be thought of as a sea hag and had "rebranded" herself back in the nineties, before there was such a thing as rebranding. Had Wes's mother invented rebranding? It seemed like a thing she would take credit for in an interview, of which she had had many in her life. The evidence decorated her office walls in his parents' home in Connecticut.

Wes made eye contact with a glossy photograph of his mother above her desk. It was attached to an interview about "having it all" from *Ladies' Home Journal* in 2006. Ulla didn't look much older than the photograph from that article. She kept her gray hair long and well tended, and her skin wasn't wrinkleless, exactly, but it had that barely lined Helen Mirren–esque beauty that women ten years younger than Ulla seemed to envy. She flicked through the PDF in front of her, the manuscript of a client Wes was considering taking on, and grimaced. "Harissa again. This is the fourth recipe in this collection with harissa."

"You don't like harissa?"

"I don't like harissa in quiche, I can tell you that much." Ulla looked up from the tablet, then slid it back to Wes. "I wouldn't take it if it were my choice. The other book, the one with the Cornish game hen and cherry recipe, that collection was better."

"Is a Cornish game hen actually its own thing, or did farmers create a fancy word for small chickens?" Wes asked.

"Just because you're short doesn't mean you can joke about short birds."

Wes wasn't *short*. At five ten, he was just not taller than many men. "Statistically, I'm above the national average. And I'd look tall to any chicken."

Ulla stared critically at him. "You're being peevish."

"I'm not."

Ulla rolled her eyes and stood. "Fine, then. Let's go."

He was being peevish, but nerves could do that to him. Sometimes he thought that being sent away to boarding school was the thing that had saved his relationship with his parents. They had a few years away from his hormones, and Wes had a few years away from their nagging. They had sent top-notch care packages regularly, every three weeks. They or their staff. If you could count on one thing from a mother who was one of the leading experts in beauty, home, and health journalism, it was a lot of freebies. Wes had grown up with very soft hands, even during the height of his high school and college boxing career. His very soft hands (he still took good care of them, especially with all the typing) were slightly sweaty from nerves, because they had an appointment for a very important tea in approximately twenty minutes.

Would he have gotten the job he had without his parents' home being close to the Morgan family estate? He didn't know. He did know that it didn't hurt that these were the circumstances he was handed. It would have been foolish not to take advantage of them. It wasn't as though Estelle

Perry-Morgan had watched Wes grow up in a traditional neighborly way: seeing him toss baseballs with his dad in the street or something. He certainly hadn't tried to sell her fundraiser candy bars. Instead, it was the kind of proximity that came from large charity donations. Knowing that your brick in the new hospital sidewalk was next to your neighbors'. Being wealthy meant knowing who gave where and checking the size of the font for their name on plaques relative to yours.

Estelle's name was usually very large.

Her house was large, too, and so was her last name on the wrought iron gate that Wes and Ulla drove through. The name broke into *MOR* and *GAN* as the entrance gate opened. The property had been E. J. Morgan's, and Estelle's grandfather's before. Built in the late nineteenth century, the house was the kind that had a title: The Hill. This was due partially to literary tourism. Estelle didn't relish large groups tromping through her yard every weekend, however, so she had a rule to limit it to school groups and special events only.

Ulla allowed Wes to drive them in her blue Maserati Levante. It handled like his daily driver, a Honda he stubbornly paid for himself, only with a panoramic sunroof. He was not enough of a gearhead to really appreciate luxury cars, but he could appreciate the way people looked at him when he drove them. He looked taller, an ex had told him, when Wes posed next to his father's Lotus Evora. The Lotus was jokingly referred to as his father's second child, one he never allowed his first child to drive without first taking a shower.

Estelle's driveway was flagstone, long and curving up toward the majestic mansion at the top of the eponymous Hill, and Wes liked the way the Maserati climbed it—perhaps it was better than his Honda. The mansion itself was sprawling and elegant, a true testament to the Georgian style. Estelle's mother, E. J. (Elizabeth Jean) Morgan née Haute, was born and raised there, though she, like the main character in *The Proud and the Lost*, had moved away during her late teens. After the death of her parents, E. J. had moved back to the estate, married, and had Estelle.

"She loved and hated the Hill," Estelle had told Wes on their first meeting. "She was fond of the gardens, but the house itself—the size of it necessitating a staff of at least ten at any given time, especially with my needs as a child—it was too much for her. She was too much of an introvert. It never escaped my notice, nor her critics, that the Hill was the kind of place that she had written Eliza escaping from. Me, though, I had always wanted a house exactly like this. Growing up here was a dream."

"This" was a sprawling ten-bedroom mansion with an elevator tastefully centered in the house to assist Estelle's coming and going. Estelle had used a wheelchair since her youth. While Estelle had been E. J.'s only child, Estelle had adopted two daughters, who both had several children, and one family or the other was usually circling in or out of the estate at any given time. Wes had barely said more than two words to either daughter, but it was likely that—perhaps soon—control would be given over to one of them. Had he not been stepping back from managing the estate, he would have gotten to know them well.

One of the updates was a large, zero-entry inground swimming pool, with a cement deck and hot tub, and a tennis court out beyond another set of large, tastefully trimmed evergreen bushes. Wes knew these amenities existed because his mother had told him, but he had not seen them personally. The Hill had twice been featured in *Ulla*, and so his mother had a more than passing familiarity with Estelle and the life she lived. With these magazine spreads in mind, Wes walked up the ramp to the front door.

Estelle's assistant welcomed them. Gary was in his early sixties with black, curly hair. His large, red mouth reminded Wes of one of those characters on the Guess Who cards from his childhood. Wes's footsteps echoed under the vaulted ceiling of the entryway. The decor would have been too much if it had been anything other than white. White flooring, white walls, and soft white light from the (white) metal chandelier above. The entryway led through a wide hallway that arced off in several directions, but they were led away from the one that smelled the nicest—Wes wondered if she was having cherry cobbler with her dinner—and toward the primary office area.

Estelle stared out the window, which admittedly was hard not to stare out of. It took up a majority of the back wall and looked out on the peony garden, whose blooms were beginning to appear for the season. The patch of peonies looked out of place, but it was beautiful. So was Estelle. She turned to acknowledge her guests and smiled with an open expression and bright, brown eyes. They softened her entire face, which could have looked gaunt otherwise. Estelle was not preserved in the way Ulla was, with that stopped-time beauty that Wes's mother was known for. Estelle had a lived-in loveliness that made you want to see her picture in black and white to see the contrast written there.

On her desk was a pile of correspondence, Wes's letter among the rest. He had told his mother neither about writing a novel nor that he was resigning as representative of the estate.

He could have, in fact, taken a meeting with Estelle solo, but having Ulla's unassuming and undeterred confidence nearby always buoyed him. Despite being glad his mother was there, he hoped for an excuse to speak to Estelle alone. Eventually.

"Please sit," Estelle said, gesturing to two white leather couches on the other side of her spacious walnut desk. She moved behind it and sighed. "It's been such a long time, Ulla."

"Too long," Ulla agreed amiably.

"Your son wrote a novel?" Estelle asked without further preamble.

Ulla's face hardly ever registered surprise, either from the Botox or a misconception that not knowing everything might appear rude. She pursed her coral lips, then nodded. "Seems like it."

"Well, not all calls can be purely social, can they?" Estelle said with a papery laugh. "In fact, I was wondering if you might take a stroll with Gary, Ulla? He's meeting with a new landscaper next week to discuss this peony monstrosity. I love them, I do, but I'm not sure how to tie them in to the rest of the property. Would you mind looking?"

"Of course, of course," Ulla said, standing again.

"We'll have a raspberry tart when you come back," Estelle said. "Your recipe."

Unless the recipe had come from the early days of the magazine, credit was due to one of Ulla's expert recipe craftspeople. In her magazine, they were on the masthead under the label KITCHEN TEAM, as if they didn't do 90 percent of the work these days.

Once Estelle and Wes were alone, she sighed and folded her hands across her lap. "Good to see you again, Wesley. Now, you've written *Proud and the Lost* again, have you?"

Wes felt for his leather side bag, in which he had stowed the manuscript in its current form in case she brought it up. His last name and connections might have gotten him in the door, and his parents' money might occasionally pay to keep that door his on any given month, but he was good at his job. His manuscript was about three hundred pages, and his hands betrayed him by shaking as he removed it from his satchel.

"Would you like to see it?"

She shook her head, which made it even more awkward that he'd taken it out first.

"Your letter was good, eloquent—I can tell your prose will be too. It wasn't your usually perfunctory diction. And your handwriting is beautiful, not that anyone would see that if you published a novel."

If. Even her use of the conditional gave him hope.

"But you're holding something back from me, Wes, and we both know that."

"Oh?" He hadn't told her about Maureen's project, despite Yuri's call. Maureen Denton wasn't his client, nor was he required to entertain every Morgan devotee who came along with fantasies of adaptation. In his two years representing the estate, Mo hadn't been the first.

"I received an email," Estelle said.

"You don't like email," Wes said, realizing it was probably rude to both interrupt and to declare someone's communication preferences out loud.

"No, I don't like email, and I especially don't like when someone has managed to find the one personal email address I use to communicate with my grandkids. I should be glad they write, but I do wish they knew how to write on paper. Schools took away cursive classes and replaced them with coding.

Anyway—" She sighed. "I've had an interesting email exchange with another agent who says she approached you about an adaptation project, and that you're familiar with and like that author's work."

"To be clear, I do like *my* work too," Wes said in a way he hoped sounded both joking and completely serious, the statement of someone who had worked for years on this book. He'd first read *The Proud and the Lost* in college. It wasn't required reading at boarding school, which considered anything published after WWI to be "a bit modern." He began writing during his first read-through of the novel in a journaling impulse to anticipate and reflect upon the material, but it spiraled into a manuscript of its own from Clive's perspective. Clive's arc from free-spirited rake to domestic tyrant was believable but excruciating.

Wes didn't know how Maureen had adapted the novel—and if he was being honest with himself, he didn't want to know. He didn't want to root for it. Even knowing its existence was like knowing a tropical fruit grew somewhere on the other side of the world that he might never taste. He had to remind himself that he was perfectly happy with the fruit here, not allow his mouth to water in anticipation of something that might or might not poison him, or at least his mind, against what he already had grown.

"I assume that Yuri Eikura was the one who contacted you. I didn't tell you because I have trust issues."

Estelle laughed at that, her face crinkling. "Well, dear Wes, I am the trust, so let's not make this a bigger issue than we must. Pardon the rhyme. Yes, it was Yuri Eikura, and whatever way she found my email, she did, and I read it. And I do want to hear more from both of you."

"Yuri and I?" Yuri had fired him. He might not have been in the right for the situation, but he certainly hadn't been in the wrong. He sucked in his cheeks.

"No, no," Estelle said. "You and Maureen Denton. I've been thinking about this for a while, and while I've extended the protections on Mother's copyright, I do have to admit that I'd like to see the next step before my death."

"Oh, Estelle—" he said, not sure how to complete that sentence, and he was grateful when she cut him off.

"I'm eighty-three now, and time is not promised to any of us. Let me be frank—I'm not good at giving up control."

Understatement.

"But I know that Talia and Flor would be far more eager to sign any project that comes along. It turns out that family wealth divided between one child—me—doesn't go as far when divided further to two children and their families. I sense a tidal wave of *Proud and Lost* after my death, and I do not enjoy the prospect. Did you take note of the quality of the last project that approached us?"

He had, of course. It was his job to, and the fact that a slasher movie adaptation of *The Proud and the Lost* had made it as far as his desk horrified him as the representative and not just as a fan. Once Estelle passed away, once her daughters took over, there would be nothing to stop that project moving forward. As her family's current representative, he should technically relish this news. If he forgot about his project and stayed in this position and if there was a rush of adaptations, he would get a cut in each of those concurrent deals. Right now, managing E. J. Morgan's literary estate was mainly saying no, every day, to everything. It was clear his agency held on to the control for the one day that the trust would begin saying yes. To him, though, it was worth saying no to maintain his position as representative, even for a chance at maybe. Maybe his adaptation *could* see the light of day.

"I'd like to invite you and Maureen here to the estate for a weekend to look over your manuscripts in detail. I'll get to know her, and get to know you on a nonprofessional basis, and find out more about the projects you've completed. After the weekend, I'll decide whether I like either of them and, if I do, I'll allow one adaptation to move forward."

Wes released a breath, staring out the window to steady himself. The ground wasn't really moving; it was his blood pressure going haywire. "A weekend visit?"

"I might decide to allow neither book, please note. But my connection to you, and your appreciation of both your own talent"—here she gave Wes a wink—"and this woman's, well, let's begin here. I'd rather have a say in the next chapter of my mother's work. Might as well start somewhere."

Later, Wes thought he had agreed to this plan, but he couldn't be sure. He might have blacked out an entire conversation after that moment. The next thing he remembered was being midchew into a raspberry tart—a delicious one at that—but he had no memory of the first few bites and nearly choked when he realized one was in his mouth. Ulla and Estelle were conversing about local politics, something that mercifully affected his life not at all. Greenwich wasn't Wes's problem. He had enough problems as it was, and one of them would include packing an overnight suitcase next weekend and returning here.

CHAPTER THREE

Mo

"What do you pack for a mansion?" Mo turned from her closet, which was approximately half the size of a refrigerator and just as useful for finding impressive, bougie clothes.

"Belle packed nothing, and things turned out fine for her," Mackenzie said.

"Whenever I've dreamed of the Hill, I cannot say I've imagined singing teapots," Mo said. "It'll be a different kind of magic."

Sloan lay on Mo's bed, kicking her legs as she paged through one of Mo's issues of *The New Yorker*. She usually scoured the cartoons and then cast the magazine aside. "I think you'd be better off shredding three thousand dollars in cash, getting it wet, and then papier-mâché-ing it all over your body than trying to shop at this point."

"Right, because I definitely have that much money, for sure. Just sitting around under my bed."

Sloan rolled on her stomach and pretended to feel around underneath. "How deep?"

Mo laughed.

Mackenzie sat on the bed next to Sloan, holding Mo's suitcase on her lap. "You need a swimsuit," she said. "And maybe some tennis whites? Do you have tennis whites?"

"I do not play tennis. Do you think Estelle Morgan-Perry plays tennis?" Wikipedia lacked details about Estelle's hobbies.

"There are lots of people who use wheelchairs who play tennis," Sloan pointed out.

"Listen, I don't know much about Ms. Morgan-Perry, but I do know she is in her eighties," Mo said.

Sloan flicked another page of the magazine. "Tennis is a lifelong sport. Like golfing, at least my dad says."

"Cannot believe you actually listened to something your dad said," Mackenzie said.

"I can pack my gym shorts."

"In case she makes you run laps or climb a rope," Sloan said. "Or there's a literary *Hunger Games* situation. How's your archery?"

"Shut up, Sloan," Mo said, throwing a pair of gym shorts at her. Mo had been intimidated by Sloan when they first met. Her roommate had the kind of face and stature to remind people of a living doll. She was tall and thin, with rich brown skin. Maureen wasn't stylish or dramatic; she was just—Mo. Middle height, pale, with dishwater-blonde hair. Sloan had once told Mo that Mo looked like if Iowa was a person. Mo thought that was vaguely offensive, but she couldn't defend herself, really. She did look like about 90 percent of her high school graduating class.

Mackenzie intercepted the gym shorts before they could hit Sloan and tossed them in Mo's still uselessly bare suitcase.

Mo sighed and folded a white blouse. "I might look awful, but I hope my words will speak for themselves."

Mackenzie patted her arm. "If she doesn't love it, she's wrong."

But as much as her roommates reassured, Mo knew they couldn't protect her from the weekend to come. *Protect* was too strong a phrase, probably, when there weren't deadly predators or noxious poisons on the horizon, just a few days at a stately home in Greenwich. The home of her literary idol, no less. The home where her favorite writer had walked the halls, dreamt, and written the best book of all time.

The Proud and the Lost was a 1929 novel that followed Eliza Wirth, a nineteen-year-old woman from high society who, after taking to the flapper lifestyle for a year, was basically kidnapped by her parents. They attempted to reintegrate her into polite society and its norms. Clive, a man she'd run with in her flapper days, had also been living this double life, though he returned by choice to his manor estate. When Clive married Eliza, they had to come to terms with personal versus societal expectations for the rest of their lives. For Clive, the freedom of his youth was sowing his wild oats before he could become what his parents assumed he always would be. After they had a baby, Eliza realized she could not conform, even when allowed to do so with the man of her dreams. But could he really be the man of her dreams if he couldn't understand her dreams? Paralleling many other novels featuring young heroines in the early part of the twentieth century, the novel ended with Eliza's suicide—or at least what was always interpreted as her suicide. Her car ended up in a ditch.

In the original version, at least.

E. J. Morgan had been a phenom of her time—*his* time, people had assumed, as the novel was accepted for publication without checking the gender of its writer. E. J. had been a young wife living in Connecticut, and once it was revealed a year after its publication to have been written by a woman, the novel became a touchpoint about wealth, power, gender, and cultural expectations. It only grew in popularity after its release, and now it was impossible to graduate without reading the novel for some English course or another.

Maureen had discovered it earlier than high school—too early? Maybe. She read *The Proud and The Lost* for the first time the summer she turned thirteen while staying with her grandparents. Her parents usually shuttled Maureen and her younger sister Anna to the farm in the county next to theirs for at least two weeks a summer to get the girls out of their hair for a while. Other kids had summer camp; Maureen and Anna had feeding troughs and mucking and the county fair. Anna had always had an affinity for animals, which was probably why she worked with dogs now, but Maureen? Nope. She'd been lucky that her grandparents didn't make her do much choring—they were a modern enough hog operation to hire staff and didn't depend on the labor of grandkids. Even though she wasn't forced to work, it was hard to really play either. At home, Mo would have spent the time playing *The Sims*, but her grandparents didn't have a computer. Modern business or not, they still did paper records all the way until Mo's grandpa passed away.

Before that summer, Mo had enjoyed the freedom to run around with Anna, swing in the tire swing, or trail along after their grandmother as she did various errands and gardened. At thirteen, though, Mo didn't want to do anything except lie around and feel feelings, feelings that suddenly felt too big for her body. She wanted someone to talk to but, failing that, would accept watching other people talk. Books fed that need. Her grandma had a few on her shelf: the Bible, of course; *The Complete Works of William Shakespeare*; some assorted Western novels, and *The Proud and the Lost*.

Maureen read the novel twice over the course of those two weeks, and though she'd started reading because of boredom, by the end of the first chapter, she was hooked. And how couldn't she be, with Eliza in the boardinghouse, rolling her fishnets over her calves for what she didn't know would be the last time before her parents shoved her into the back of a Mercedes?

Since that summer, Mo had read the novel more than fifty times, so much so that her early writing efforts were stilted E. J. Morgan knock-offs. Once she started reading more broadly and writing more stories of her own, Maureen found her own sure footing with a voice that wasn't from 1929. Even today, though, Morgan's novel—her only novel—was a favorite. When Mo turned nineteen, she'd gotten a haircut like Eliza's from the cover of the edition her grandma owned. Eliza's hair in the picture was black, whereas Mo's was a fawny blonde. She'd kept it short for years like that, but ever since beginning her adaptation of *The Proud and the Lost*, she'd been growing it out. She could mark the time—two years—in terms of growth of her blonde, past-shoulder-length cut.

Mo's life had never been the same since she read the novel for the first time, and now she dared to compare her book to her idol's. She shivered, running her hand over her measly collection of clothes hanging in the closet. "My dresses are mostly from Target. I feel like wearing a Target dress would be worse than wearing no dress."

Mackenzie laughed. "I mean, not *no* dress. I don't think it's that kind of party."

In the end, Maureen packed too much of what she was sure was the wrong thing. Every item she placed in the suitcase rebelled against its inclusion—unfolding from its neat square—except her manuscript. She'd had her book printed at the print shop down the street and enjoyed the heft of it. Beforehand, she'd read through it an additional time and changed about three words. What if those three words were the ones that made Ms. Morgan-Perry—Estelle—fall in love with it, though? Yuri had also emailed the full manuscript to Estelle's assistant so that she could read it in its completion after the weekend was over. Yuri told Mo this was her chance to meet Estelle and let Estelle really meet her project. A whole weekend felt excessive, but if that was what it took for Estelle to understand that Mo loved and respected her mother's work well enough to write in conversation with it, then so be it. Amy, her boss, hadn't been thrilled that Mo would miss a weekend, as the wedding season was starting, but Mo promised to make it up with double shifts the next week if she needed to. Anything to give this book a chance.

Mo knew she didn't have enough of a platform to be an automatic bestseller. She wasn't well known and didn't have a zillion Instagram followers. Her short stories had gotten awards that no one cared about outside of a small group of twenty people she loved on the internet, but she hoped that E. J. Morgan's daughter would see something in this retelling that spoke to her. The whole situation felt like an extended job interview, or a corporate retreat, except one for a very small corporation.

Mo finally shoved the last thing inside the suitcase, and Mackenzie zipped it closed. "You have deodorant? Toothpaste? Toothbrush?" she asked. She was so used to working around children that sometimes she became mom-ish without realizing it.

"I'd worry more about bringing some edibles," Sloan said.

"What?"

"Oh, come on." Sloan sat upright, stretching a long arm above her head. "You can be totally uptight when you first meet someone. A gummy could be a shortcut that doesn't require a Valium or a bottle of rum, and it'd make you less sloppy."

Maureen rarely got sloppy, but she knew what Sloan meant. "I haven't really had edibles."

Sloan rolled off the bed and left the room. When she returned, she held out a small plastic bag tied off with a green twist tie. Inside were ten gummy bears. "Have you ever gotten high? Ever? Do they do that in Oklahoma?"

Mo rolled her eyes. "Iowa, and yes, I have smoked weed." Only once, she didn't say. She felt like that old Bill Clinton quote "I didn't inhale." She had smoked it in someone's bong in college, mixed with some herbs, but she thought she did it wrong because she felt nothing.

Mackenzie got an expression that Mo could only describe as worry eyes. "Only take one. Or half of one. They're stronger than you think," she said. "Don't . . . don't go *all* the way loose."

"What would that even look like?" Sloan asked, laughing. "She might wear mismatched socks. Oh nooooo."

Mackenzie snorted at that, and Mo laughed too. "It's a good backup plan. And thank you. I'm . . . I'm nervous."

"It can be nerve-racking to be given an all-expense-paid trip to a rich person's house for a weekend. I totally understand that," Sloan said. "Consider the gummies a vacation from your vacation if you need it."

Five minutes later, Maureen got the text that the estate's representative was waiting to transport her to the house in Greenwich.

CHAPTER FOUR

Mo

The car wasn't as fancy as Mo had imagined. It was a mid-sized Honda Civic. Newish, sure, but very much a dad car. The man driving the car didn't look like a dad, though. He was Mo's age, with wild brown hair twisting in an untidy nest above his broad forehead. He had a thick build, with shoulders like a breadboard, and wore a white ribbed sweater. Before they pulled off the curb, he raised his sunglasses to check his mirrors.

"Thanks for the ride," Mo said as she buckled her seat belt.

"You're welcome for the ride," he said. "I'm Wes, by the way."

"Mo," she said. "Which you probably know. Sorry, I'm just nervous."

She pulled out her phone and texted Mackenzie. *Reminder to feed and adore Perkins while I'm gone.* Perkins was her hedgehog, and he was extremely nocturnal and snuffly and generally all the good things to expect in a hedgehog. He'd been an impulse-adopt from a Facebook posting soon after she moved to the city. Someone's kid had not understood how much work pet ownership was, and she had gotten him very cheap. All Mo wanted was a big, slobbery dog to cuddle with at night, but the lease agreement plus their work schedules could not handle that. Instead, Mo had taken on the opposite of cuddly with Perkins.

In response, Mackenzie texted a picture of him. He was, as expected, sleeping in an adorable ball.

"Is that a rat?" Wes asked, his sunglasses directed squarely at her phone screen.

Her mind skidded suddenly to the rat and the rose peeking out from the garbage can. Her driver probably didn't want to hear her ratport. "I don't want to distract you."

He gestured at the stopped traffic around them.

"It's a hedgehog. His name is Perkins."

He snorted. "Like Clive's friend Perkins?"

Of course, as the estate's representative, Wes would know everything about the book. In the novel, Lieutenant Samuel Perkins and his wife Charlotte came over for a dinner party, which served as the climax of the book, where Eliza first lost control of her temper. Morgan described Perkins as having a long nose and pinched face, and once Mo saw her hedgehog, well—sometimes a name stuck.

Traffic finally moved again, and the Bronx slid past at a pace a little faster than walking. As they crawled, she toyed with the name Wes in her head, flipping it here and there. Something about him pinged in her, like they'd met before, but she couldn't place him. Then, finally, it clicked. She glanced sideways at his profile, then typed into her phone. She searched for his name and found him instantly on LinkedIn.

Wesley Spencer was a literary agent, and on LinkedIn he wrote about trends and pointed out publishing scams. He also spoke openly about being a bisexual man in the publishing world and the need for more and better representation. Mo had been following him for a few years, in fact, along with his other half a million followers.

With his LinkedIn headshot in front of her, she had to admit he was more handsome in person. His mouth was nice, Mo noticed. He had perfectly symmetrical lips, something she hadn't realized other lips lacked before. It was easier to look at his lips, since his eyes were obscured. Covered or not, Mo could still see his eyebrow jutting up above the sunglasses.

She looked away before she made it obvious, but she felt him glance over at her, curious.

At a stoplight, Wes asked, "Do you think Perkins is gay coded?"

"My hedgehog?" Maureen had never considered her hedgehog's preferences before. Then what Wes meant registered with her. "Oh, in *P&L*? I've never really thought about it."

Wes *hmm*-ed. "I've always thought of Clive and Perkins as a did-they-or-didn't-they thing," he said, then ran a hand through his hair. Somehow, despite the sunglasses, it seemed to be falling in his eyes.

"I never really read Clive as gay," Mo admitted.

"He's bi," Wes said with surety.

"Like you." Mo froze, embarrassed. "I mean, I know from the internet. From you posting about being bi."

Wes laughed. The sunglasses came off and he glanced toward her, waving an SUV in to merge. "So you know me? Threads or BlueSky?"

Rivals to Lovers

Every pubescent horror or gaff in front of a class had been erased to crown this moment. "I follow you on LinkedIn."

He laughed. "We can make that a formal connection after this weekend," he said.

The word *connection* snagged her brain. The sound of the word with *neck* in it, said from his perfect mouth, made hers get warm. "Should we listen to something?" Mo asked, changing the subject.

"Should I trust you with the aux?"

"Hey, I have very good aux sense."

"Fine."

Mo scrolled through her phone. She couldn't read him, but she didn't want to put on something he hated either. "How about aughts alternative?"

"How alternative?"

Instead of answering, Mo started the playlist. She wasn't going to give him a doctoral thesis on her music curation. She started with the New Pornographers, then led into Matt and Kim, transitioning into Tilly and the Wall.

"Interesting percussion," he commented.

"Live tap dancer. Their concerts were amazing."

When he didn't complain about the first few songs, she settled in and looked out of the window at the passing scenery. New York had slipped behind them. More comfortable with her music behind her, she said, "The Clive/Perkins discussion reminds me of the Frodo/Sam headcanon in *Lord of the Rings*. I never really considered them as a couple until I started reading fanfic."

Wes glanced at her. "Read much LOTR fanfic?"

She was not going to tell this stranger, this big-deal agent, this possible LinkedIn connection that she had *written* fanfic, and that Sam had been her crush since—forever. "Some. But after I started reading more of it, I couldn't watch the movies in the same way. It really was the most tender relationship in the films, and there was something more than friendship there."

"We agree on that. So can't you see how that scene in *P&L* . . ." He tapped the steering wheel, nervous energy thrumming through him. "You know the scene I'm thinking of. That level look they give each other over the dinner table. Clive and Perkins, I mean. The way Morgan describes Clive writing the letter to Perkins, the way he labors over it."

"I always thought that was because of their shared war trauma, the way they didn't get a chance to fully have an adolescence, and so when he, you know, joins the party scene a bit later than everyone else, he never fits in there. But he never fit in with his unit either," Mo said, working things through aloud. It was surreal to be having a deeply literary conversation in the car, with a hedgehog starting it all.

In Maureen's retelling, Clive was a man who saw people as stepping stones. People were valued based on their utility to him, and if those people dared to step outside of those norms, well—consequences. It was only too easy to recast him in the modern day as a Wall Street bro. Yes, he partied, but then again, how could he not want the familiar world order that supported him, making as much money as he could and having a traditional family to boost his image as he earned it? After a moment, she cleared her throat. "I could see a Perkins-and-Clive thing. The way Clive touches his jacket in the hallway. I always read that as acknowledging the medals of valor they shared, but the intimacy is something."

"Exactly," Wes said. He tapped the steering wheel and looked over at her. "It's nice to talk about the novel with another fan."

"I'm guessing, as the estate rep, you get to do that a lot," Mo said.

"Not with another writer."

"You write too?"

He gave her a look. "Yeah." He seemed to be about to say more, but instead he tapped his fingers on the steering wheel to the beat of "Read My Mind" by the Killers.

Was she supposed to know his writing? All she knew about him was his emblematic and usually funny posts on a social media site usually designed for cringing your way through the job market. The buzzing of her phone conveniently drew her attention away from him. A text from her sister, Anna, with a link to the proofs of her wedding invitations.

For the moment, Mo put that text aside and opened one with Sloan. She couldn't easily Google Wes in any depth from the car, but her roommate was a regular internet sleuth. *Who is Wesley Spencer?* she texted.

Wes didn't seem to notice the pause in conversation. I-95 N was heavy with traffic, but at least it moved. The Civic hummed along and rain tinked lightly on the windshield, barely a drizzle. It couldn't seem to decide whether it wanted to be there or not. While waiting for Sloan to text back, Mo clicked on and reviewed her sister's wedding invites. They were perfect, much like her sister. She sent back a heart emoji. By the time she looked up again, they were in Connecticut.

Mo hadn't had any reason to visit Connecticut before. She had friends in Baychester and Harlem and Roslyn Heights, but not *Greenwich*. Even its pronunciation seemed like it would cost you money to say it.

Wes went through a tollbooth, slow enough to ensure the E-ZPass scanned. She watched his hands on the steering wheel, trying not to be obvious she was watching him. Observation was an important part of being a writer. He had nice arms under that shirt and shoulders that could support a wall. That wasn't exactly the stuff of Alice Munro, but it was something.

Suddenly, Wes glanced out his side window, then back at the road. Calmly, he said, "The bridge collapsed."

Mo's stomach dropped and she grabbed for the oh-shit bar. She'd been an adult before she realized its actual purpose was for people (fancy people) to hang dry cleaning on. She held on tight, heart pounding, and looked out the window, prepared to see the gaping hole that was about to swallow the car.

Only to see a perfectly normal bridge.

Wes finally took off his sunglasses, lazily with one hand, leaving the other on the wheel. He caught her reaction, and the side of his mouth quirked up. It shouldn't have made him more attractive, but it did. "Not now. In the eighties. It was a big deal; several trucks and cars went over the side. One of my authors' books talked about it, used that incident to illustrate the failure of infrastructure on a national level."

Her heart hadn't caught up with her brain, which was still marching-banding in her chest. "Can you see why it might be, I don't know, disconcerting to talk about while driving over the bridge?"

"Do you honestly think I would toss an offhand comment like that? And not slow down or try to stop?"

"I don't know anything about you!"

"LinkedIn says otherwise, and LinkedIn doesn't lie."

"People on social media certainly lie." Her phone announced a text from Sloan, and Maureen opened it, turning toward the window. If it had been embarrassing for him to notice her hedgehog on her screen, it would be a thousand times worse to have his own face there. She scrolled through the six screenshots Sloan had shared. The first, the bio page from his literary agency. Standard stuff, exactly what she'd seen from his profile. The second and third were other social media profiles, where his follower number dwarfed small midwestern city populations and his bio, like the bio of any person who didn't need to be clever to get those followers, was simple. "Book person," it read. The fourth through sixth shots, however, were more surprising. The fourth was an article from a tabloid, with Wes beside an older woman at a gala function. He wore a tuxedo, which, had she had more time, she might have lingered and zoomed in on. As it was, the person next to him piqued her interest. She'd seen that face before. The caption read "Ulla and her son, Wesley Spencer, both in Versace."

Ulla. Of *Ulla*. He had never talked about Ulla on LinkedIn. She was one of those one-name celebrities like Beyoncé or Bono, so how could Mo have known? It clicked, then, the whole thing. The media nepotism baby and his zillions of followers. She'd had enough friends try to break into the publishing world to know that the connections didn't hurt, and neither did inherited wealth. She flipped through the last two images, one of an unflattering tabloid article about a breakup and one of him posing next to the woman they were about to see, Estelle Morgan-Perry. Maureen took a deep breath, refocusing. She wasn't here to figure out the backstory of Estelle's agent. She was here to share her vision of the novel with her.

She must have taken longer gazing at the tuxedo than she thought. When she glanced up, they had moved into Greenwich proper. Even the trees were different here. Mo wasn't sure if it was the slightly less polluted air this far from the city, but she swore even the blossoms on the apple trees were whiter and the cherry blossoms pinker. She wondered if Wes noticed the difference or if he was so accustomed to having good things that they flew right past him without notice.

Her phone buzzed again, and she expected a follow-up from Sloan with even more bombshells. Maybe that Wesley owned *The New Yorker* or something. Instead, it was a text from Yuri: *Have a good weekend. Don't stress.*

Don't stress? About the biggest opportunity of her life? Maybe someone like Wesley Spencer wouldn't have to stress if he were in his shoes. Mo wished Yuri could be there with her. Yuri was a dynamo—110 pounds of concentrated authority in a pantsuit—but somehow she wore that confidence in a way that put Mo at ease. Yuri would not be present, she had confirmed, but she could get to Greenwich within two-ish hours if Mo absolutely needed her. An agent-client relationship was a strange thing, because her agent didn't make any money unless Mo did—and Mo hadn't made any money yet. It was like having an employee on spec, except an employee who technically had more power than you did. Someday, Yuri must imagine, Mo would be a lucrative enough client to justify a promise like this, but for now Mo had made her exactly zero dollars and zero cents, almost the same as what Mo made in writing for herself.

The gate for the Morgan estate opened before the Honda, splitting in half. She had never been in a place that had so much wrought iron before. It was called the Hill for a reason: Its elevated placement rose into view ahead of them. She had tried, when she moved to New York, to get a tour, only to be told it was open to high school tour groups and benefit events only. The first category disqualified her, and the second had a thousand-per-person price tag on the only occasion she'd checked. She'd given up on ever seeing this estate, tried to comfort herself with the idea that walking around a person's house wasn't walking in their shoes. It wasn't like holding a literary séance and being present with the genius. Now that she had the property a thousand yards away from her, her knees shook. She didn't know what she could learn about her favorite author from walking around in her house, but she couldn't wait to find out. "It's massive."

"It is. Not unlike my ego," Wesley said.

She laughed at that. "At least you admit it."

"I think a healthy ego is important."

"A topic for another one of your famous posts," she agreed.

As the car crept down the driveway, she steadied herself. The sun was setting behind the house, a convenient and luxurious backdrop that felt staged for Maureen's benefit. She imagined E. J. Morgan's father standing on this hilltop, finger-squaring the plot of land where their mansion would go. Mo wondered what kind of coating they had on the windows to reduce this kind of evening glare. If she had been building the house, she would have placed the dining room in the rear to stare out at the vast back lawn—at least she presumed it was vast. It was funny that so much about a stately house could be presumed. As a writer, she had spent a lot of time on Zillow looking at fancy homes to write her version of *P&L*, and the houses blurred together after a while to become a monotonous blah of white walls, subway tiles, white-painted bricks, white columns, sweeping double staircases, and white people, generally. Not to stereotype. Okay, yes, to stereotype.

The mansion recalled British historical manor dramas, maids, and little white hats. Bells being rung for dinner and tea. If she were cast in a drama like that, she'd be entering through the service entrance, not the front door. She had always been solidly middle class growing up, and now that she was on her own, she was a few notches below that. Still, she knew how to be around the upper crust when she was working for them. That term: the upper crust. As if the rest of the world were the soggy-ass bottom of the pie mush that people usually shoved to the side of the plate. To not be shoved aside, she had to decide what parts of herself she wanted to pack for this trip, alongside her nonexistent tennis whites and Sloan's weed gummies.

The long driveway ended in a roundabout with a fountain at its center. The fountain was granite, but at this point in the season it was only full of blown leaves. Standing in the driveway, she realized that the air felt cooler here, probably because of the sun setting. She shivered, arms goose-bumping under her nicest cardigan. First impressions were hard, but she'd settled on a green wrap dress that accentuated her hips, paired with a pale-yellow sweater. She looked like a just-opening daffodil if a daffodil taught preschool. Her braided blonde hair completed the perception. Her shoes had a little heel to them, enough that she was eye to eye with Wesley as he unloaded her bag from the back seat.

He handed her the suitcase, and she pulled the handle straight to roll it behind her into the house. He slid his own bag out next, a leather shoulder satchel that looked as soft as a kitten. She wondered if Ulla had picked it out for him. She had a sudden urge to press her hand to it. She had a thing about textures. Especially as a kid, she'd had to feel everything, run it between her fingers. Certain textures gave her intense pleasure, almost like what Sloan described as ASMR, but for feeling things. She'd tried to work in a clothing shop in college but was too easily distracted. Catering had fewer sensory distractions: the same reassuring hardness of a plastic tray, the cool firmness of an ice-cold glass—these things centered her. But no, she would not pet this man's obviously expensive bag or his well-knit sweater, as much as she wanted to.

She followed him up the front ramp to the double wooden doors at the entrance. "I feel a little like I'm walking into the Clue mansion," Mo said. "At least the rain stopped."

He rang the doorbell and gave her a tentative grin. "I am your singing telegram," he half sang.

"You might want to duck, if that's the case," Mo said. "Just in case Tim Curry is inside."

"Oh God, I wish," he said.

"Same." *Deep breaths, Mo,* she told herself. *You can do this. Pretend this isn't the beginning of the biggest interview of your life.* Her heart thumped as loud as any door knocker.

A man opened the door and introduced himself as Gary, Estelle's assistant, and ushered them inside. Taking their bags, he gestured down a long hallway. "I'll take these up to your rooms. It's about thirty minutes until dinner, if you'd care to freshen up."

Gary took their bags upstairs, leaving Wes and Mo together in the entryway. Long, paneled corridors led down either way toward different wings of the house. Amazing to be in a house with *wings*. It felt almost as likely as being on top of an eagle with them. She stifled an internal image of Gandalf atop an eagle. She didn't know why her anxiety manifested as *Lord of the Rings* references. Gazing upward, she pictured herself back in time. This was the place

E. J. Morgan had lived when she wrote *Proud and the Lost*. This place might have inspired some of the caged feeling of luxury, but E. J. hadn't moved out of it from her birth to her death.

Don't think about the fact that E. J. Morgan died here.

Mo cleared her mind, breathing deeply, and turned to Wes. He was designated to be the receptacle of her non–*Lord of the Rings*–released anxiety because, hilariously, she had known him the longest of all these strangers. "I can't believe I'm here in her house."

"It's surreal to be in the house of a person whose book you're adapting," he agreed, and she suddenly felt how perceptive he was. He might be rich and powerful, but he was insightful too. How lucky for your emotional conduit to have that kind of empathetic sense.

"It is beautiful here."

Wes shrugged his acknowledgment. "It's beautiful but not charming, if you see what I mean."

Mo did, and agreed, but also wondered if that was how Wes saw her too. Or maybe if that's how she saw him.

When she got up to her room, she texted Yuri. *Here safe. Wes Spencer gave me a ride.* She would also not mention the LinkedIn embarrassment, how cute he was, or how much she wanted to rub her hands along his finely knit sweater.

Be careful around him!! was Yuri's instantaneous reply.

Double exclamation marks. She bit her lip, wondering what more dirt another publishing insider could provide on this man. She noticed the three dots and waited for more details. She wandered around her room and marveled at its lovely simplicity. The windows looked out over the large front lawn. She pictured E. J. Morgan crossing that lawn and walking up the stairs she just had. Even, perhaps, sitting in this room. Writing here? Anything was possible.

The room included an en suite bathroom and a plush yellow bedspread. She ran her hand over it and felt the soft release of the down under her fingers. After rinsing her face and reapplying makeup, she checked her phone again. Yuri had left her a paragraph response, whose first few words were *Okay, so don't hate me, but here's what's going on this weekend—*

Mo sat back on the bed and stared at the ceiling. She wasn't here to wow Estelle. She had competition, and that competition was in the room across the hall.

CHAPTER FIVE

Wes

For dinner, Estelle's chef had made roast pork and pineapple with a side of roasted brussels sprouts and a chewy, fresh baguette. So chewy that Wes had difficulty speaking, which was fine, because Estelle and Maureen seemed to be hitting it off famously without him.

It had to be pork, of all things. They couldn't have eaten chicken to give this rival less ammo to charm Estelle with. No, it turned out that of course Mo would basically have read the tarot cards of the pig they were ingesting.

"I wasn't raised on a pig farm," Mo clarified after the first five minutes of the discussion. Wes couldn't stop watching her, not even when she unselfconsciously put a bite of the former Babe in her mouth. A tiny little Gordy covered with sauce. A delicious little Wilbur . . . the more Wes spun out the thought, the less hungry he was and the more curious he was about why kids were so fascinated with pigs.

Maureen had been a little quiet at the beginning of dinner, shooting Wes sideways glances that made him wonder what she had Googled about him upstairs. Something had happened, that was for sure, but when the main course was brought out, pork talk began. And, it seemed, was never going to end.

"My mother was raised on a hog farm, and she and my dad took over the farm after my grandparents passed. So I wasn't raised around hogs, but I spent summers with them. My parents took over the operation after I left for college."

Wes did not interject with an anecdote about where he summered, mostly because his May-through-August periods were bougie enough to use the verb *summer* for. He imagined the conjugation on a blackboard in chalk: *I summered in Tuscany. You summered in Tuscany. He/She/It did not summer in Tuscany. We summered in Tuscany, but sometimes also in Laos or San Pedro Island. They summered near pig excrement.*

Estelle was charmed by the description of a life completely unlike her own. Rural exceptionalism, that's what it was. Just because Maureen was brought up on or around a farm didn't make her somehow more moral or worthy, although Wes had to admit he couldn't think of anyone he knew who grew up on a farm. He represented a diverse range of clients in terms of race, sexuality, genre, and education, but he didn't send any of their royalty checks to a soybean field.

"When I was growing up, my grandparents kept about a hundred hogs, but that's more like two hundred today. And my dad is in construction, always has been, so he helped build the new facility for them." Maureen's voice was steady, but fifteen minutes into the discussion, even she sounded a little bored by the topic. She pushed a brussels sprout around her plate.

"Can you smell them from the house?" Wes asked. His appetite for pork was completely gone, but both Estelle and Maureen had eaten their portions without issue. His three rounds of pale flesh stared up from a bed of cranberry dressing. Tiny Peppa covered in red sauce. He might never eat pork again.

"Yes and no. The buildings are better ventilated than they used to be. You can be within a hundred feet of the confinement and not smell anything. And it's not like we do the processing of the hogs on-site, so there's not—" Maureen paused. "Anyway, pigs aren't really a passion for me. That's why I'm here. Well, *here*, yes, but also why I'm in New York in general."

The dinner plates were cleared by one staff member as another put down a small crème brûlée in front of each guest. The tops were perfectly toasted to a coconut tan, and Wes tapped the top with the back of a spoon. The sugar top gave with a crack, and he dug into the rich custard.

"Does all of your family live in Iowa?" Estelle asked, her brain unwilling to move on from the topic that both Maureen and Wes were obviously over. Maureen looked across the table from Wes with a complicated look. In it, he read how apologetic she was about the continuation of the conversation, but also how trapped she was. He smiled at her, chest warming. At least she realized it, and he wasn't envious of the attention. He knew only too well how much it felt like being consumed to have your family life picked apart.

Maureen put a spoonful of dessert in her mouth before she spoke. She closed her eyes while she tasted, and Wes realized how long her lashes were. When she opened them again, the spoon was still in her mouth, lightly held in her fingertips. She pulled it out smoothly, tongue peeking barely from between her pink lips. She did have a farm girl freshness in her looks. That braid down her back, blonde and sweet, was something he could picture parted. Two Pippi pigtails, braided across her shoulders.

Finally, she spoke, putting the spoon beside the custard. "Yes. We're sixth generation or something like that. My parents were high school sweethearts. To find the love of your life in a high school with a graduating class of about forty is incredible luck. And my little sister lives about twenty minutes from my parents. She's getting married this summer."

"Do you get to see them often?" Gary asked.

"Not as often as they'd like." With a forced effort Wes could see from across the table, Maureen's brow furrowed, then smoothed again. She picked up her spoon again, angling it into the custard. "So, what is on the agenda for the weekend?"

Wes turned to Estelle. "Yes, I guess we should discuss how you plan to put us through the ringer."

Estelle lay her spoon on top of her empty dish. "We'll get down to business in a minute. I'm going to attend to a few needs, and while I'm gone, feel free to have a little more coffee."

She held up a finger, and a staff member refilled her cup. Estelle and Gary left the room. The gravity of the room changed without Estelle at the head of the table. Wes shook his head at the offer of coffee.

Maureen asked, "Decaf?" The server shook her head, and Maureen said, "Thank you, Angie. I'm okay."

Angie left them alone in the dining room, the first time they had been alone since the car. "Do you know her?" Wes asked.

"She has a name tag, and that means she has a name."

"I know she has a name." Wes knew he sounded defensive. He shouldn't be embarrassed that he hadn't taken note of the staff members' name tags. Should he? He realized, suddenly, that Maureen had not looked at him more than twice the entire meal. This lack of eye contact only made itself known now that they were alone. "You don't need to know everyone's names."

"If we're going to see Angie all weekend, I'd like to use her name," Maureen said primly, examining her mug.

In the bustle of the past few hours, Wes had barely had time to consider his impression of Maureen. Not really a first impression, since he had fallen for her manuscript two years ago, but a book isn't a person. He found himself curious about this woman who followed him on LinkedIn and shipped Sam and Frodo; this woman who had grabbed onto the dry-cleaning bar in his car for dear life an hour ago and was now staring into what he knew to be an empty mug in her hands. "No coffee past six PM for you, huh?" he tried.

"I don't want to have more reasons to not sleep. I'm just—"

"Just what?"

She glanced behind her, probably checking for Estelle. When it was clear they were still alone, she spoke. "I'm mad at you."

"Me!"

"Can you blame me? You could have said something in the car that we were up against each other." She had no issue looking in his eyes now.

"I don't represent the estate anymore, if that's what you're worried about. As of this weekend, my boss took that position over. I'm in the same situation you are."

"Oh, sure," she said with heat. "A publishing insider with a famous mother, a close connection to the estate, and a large social media following versus the pig girl. Absolutely square."

"I can't help any of that."

"I thought this was a one-on-one type of thing, not a *Hunger Games* situation." Mo laughed coldly. "Not that I'm going to go shooting you through the heart or anything."

"Maybe a little competition is a good thing. I'm not nervous," he said, finding it was true. "I am anxious."

Mo scoffed. "Same thing."

"Oh no. One hundred percent not." He was on firm ground in arguing semantics. "Nervous implies some amount of control over the situation. Anxiety is an acknowledgment of your lack of control."

She *hmm*-ed. "Well, I'm not good at not being the one in control." Her voice was suddenly low and rough.

"I prefer someone else to be in control," he said.

"Seems like a strange temperament for an agent."

"Oh," he said, "being an agent means being able to accept how powerless you really are. I'm good at making that personal connection and marketing projects, but I'm not sure I could ever be an acquiring editor. Or a politician."

"Are those two jobs so alike?"

Her heard the thaw in her voice, wanted to keep it going. "Well, both jobs have to get used to asking for more money and disappointing people, so I'd say yes."

"Agents disappoint people all the time."

"Fair," he said. "But publishing on the agent side doesn't raise my anxiety like publishing on the writing side does. This is—well—torture paired with a nice dinner."

"It is, right?" She bit her lip, glanced at the door again. "My roommate gave me some weed gummies. I don't know if they will make things better or worse. I've never tried them."

But before he could reply to that interesting bit of information, Estelle rejoined with Gary in tow. She placed herself at the head of the table again, and Gary sat in the empty chair to Wes's left. Their appearance on the scene was like being given a new script to read from. The tension shifted. Wes wondered what it was like to be on a reality show, suddenly. If sometimes there was real banter between the contestants that went unfilmed.

Gary tapped a folder on the table and smiled. His graying beard was neatly trimmed, and so was his jacket. "All right, procedures for the weekend," he said, handing each of them a printed formal agenda from the folder. The top page held a schedule of events for the next two days, including what appeared to be the dinner they had finished eating. In fact, the conversation they were having was included on the schedule as an "introductory session," and like a chess piece laid on the board, he sensed himself being moved against his will.

Wes skimmed the paper until he got to a three-hour block after breakfast the next day. Another block after lunch, then dinner. "Wait," he said, "these are marked as readings?"

Estelle nodded. "You will read portions of the book out loud. I am an avid reader, but I can't finish two novels in a weekend. You'll leave a copy with me after the weekend ends to enjoy in their entirety."

"These post-meal readings are an audition?" Maureen's voice was small.

"Of a sort," Estelle said. "After breakfast, you will read your first chapters. The first, say, twenty pages or so. After lunch, you can select any middle chapter you'd like to share, and after dinner, the ending," Gary explained. "We have tea and lozenges on hand if your voice gets tired."

"I can talk," Wes said. "That's not the issue. My issue is that reading random chapters spoils the ending!"

Estelle only smiled. "It shouldn't if you did an adaptation right. I'll still be surprised by the journey."

Wes had been surprised by this journey so far, that was for sure. If only he knew how it was going to end.

CHAPTER SIX
Wes

After the orientation, Estelle—and the official paper schedule—dismissed them for the night. Wes went back to his room and lay on his bed. Estelle had given them free range of the grounds, but the sun had set more than an hour ago, and right now the only sightseeing he wanted to do was the back of his eyelids. But again, it was only eight thirty, and he hadn't gone to bed that early since he thought Tamagotchis were cool.

The bed was comfortable, with a forest-green duvet. The same green echoed the leafy decorations of the room—botanical prints, as if from some ancient textbook on the subject, the kind with the hand-inked sketches. There was always something sexual about the reedy flowers in those textbooks, or maybe he was a pervert who saw necks and slender legs in everything.

It had been a while since he'd had sex, to be fair.

The bed frame was deep mahogany, with a matching desk and bureau. He placed his bag on top of the bureau and unpacked his laptop and manuscript on the desk. The print shop had bound the book with those irritatingly fragile plastic rings. It stared at him as if it too were restless. He was about to fetch the laptop to bring to bed to peruse a client's manuscript—he was nothing if not a workaholic—when he heard a tap on the door.

Maureen had changed from her dress into jeans and red Converse sneakers. She wore the same yellow cardigan, a jacket draped over her arm. "I'm going for a walk," she said, "If you want to come."

"You're not still mad at me?"

"I am. I just don't like to be alone in a new place."

On one hand, he should get to know the woman he was competing against. On the other hand, he worried that knowing her better might dull what competitive spirit he possessed. Wes hadn't found passion in sports until discovering boxing as a teenager. He never saw the point of winning at games that he wouldn't remember tomorrow. If he put something on paper, he could return to it, relive it. Watching an old game never had that feeling, and his muscles forgot the strain of exercise after a few hours. At least with boxing, there were bruises that forced him to remember the bouts.

Like in boxing, it might help to know his competitor this weekend. "Okay. Give me a minute." He slipped on his gray pea coat and followed.

The stillness was unsettling, as was the darkness. Gary informed them that the lights were on a timer system, set to turn off after the staff were usually gone for the night. No one lived in the huge, sprawling residence except Gary, who had a main floor bedroom, and Estelle, who had the large room near the elevator upstairs. They left through the French doors at the back of the kitchen.

It was strange passing from the gleaming chrome of the kitchen to the cold expanse of flagstone patio outside. The zero-entrance pool hadn't been filled yet for the season and sat like an empty, white hand. Lights inside were also lit so the cavern of the pool glowed eerily.

Keeping pace beside him, Maureen buttoned her pale-pink coat. She had what Wes's dad would have called "a classic figure"—shorter than he was by a few inches, with an hourglass shape accentuated by the cinched belt. "It's hard to believe this is where she wrote the novel, isn't it?"

"Not exactly humble beginnings." He suddenly needed to prove to her that he had been here before. "There are some new gardens around this way," he said, gesturing. The classic English gardens, with winding paved paths stretched out in the distance. Wes remembered the side plot of peonies he had seen from Estelle's office last week.

"Oh?"

"I was here with my mother last week," Wes said.

"Is Ulla working on something with Estelle? How convenient for you."

"No, no," he said, glad for the confirmation that she knew. He didn't post about his mother on LinkedIn, but Maureen still knew somehow. He decided to answer with a partial truth. "It was a personal visit. Something about these peonies."

"How lucky for you, to know your way around here." She glanced away. "Maybe you can give me the full tour. Or perhaps we could wait for Ulla to arrive."

"It's not like that," Wes said.

"Of course not. I'm sure it means nothing that you're probably neighbors. Am I right about that?"

Silence settled between them, him a step behind for a moment. She shook her head as if to free something. "Well, might as well enjoy the weekend away while I have it."

The peony beds came into sight now, wavy lanes of buds. They still weren't in bloom, and he suddenly felt foolish for leading her this way, as well as for leading her into the conversation they were having. He had wanted to see if her demeanor changed when Ulla's name dropped. Typically it did. He saw friends' intentions change and dates' eyes fill with calculations. Even worse, if they had known before he brought it up, it was always obvious in their poorly feigned surprise. From that point, there were soft asks for contact info, for ins, for a nudge to this department or that or for her to try this new product.

Instead, Mo was obviously angry. Frustrated? Both? It didn't matter, because he wouldn't see Maureen after this weekend. This was the big match. This was the chance to duke it out, and one author would bow out and go home. Nevertheless, he wanted to win because he was good, not because of some impression that Ulla pulled strings.

In the still night air, he enjoyed the smell of freshly mowed grass and the peace of the scattered exterior lights. Maureen's face was shadowed, but he wanted her to catch his eye. He wanted, he realized, for her not to hate him. "Peonies are traveling plants," he said, breaking the silence.

"Like Ents?"

Her reply was so immediate that he had to laugh. "Is Tolkien haunting you? Seriously. No, another client wrote about it, about how species of plants are sent all over the world. It was part a treatise on colonialism but part an exploration of the adaptations of nature and beauty. Peonies from China and Japan are more treelike—shrubby. Is shrubby a word?"

"It should be." Her tone was now softer, almost sweet, and she almost had a smile on her face. "But maybe some of the Ents were peony trees. I bet they would still kick Orc ass."

Was she messing with him? He hadn't been thrown this far off his balance since, well, probably dinner tonight, but before that, it had been years. She lazily touched a bud with a finger, the stem moving under her hand. He did his best not to notice her arms, the gentle curve of her body. He absolutely did not think about the botanical drawings upstairs. When Mo pulled her hand back, she brought her wrist to her nose and sniffed delicately. "Natural perfume," she said, and extended that wrist to Wes.

Yes, she was messing with him. Wes found that he couldn't help but be messed with. He placed his nose near the base of her hand and took in that echo of a scent. He also took in the scent of her skin. He realized what a forward gesture this was for a stranger and took a step back. When she smiled crookedly in return, he had flashbacks of Penn and smoky frat houses. Suddenly everything fell into place. "You took those weed gummies, didn't you?"

She pulled her hand back as if burned. "What?" But her voice held guilt in it, and so did her open expression. A thin smile, lazy and unaggrieved, caught in the partial light that bathed the garden through the wide glass windows behind them.

He laughed. "You thought you could sneak your high? Come on. You are less mad at me. And you're talking about Ents."

"Why don't we talk about Ents more is the question." Maureen's voice was wry enough that Wes thought she wasn't too far gone. Her next step faltered, though, and she touched his arm lightly for balance. When he looked down at her hand on his arm, she said, "Nice coat. It's a nice texture, like your sweater. Sweaters and coats are so good when it's chilly."

It was chilly. "Still want to walk? You look a little wobbly."

She nodded and removed her arm from his coat. She took a few steps forward, then glanced back at him. "I feel—uh. Yes. Walk. So, I haven't had weed gummies before. I needed some air in my lungs. Not an exact measurement of air, just some."

And then she fell face first onto the dirt path.

Once he got her sitting up, Wes ran back through the kitchen door and retrieved a glass of water. In the meantime, she had managed to crawl toward the patio. He intercepted her halfway to the door. "It's like my legs are asleep," she said in what she must have thought was a low voice. It was not. "Do you want some gummies? I have them in my pocket."

With her safely drinking water and back within view of the house, Wes considered his options. He should find out what exactly he was dealing with here. "Sure. Let me see them."

She handed over the bag, which had no markings on it. Inside were six gummy bears. He'd had edibles before and knew how little you needed to get the effect. "How many were in here before?"

"A clan. Is that how you measure bear amounts? A clan of gummy bears?"

He sat next to her. "Do you remember how many bears were in this clan?"

"Eight. Like *The Brady Bunch*. Oh my God, what if I ate the Greg and Marcia ones. Marcia, Marcia, Marcia!" she cried.

"That is a really old TV show."

"I'm a really old soul."

He looked at the remaining bears and did some mental calculation. One gummy usually had about 10 mg of THC, enough for any beginner—and she had to be a beginner, right?—to feel something. But with two?

"How you doing, champ?" he asked.

"My legs no longer work."

"I noticed that." Suddenly, the kitchen light, by whose glare they had been talking, shut down. It must be nine o'clock.

"Do you think Ulla would hate me?" she asked. "And it's dark. It's dark now."

"Yes," he said, then paused. "Yes, it's dark, not yes that my mother would hate you."

"Do you hate me?" she asked.

"I don't know you," Wes said, though he wondered if he could admit now that he did, in one way at least, know her. The Google alert. The first book she'd written. But it didn't matter, and he didn't want to freak her out or even let on how deeply curious he was about her. Her book, that is, not the woman sitting next to him, leaning into his shoulder. She probably didn't know that she was doing that last part.

"I think I hate you. I should unfollow you on LinkedIn."

"That would be fair."

"Like you'd even notice."

He sighed and tried not to look at her lips. "I'd notice."

"If only you weren't cute, in a Sam Gamgee kind of way."

He did what he did best: deflect. "Do you usually make a lot of *Lord of the Rings* references when you're high, or do I bring that out in you?"

"Oh, I don't know, but if you eat some gummies too, we can see if it's the batch." This suggestion made her laugh harder.

Despite her silliness and lack of control over her legs, he was enjoying himself. Despite her yelling at him, they'd had a better conversation that he had at most parties. Many of his friends were famous-adjacent children like he was. That set weren't necessarily based on kinship or similar interest, just the mutual annoyances they all put up with. A nepotism collective, maybe. He had work colleagues he was friendly to, clients he was collegial with, and then he had his family. Someone who could swing wildly from seventies-era television to fantasy to *The Proud and the Lost* seemed like Wes's kind of person. Plus she was attractive—that fact was undeniable.

He couldn't tell her any of that, whether she was sober or otherwise, because he'd read her book and chosen her from the slush, then left the agency he'd chosen her for. And now they were rivals for the same book deal, which for either of them would be life changing. The sooner he got her back to her room, the less he would learn about her, and maybe that was for the best.

"Can you stand?" Wes asked.

"Can you?"

"I haven't had any controlled substances," he said. "And yes. I can."

"We should go to the hot tub," she said. It wasn't even in a suggestive tone. It was an almost too-sober tone, like suggesting they should go to the grocery store to get snacks. "The one off the patio. I'm so cold. That would be fun."

Wes chewed his lip, trying not to imagine unwrapping that belt from around her waist, the curve of her body underneath. He might not accept her statement that he was cute, but *she* undoubtedly was. He'd noticed in the car, and agonized about it over dinner, and now that tug was worse than ever. She had dimples in her cheeks and sparkling hazel eyes. He could tell those eyes were sparkling, even in the dark. "No. I don't think we should do that tonight. Let's get you upstairs. Can I . . . help you?"

She grunted something that sounded like an affirmative, so Wes knelt next to her and put out his arms to raise her up. She was unsteady, almost falling again, but he circled one hand underneath her armpit for support. The kitchen was dark, but a rope of light from near the baseboards ensured they didn't slam into anything. When they got to the bottom of the long, curving stairs, Wes paused. She had already slipped from his grip once, and he didn't want to chance things. "Let's try the elevator."

The elevator was down the hallway underneath the stairs. Wes held on to her body with one arm, using the other to press the button. The door opened with a ding, and she turned to it in acknowledgment. "Thank you, Jeeves," she said.

The door closed. "Am I supposed to be Jeeves?" Wes asked. Now that they weren't moving, she leaned against the wall, then used his shoulder for extra support.

"No, no, the elevator is Jeeves. Doesn't it seem like someone in this house should be named Jeeves?"

In a movie, the elevator would have gotten stuck and they would have had to figure a way out of this situation.

Luckily, with no cameras or producers around, the journey upstairs went smoothly. He didn't think she noticed that during that short elevator trip her hand began to rub his arm—or rather, pet his jacket—in an absent way. His arm hair prickled.

As they got out of the elevator, Maureen stumbled ahead before Wes could get ahold of her. She began to topple again, but Wes jumped forward, catching her before she slammed to her knees. He'd stayed in the routine of starting the day with fifty push-ups ever since college, and that practice paid off as he hoisted her in his arms. At this new vantage, her eyes opened wider. Close range, Wes could see the flecks of light brown in her irises and take in that scent. Just her, with a bit of peony.

And then Estelle's bedroom door opened.

Wes glanced from Mo's body in his arms to Estelle's curious, flushed face behind the door. Gary was behind her, both of them in bathrobes—which was interesting, to say the least. He might have been helping her get ready for bed, but then again, why was he dressed for bed too? Wes looked at Gary and Gary looked at Maureen, and suddenly Wes wanted the elevator to have gotten stuck after all.

"She's not feeling so well," Wes said, overlapping Gary's explanation of "We were having our nightly chess game." Wes didn't think either man believed the other one. Gary waited for Wes to get to the door of Maureen's room before Gary waved at Estelle and left, closing the door behind him.

"Well, that was awkward," Wes said as he closed the door to Maureen's room.

She made a humming noise and found her footing again, tottering toward the desk. Her room was like Wes's but themed around foxes instead of botanical prints. A line drawing of a fox kept watch over the bed that Maureen fell onto, still fully dressed. He moved to her, dimpling the bed with his weight. He tugged off her shoes and socks.

She murmured, "You're very handsome, and I'm sorry I thought you were going to let us drive off a bridge. Your mouth is a good mouth."

Wes didn't know how much she would remember tomorrow, but he didn't want her to dig herself into memories that might be embarrassing if those memories stuck. "It's time to sleep."

"What if beds were stuffed with marshmallows so if you got hungry, you could just eat them while you were dreaming?" she asked.

Wes moved Maureen so that he could tuck the sheets around her. "That might get messy."

"That's what she said."

"Definitely bedtime," Wes said.

Maureen closed her eyes and lay back on one of the uncomfortable-looking decorative pillows. He removed that one, then fluffed the softer pillow behind it before she settled back down on it. On his way out of the room, Wes turned off the light and said, "Good night, Maureen."

No response came from the bed. She might have eaten a pillow, for all he knew, but he hoped not.

In bed, after he'd brushed and washed, he tried not to think about the length of her neck, her weight against his shoulder in the elevator, and the softness of her body in his arms. He wasn't used to carrying the full weight of a person, and his muscles still resonated with some of that effort, the pressure of holding all of one person in his grip and the pleasure of it, too. It was the kind of muscle memory that boxing had always given him, the glowing feeling of use afterward. He hoped he'd be able to feel it tomorrow, ache from it a little to relive the moment. The proof that he could hold her, and that when he did, she would be close enough for him to see that gold in her eyes.

CHAPTER SEVEN

Mo

Ah fuck.

When you wake up in your clothes from the night before, you know things went wrong. Mo's coat was carefully draped across the back of the chair, but she could hear the phone in its pocket vibrate all the way from the bed. Rolling sideways, she ran a hand across her brows and found mud. It was ironic for the outside of her to be as messy as the inside of her head felt. Was there actual gravel in her skull? Because—

Right, the phone. She scooted as far as she could to the edge of the bed and snagged it from her coat pocket. It was her sister.

Mo paused for a moment, considering whether to take Anna's call or not, but if Anna was calling at almost six Central Time, then Mo should take it. "Hey, sis," Mo said, falling back on the bed, phone cupped to her ear.

"Sorry it's early—" Anna's voice sounded like their mother's but slightly higher and sweeter, like she was always smiling. Maybe she always was these days, with her life so perfectly arranged.

"It's even earlier there. What's up?"

"Well, Midge went into labor last night, so I technically haven't gone to sleep yet, and you know how hard it can be to lay down when you're overtired. But anyway, Mom and I have been talking about timelines for June. Have you bought your ticket home for the wedding?"

"How's Midge?" Mo asked, quick to change the subject. Midge was one of the Bernese mountain dogs that Anna bred for Bernedoodle puppies on her farm. Anna had gone through ethical breeder training to ensure that her puppies would not only be safely bred but also well trained and properly homed, and in her limited free time she volunteered at the local shelter, training the rescue dogs to assist in placing them with new families. She was, in short, an angel in human form. Mo had never had the kind of single-minded drive on anything except her writing. It was strange to look up to her little sister, but sometimes she felt jealous of her for having everything figured out—not only a five-year plan but a fifty-year one.

"Midge is understandably more tired than I am." Anna laughed. She could even laugh at six in the morning. How were they genetically related? "All seven puppies are healthy, so that's a mercy. But June? Have you bought your tickets?"

Mo closed her eyes, which probably had dirt like eyeshadow all over them, with her luck. How did she get dirt all over her face again? "I haven't, but I promise I'll be there. I've already requested the weekend off." Her boss, Amy, had only been too happy to accept this proposal, since Mo had promised to work the whole week of the Fourth of July.

"And the shower is the second Saturday in May. And have you been thinking about the bachelorette party? Or—"

"You shouldn't be worrying about any of this," Mo interrupted. "You have enough to plan. Mom has the shower under control. I know you're not privy to her Google Doc master plan, but it's well organized, believe me." Not as organized as it would have been under Wes's mother's control. Mo wondered if there was a section in Ulla's very popular website that talked about edibles. Maybe a gallery of images of artistic fainting couches to pass out on after overdoing it.

"Listen, we'll catch up more later, Anna-banana. It sounds like you need to go to sleep, and I need to get up for the day."

"Big plans?" Anna asked, but her voice had a yawn in it. "You hanging out with Aaron this weekend?"

"No, but still gotta go."

They exchanged *I love you*s and hung up. Mo hadn't told anyone back home about the weekend, or about her new book at all. She also hadn't told them that she'd broken up with Aaron nearly a year ago after he proposed and she said no. She couldn't pretend that the book and her failed relationship weren't mixed up, but it wasn't a clear linear choosing of one or the other. Maybe she would inform her family when she RSVP'd for the wedding and wouldn't be bringing a date. Slipping that detail in among three thousand others could let it slide by unnoticed, right?

It wasn't that Maureen didn't want to marry Aaron because she loved the novel so much. She didn't have that kind of reductive view of marriage as an institution. Her parents, for instance, had been happily married for nearly forty years, or at least as happy as marriages seemed to be from the point of view of a child. Her grandparents on both sides had remained married for life, as monogamous as swans. But in a few months, Anna was marrying a man Maureen didn't really know. She was binding her life to some dude who looked good in a plaid shirt and liked the Iowa Hawkeyes. Mo couldn't see what Anna saw in Kyle. Mo went home for some holidays, but he'd been there for such a limited time that Mo had barely met more of him than his smile and firm handshake. "Whoa," he'd said the first time they shook hands. "Nice grip, cowgirl."

Technically, Clive and Eliza's marriage had remained in place until death did them part too, but that was a different situation. Mo didn't fear that what stifled Eliza would stifle her, not really, but she didn't like to be caged or held back. If being unflappable was one of her goals in life, then she needed to make sure to only be with people who couldn't flap her. Letting someone close enough to really know her, enough for to promise her life to them? She didn't know if she could do that.

Maureen wasn't looking for love when she moved to the city. She wanted one thing: this book to be a book in the real world. Well, okay—that was the beginning of it. She wanted to be a writer, who could sustain her living that way. Everything else in her life had been put on hold to make space for that dream: any kind of other meaningful career, serious relationships, and even coming home as often as she might like. This book was her best shot, and in adapting *P&L*, she truly believed that her ambition gave more shape to Eliza's. In the original novel, it was unclear what Eliza needed. Mo's adaptation reimagined Eliza, gave body to her wishes, in a new time period. Mo knew it could speak to people the way *P&L* in its original form had spoken to its original audience, expanding the conversation.

Did Mo turn every thought about Aaron away from their relationship and back into her work?

Maybe.

Perhaps she should have told her family about Aaron, or even about the book. There were so many uncertainties in publishing, so many *maybes* or *somedays* that it was hard to talk about with people not in the business. Relationships were the same way, honestly. She had spent years of her life writing a book that might never see a bookshelf. She'd spent a year dating a man who hadn't, essentially, understood her at all. In life, so much effort went into something that might really end up being nothing. If Mo thought too long about it, it made her want to lie on the floor and not get up for the rest of the day.

But she had to get up. She brushed her teeth, then hopped into the shower and soaped down. There was dirt under her fingernails. Her hands remembered what last night had brought, but she didn't. She did remember Wes's presence and the way his face loomed in front of her. She remembered the smell of him, like cedar and pine. She remembered his lips looking very close and very good and—

Mo shut off the shower and stood there, dripping onto the white tiles. Had they kissed? They wouldn't have done that. He was a narcissistic, nepotistic jerk who thought he'd already won before they began. The fact that she was attracted to him was unrelated. Or, if they had kissed, she would have remembered. She *would* have remembered, right? It wasn't like there was some sort of tangible evidence of a kiss that could be put on or washed off, but she put a finger to her lips as if to feel if they were different. No, they were just wet from the shower. Mo wouldn't have done that, though, even if she did think he was frustratingly handsome. When Wes held her, because she remembered that, his arms hadn't been ropy. She remembered the cabled muscles under his coat, their firmness. It was . . . a lot to think about.

And she needed to stop thinking about it, especially dripping wet and naked on the rug in a guest bathroom of a mansion that served as the backdrop for the biggest day of her life.

Whatever had happened had happened. They were adults, and she could pretend like everything was normal.

Mo toweled off and dressed in black fitted slacks—they were from catering—and a thin pink sweater that matched her naturally rosy complexion. Her bangs hung slack in her face, and she brushed them with a rounded brush, scolding herself for forgetting a hair dryer. She looked okay. She also looked a little nervous, but picking up the manuscript from the desk, she noticed that she'd accidentally coordinated with the rose-colored front and end paper that they had bound it with at the print shop. Even the binding looked like bangs curled over on themselves. She took a breath and left the room.

The agenda said breakfast would begin at 8:00 AM exactly, and at 7:55, Mo was still the last person to arrive in the formal dining room. Unlike the night before, sunshine streamed through the windows facing the front of the estate, illuminating intricate floral wallpaper. She imagined this room on a tour route now that she saw it in the daylight. As if to set that thought even more firmly, she noticed velvet stanchions and poles near the wall. After saying good morning, she helped herself to the spread of breakfast treats on a wine-red table runner in the middle of the long, reclaimed-wood table. "Are there any tour groups coming through today?" Mo asked as she seated herself.

Estelle shook her head. "Oh no. I try to limit those to weekdays and one Saturday a month. The things people do on tours sometimes. They seem surprised that someone lives here! Can you imagine someone tromping in and out of your house, poking around?"

Mo laughed. "I think there's barely room in my apartment to tromp, let alone poke." Then, without meaning to, she caught Wes's glance. Why. Why did he have to be here? "Anyway, yes, I bet that's annoying."

Estelle's plate featured a delicate grapefruit half and piece of buttered toast, and Gary had a large sunny pile of scrambled eggs with mixed fruit. The group ate in companionable silence, except that Wes kept looking at Mo.

Mo focused on anything except Wes, including the fact that this breakfast dish was nicer than any place setting in her parents' house. She wanted to ask suddenly if it had been used by E. J. Morgan herself but was cowed by the idea of being compared to a tromping tourist. She used tiny silver tongs to put a pain au chocolat on her plate alongside a grapefruit half.

Mo picked up her spoon and managed only to squirt herself in the eye on the first attempt. Wes handed her a serrated spoon from his setting. "Try this." When she gave him a look, he said, "I haven't used it."

Mo cut into the grapefruit with this perfectly made tool and scooped a triangle into her mouth. The bright sourness was mixed with something lovely—the top had been broiled with brown sugar and had a crunch to it like the crème brûlée last night. "Forgive me for not knowing the spoon etiquette."

"There's a whole semester in utensils if you attend boarding school," Wes said with a straight face. He stood and retrieved another grapefruit spoon from the end of the table. "Butter knives have their own week."

"Well, at my public, non-boarding school, butter had its own week, so I guess we're even." Mo took a bite of the pain au chocolat and a sip of dark coffee. The mixture was heaven, and she let it soothe the snark from her. She would not snipe at Wesley Spencer, at least not in mixed company. She turned back to Estelle. "Have you ever seen a butter sculpture?"

"No," Estelle said, seeming to rouse herself. Mo had noticed this trick about Estelle last night—her delight in what Maureen took for granted back home. "Have you carved butter?"

"Oh, no," Mo said. "But the Iowa State Fair has had a butter cow since the early 1900s, and we went to see it every year I was growing up. And I love that they have different butter sculptures every fair to go with it—famous characters from *Peanuts* or *Star Trek* or *Sesame Street*. I remember one of Da Vinci's *Last Supper*."

"And they say Iowa doesn't have culture," Wes said.

"It's butter, not yogurt," Mo said, before she could stop herself. A pun was better than slamming him for his coastal elitism.

Estelle chuckled, like they'd planned an Abbott and Costello routine for her.

Wes narrowed his eyes. "Butter sculptures. That's—interesting." His tone made *interesting* sound like he meant disgusting. "And do you . . . eat the butter after? I mean, what happens to all that butter?"

"Yes, Wes. I personally eat an entire cow of butter. They bring a semi to my house and drop it on the lawn."

Estelle chuckled harder and looked at Gary, who laughed too. "Oh my," he said.

Wes made a sour expression, which annoyingly didn't make him less handsome. "What do *they* do with it."

"*They* reuse most of it," Mo said. "It goes into cold storage and gets recarved. For years and years, I'm pretty sure."

Wes took a sip of coffee. If sips of coffee could be judgmental, his was. Had she kissed this asshole? Who was he to judge someone else's art? Just seeing Wes in Mo's peripheral was making her uneasy, and that uneasiness doubled when Gary broke the momentary silence. "Are you feeling better this morning, Maureen?"

She swallowed a mouthful of burning-hot coffee, trying not to choke. She didn't remember seeing anyone except Wes last night, and she had the embarrassing sense of wishing she had seen more of Wes. She had even dreamt of him—wearing his soft gray coat but nothing underneath. She was sure that was her subconscious trying to sabotage her. "I'm fine, thank you."

That set off another round of stares around the table. After a second, Wes picked up his manuscript from beside him. "So, opening pages?"

Angie cleared Estelle's plate, and Gary produced a tiny notepad and gold pen. Estelle took them and smiled. "I'm ready," she said.

Wes offered to read first. Mo didn't realize how much she had been looking forward to hearing his adaptation until he flipped open the front cover. She wanted to know, without a doubt, that hers was better. She couldn't wait to discount his place here this weekend as preferential treatment, pure and simple. The way he'd said *boarding school* like it was nothing. The way he had worked within the system, literally with Estelle, for years. She was ready to reply to him with cool confidence that his adaptation was *interesting*. Despite her readiness to hate his book, her body reacted, tightening, as she saw his face change in preparation to read, his brown eyes scanning the words in front of him. He was nervous. He took a sip of water and began.

His adaptation started at the party where Eliza and Clive met but was told from Clive's perspective. Mo fell into the rhythm of his words easily—too easily for her comfort. She wanted to keep emotional distance, but it was hard not to get lost in the words. His opening chapter was resplendent with 1920s charm. Clive adjusted his spats and ran a hand over the beading of Eliza's dress as they stood in line for punch at the party. And when he spilled some on himself—sometimes called the twentieth century's first meet-cute—she took him into the kitchen at the party and tended to him. The moment, recast through Clive's eyes, probed the tender domesticity of this action from a character who was obviously so independent, and showed why he wanted her so much. In Mo's readings of the original scene, this desire felt almost predatory—Clive's eyes on Liza's as she patted at his jacket with club soda—but Wes took a different tact. He wrote something tender in Clive's gaze. As someone who had read the whole book so many times, it was hard for Mo to think about the scene differently, but he managed to frame the interaction as fresh. The way the light caught Eliza's sleek bob, the smell of lilac in the air.

When Wes finished, he took a deep drink of coffee. Mo did the same, realizing it had gotten cold while she listened.

He was a good reader, confident and expressive. Maureen wasn't quite so confident in her speaking voice, but she knew her voice on the page—and of the character—would come through. She waited for Estelle to give some sort of signal that it was her turn. Estelle finally looked up from the notepad on which she had been taking copious notes and smiled. "Go ahead, Maureen."

After a steadying breath, Mo began. "'Liza didn't have many friends, but the friends she had were also named a form of Elizabeth—Lizzy, Beth, Ellie—and the many forms an Elizabeth could take made her hopeful that she too could take a new form as easily as adopting a new name. As easy as changing her clothes. As easy as rolling her crop top off in a stranger's bathroom to put on a new shirt and pretend that this party, this next party, would be the one that would change her life.'"

Mo kept reading, steadier with the first paragraph behind her. She'd centered her narrative in the early aughts. The post-9/11, halfway-through-the-endless-war period was defined by McMansions and "We are the 99 percent" rallies on the streets of New York. For Mo, Eliza's counterculture appeal wasn't limited to the flapper era. Mo pictured Eliza as a sheltered girl shot-putted into the real world for the first time, struggling.

Once Mo had started reimagining the novel, there were so many threads there to pull on that she'd had to limit herself, and she knew later adaptations would have so much to say. The original text wryly called out the sexism of Eliza's situation, which was doubly wonderful in retrospect, since it was published without people knowing the author was a woman. Feminism had changed so much since the twenties, though. Something Mo noticed while listening to Wes's first chapter was a lingering classism, one of the reasons Mo wanted to retell the novel in an updated context. Here in this hall of money, she thought about this same irony of class barriers. In her book, Clive came from a working-class family but had clawed his way up the Wall Street bro hierarchy with a mix of charisma and smarts. And how much more countercultural could it seem to an independent twentysomething to fall headlong into a serious relationship with him—an elopement and the sudden recentering of the traditional values that she didn't know were expected of her?

Mo finished reading the chapter. At the end of it, Clive and Liza had made their way into the bathroom at a party after she spilled a drink on him. Instead of merely touching hands, as in Morgan's novel, the characters kissed. She didn't like to think of it as *making* the characters kiss, because it hadn't felt that way when she was writing. The kiss felt inevitable, necessary. When Mo reached that point while reading, she glanced up at Wes and took in his set expression.

Mo read, "'His hand met mine on his chest, and that press of skin on skin made the next press easier. Our lips met. His tongue explored my mouth and I let it, leaning against the pedestal sink and feeling like I was on a pedestal myself.'" She didn't want to see how Wes took the decision she had made to move their kiss up, and to write it explicitly on the page. Mo wanted to keep many touchstones of the book in place—the drink spill, the wedding, the dinner party, and the argument at the climax of the book. Without them, it wouldn't be an adaptation. She wanted readers to feel the anchor of Morgan's novel but still feel a bit adrift, unsure how Mo would twist things. Mo had felt adrift while writing it—it was only fair.

The chapter ended on that kiss, with Mo suddenly feeling as breathless as her character was. When she looked up from the manuscript, Estelle and Gary were both smiling. She smiled in return and glanced at Wes, whose face was less friendly. And why should it be? Just because she had imagined kissing him didn't mean they were friends. She wondered idly how Wes's mouth would feel—had felt?—against her own. The shape of that tongue that had helped him speak so well minutes ago and the other tricks it could do.

Deep breath.

With a calm smile, Estelle dismissed them for the morning, explaining that dinner that night would include some company—her two adult children. "We thought a little party would be fun, nothing fancy."

Wes took this in stride. "Of course," he said. But internally, Mo panicked. She had already worn one of the two dresses she'd packed for the weekend, and it had arguably been her nicer one for first impressions' sake.

"I'm afraid I don't have anything party appropriate," she said.

"Oh, don't worry about it," Estelle said, waving a hand. "It's a family dinner."

As Mo and Wes left the dining room, he touched Mo's arm lightly. "If you want to go shopping, we can. If you're nervous."

"I'm not nervous," Mo said, once she knew they were out of earshot. She stepped back to lose the faint touch of his fingers, then immediately missed the warmth. "I'm not nervous or anxious."

He gave a small shrug. "It's okay to worry about how you look."

"I think I look fine."

"You do," he said, then blushed. It might have been a blush, or it might have been a trick of the light. Before she could look closer, he had turned away, moving down the hall, and continued the conversation. "How are you this morning?"

She took a hint from his careful tone that he remembered a lot more about last night than she did. "I'm fine. Thank you for . . . helping me when things went wrong."

"And how about Gary and Estelle?" he asked. "I . . . didn't expect to see him."

"I thought it was fine," Mo said, unsure of why he was so thrown off. They had been perfectly polite through both readings. Gary had even nodded during a part she'd rewritten a dozen times, a satisfying sight from an audience member. "I assumed he would be there, to be honest."

"You did?"

And there it was again, that sense of exclusion, of exclusivity. Gary obviously was "the help" to Wes, and therefore somehow unworthy of what—hearing their drafts? Mo felt her cheeks reddening. "You wouldn't have been that way if it had been one of her daughters in there, would you?"

He looked shocked. "Of course not! I would have expected it, even. I was surprised, that's all—"

Mo took a deep breath, scanning his face. It was too easy to get caught in his brown eyes and in the curl of his lips. "I need some fresh air." Mo knew her voice was cold, but she didn't care. Let him figure out what an ass he was. He'd had how many years of private school? He could educate himself on this one.

She slipped upstairs to get walking shoes. The day outside looked clear and bright, but by the time she had gotten into the hallway, Wes was standing, waiting for her. "I thought you might want a ride somewhere," he said. His tone was careful. "I'm grabbing coffee downtown, if you'd like to get out of here for a while."

Mo hadn't had a clear sense of her goal for the morning. She'd optimistically brought her laptop to write, but her nerves had jammed any creativity. Her true goals were to keep it together and not make a fool out of herself, and it seemed easier to do those two things away from the person whose choices controlled her future. At least if Wes was out with her, it wasn't like she was losing some prime bonding time with Estelle that he was taking advantage of.

She sighed, then nodded. "Okay. Sure. Let me get my non-designer purse and we'll get out of here."

CHAPTER EIGHT

Wes

Things had gotten decidedly chilly between him and Mo, just as he hoped they might get warmer. He had brought up Gary and Estelle as a point of common knowledge—seeing two people in the act of something seemingly illicit. He'd always found that a little shared gossip was the fastest way to create a friendship, much like social grooming with other primates. Not that he and Maureen would be friends, but he didn't want her to hate him.

It would be easier if she weren't, well, cool.

Wes wasn't jealous of her talent. Her authorial voice was so different from his that it couldn't be that. His novel was about being a man, wanting. Being destroyed by wanting. Besides the adaptation being told from Clive's perspective and remaining in the time period, Wes's Clive was explicitly bisexual. In the original novel, Wes couldn't help but see Clive as bi coded.

Wes's own sexuality aside, he didn't assume anything of the people around him or most of the characters he read. But there was a latent, charged maleness in Clive, and desire was an undercurrent in his relationships with his compatriots. In the dinner party scene with his old war buddy Perkins and his wife, their exchange about "modern games" read as flirting. Wes didn't know what Estelle would say after hearing his book. It wasn't as if he'd set out with the premise "I took your mom's character and made him have gay feelings," because he didn't think he'd really *made* Clive do anything. The characters' choices naturally flowed from themselves, sparks catching line to line as Wes wrote the book. Clive didn't end up doing much more beyond just longing, but this longing created a negligent tyranny over Eliza.

But Mo's first chapter had caught fire in his brain. He couldn't stop thinking about how the rest would go. It was maddening not knowing how she'd approach the wedding, for instance, something that would come early in the manuscript before the halfway point they would read over lunch. So yes, Wes had moved his coffee date with Ulla downtown to a public location to make excuses to spend more time with Maureen.

Mo slid into the passenger seat with the same pink jacket from last night wrapped around her. She'd obviously tried to scrub off some of the dirt from the cuffs and collar. Wes wasn't going to mention to her that those spots reminded him of the feel of her in his arms. How different would this morning have been if he hadn't tucked her responsibly into bed last night, if he'd let her kiss him like she'd wanted to? He would have felt horrible about it, but maybe the sexual tension would have broken, because that's what it was.

Stop thinking about her, he scolded himself as he pulled out of the estate. He had to acknowledge the unbearable singing tension of someone who was undoubtedly attractive—her hair was lightly curling in the morning's humidity—and whose brain you wanted to open and examine for all its weirdness. Instead of last night bonding them, it was clear that she regretted everything about it, and her icy attitude was jarring.

They passed the gates, which latched closed behind them. Veering down the familiar streets, he tried not to notice her blank expression as she stared out the window. He wasn't used to people saying no to him or turning down attempts at friendship. He was a well-connected, well-liked person with a famous mother and money besides. He was so used to having to push people away, or freezing them out if they got too close, too fast, that he couldn't imagine someone doing the same right back to him.

Well, fine, he thought. But he didn't feel fine, and he couldn't leave it at that. They'd driven much farther yesterday, but it hadn't felt awkward. Now, even with the music as a buffer between them and only a few miles to travel, it did. He had to say something or it would needle him the whole day. "I don't know why you're frustrated with me," he said. "But I hope you can clue me in."

"No idea at all?"

"It's got to be about a butter cow."

She laughed, as he'd guessed she would. "Clearly," she said.

That laugh buoyed him, made him want to push harder. "Or besides the obvious fact that I'm beating you in a literary competition."

That earned a narrowed glare from the passenger sea. "You wish."

He continued. "But besides that?"

"I don't think you really want to know."

"I do or I wouldn't ask."

"Fine." She turned toward him and huffed a breath. "If I'm being honest, you have this whole entitlement thing going on, and it's getting to me."

"Is this about the . . . server?"

"You don't even remember her name."

Damn. He coughed to buy himself time, then swallowed. "Angela."

"Angie, but no, that's not it. It's Gary."

He nearly slammed the Civic into a mailbox. "What? Gary? I love Gary. I've worked with Gary for years longer than you. That's *why* I was so surprised."

She paused. "Surprised about—"

He laughed, making a right turn onto Greenwich Avenue. "Gary and Estelle are obviously doing it." Luckily, they were stopped at a stoplight so he could catch her expression.

It was worth it. Her lips fell open in shock. "I guess I *really* don't remember a lot about last night."

He explained what they had walked into—not exactly walked in *on*, since everyone had met in the hallway like some Noël Coward production. The story expelled some of the tension between them, thank whatever deity was responsible for such things. By the time they parked in front of a brick-front café downtown, Mo was rooting for the relationship that might or might not have been completely imaginary.

"I love stories when someone finds love late in life," Mo said.

"Or lust."

"I think lust finds you. I don't think that's something you look for," she said, then glanced away. The sun must have been in her eyes.

"What makes it lust, then?" he asked, wanting to press the issue. What would make her turn and look at him in that less careful way she had last night?

"Oh, pheromones and hormones, probably," she said, taking the question academically. "I could ask my sister."

"What?"

"My sister. She breeds dogs, so she thinks a lot about mating, compatibility—"

He stepped faster to catch up to her. How she could walk so quickly was a testament to her having become a real New Yorker. "But humans aren't *dogs*," he said.

"Most aren't, but I've met some exceptions." She stared at him with an eyebrow raised.

"That's a rough assessment."

It was her turn to stop on the sidewalk, and he was gentleman enough to stop next to her. "That was a bad pun." She elbowed him. It was a light jab, but her elbows were ridiculously pointy.

"Ow. You got a permit for those elbows, Ms. Denton?"

"No, but I am always armed."

"Terrible," he said, but grinned. He wanted her to like him, he realized. He wanted to claw his way into her good graces to see what it looked like to earn a real smile from her.

The café bell dinged as they entered. This place was one of his favorites and baked the best lemon poppy seed muffins he had ever eaten. Wes took in a deep, fresh-roasted sniff and glanced to see if his mother had taken a table yet. Ulla was, as usual, precisely one minute ahead of whatever internal schedule he was running. She had a tablet in front of her and was delicately scrolling through some proposal or another for a product that she would find a way to sell to the masses. He stopped by the table before ordering, leaving a kiss on her delicately powdered cheek.

He asked after his father.

"Well." Ulla gestured with her eyes over Wes's shoulder.

Maureen stood, wearing the familiar fish-out-of-water look he had observed more times in the past twenty-four hours than her smile. "Hi," Mo said. She introduced herself, and Ulla reciprocated.

As the two women fell into stilted small talk, Wes excused himself to get a coffee. Standing in line, he felt the guilt roil in his stomach. He and Mo had been so busy talking about the October/December romance unfolding in the bedroom down the hall that he hadn't warned her that Ulla would have coffee with them. Ulla never expected much from Wes and wasn't the type to meddle, but if he was back in town, a coffee date was an expectation. He'd forgotten to share that plan with Maureen—or his mother, for that matter.

He ordered a latte—oat milk and an extra shot—and stood at the end of the mahogany bar. The frother hissed and the door tinkled again as a huddle of women entered, gabbing gleefully. They passed the table with Mo and Ulla, who seemed to be deep in conversation now.

He might have made a mistake in leaving them alone together. Ulla had a forceful personality. She tended to steamroll people with meaningful silences and solid smiles and had a way of enforcing her point of view by allowing you to come around to it. This kind of expected mind reading was a conversational curse that Wes had inherited and one that had meant the downfall of some past relationships, both professional and personal. He had trouble asking for things from other people—that would be rude. Better to let someone figure out his desires through watching. He didn't act this way in business relationships. His editorial letters to clients were clear and to the point—he didn't bullshit them, and it served both parties well—but in personal relationships, he had a way of assuming both the best and worst in the other person simultaneously. The best in that whoever he was with was the absolute perfect person for him—at least for two weeks. And the worst in that they didn't know how to love him without all the connections he brought along. It was easier to assume temporary status for any relationship. It was easier to accept the mutability of the heart than to let himself be hurt.

Ulla and Mo were chatting like old friends by the time he got to the table, and amazingly not about pork or butter—or any kind of animal product that he could determine. Instead, horrifyingly, it was obvious they had been talking about him. Ulla smiled in an *I just showed your baby pictures* kind of way when he approached, and he saw her reach for her phone again. It was surreal to see Mo unfazed by Ulla. In the past, new friends were showing work samples by this time, but Ulla had paused her embarrassing story about him to check something on her phone. Of course, Mo was not a new friend. Perhaps Wes needed to make and bring around more enemies to the estate.

Suddenly, Wes's own phone buzzed, and he reached into his pocket. The message was from Ulla. *She is sweet. I like her, but can we talk alone?*

He texted back. *I'm her ride.*

Instead of replying to the text, Ulla pursed her lips and turned to Maureen. "There are several lovely shops around here. How about we walk around together, and we can show you the circuit?"

Maureen glanced uncertainly at Wes. "I don't want to intrude."

Ulla, who clearly had won over Maureen more in five minutes than he had in a day, touched her lightly on the arm. "Please do me the favor of letting me show you around. I never get to play hostess to Wes's friends."

Mo seemed about to argue again but cast a look at Wes. The word *friends* sat as heavy as an anvil between them. "Sure. Of course." Two minutes later, the three of them set off again into the chilly morning air. Ulla led the way—she usually did—and Mo walked in step next to Wes. "I'm not planning on buying anything."

"That's fine," Wes said. "It's always fun to look." Even though he didn't believe that at all, especially not at the women's clothing stores that he had been dragged in and out of too many times. Before he left for boarding school, on days when his nanny was sick, he remembered sitting outside changing room doors or hiding in the giant metal circle racks of women's skirts and dresses, waiting for Ulla to find the right outfit. He hated to shop even for himself and subscribed to one of those "order for me" men's clothing services.

The first stop was a consignment store for luxury clothing. The window display showed mannequins decked out with entire ensembles, one in what looked like a navy-blue Victorian jacket with tasseled trim and padded shoulders. "Looks like Miss Havisham out on the town," Maureen whispered. Wes grinned at her.

The other mannequin wore a pale-pink sateen dress with a ruched flower at its waist. "Jason Wu," Ulla pointed out as they passed it. "And the shoes are Jimmy Choo." How she could tell one pair of beige pumps from another was a mystery to him.

Inside the store, long racks lined the walls, color coded and separated by type of garment. The coats hung out together near the front of the store, while couture dresses lined the back wall. Shelves of purses hung above the clothing racks to crown them off. Ulla immediately separated herself, now distracted from the need to talk by the need to browse. Maureen seemed as frozen as Wes was.

"I really don't need anything," she said again, not looking at him.

"Neither do I."

"I mean that I'm not uncomfortable about what I packed."

"Trust me, we're here as an excuse for my mother to gab as much as for anything else. This is her exercise. Some people do yoga, she does shopping." Ulla was deep in conversation with the attendant at the counter, gesturing at the bags. They would be here for a while. Ulla could buy anything new, but she loved the thrill of the hunt, and upscale used-clothing stores offered that to her. Try as she might, she could not escape her upbringing as the child of a child of the Great Depression and always appreciated what she thought to be a good deal.

Maureen turned toward the closest rack of blouses and fingered a red cap sleeve shirt. "Look at this," she said, pulling him toward it. "It's a leather blouse. Who would wear a leather shirt?"

He checked the tag. "It's lambskin leather with a silk lining. And oh, look at the care instructions."

Mo maneuvered closer, turning against his chest out of necessity to glance at the label. His heart sped up as her hair pressed against his face, the smell of rose filling his senses.

"Dry clean only by a leather expert?" She snorted. She took a step back, much to his relief. "How do you even determine that? Do you go into every dry cleaner until you see one in leather chaps?"

"If my dry cleaner is wearing leather chaps, I think they probably have a better social life than I do."

When she wandered off to browse, he noticed her expression change when she stumbled upon something she liked. Her eyes widened as her fingers reached out tentatively toward a dress. Her lips, which were very pink and had a shape like they were always about to pout, opened slightly. His mouth went a little dry and he had to look away. He didn't realize he'd wanted to be looked at like that.

He took out his phone as a buffer but found himself staring at the lock screen without typing anything. What did Mo's daily life look like? Maybe he'd passed her on a jog in the park and never noticed. Maybe she'd been at a literary party he'd been dragged to. The Google alerts hadn't told him anything about her, other than a few short stories she'd published in the past few years. In trying to picture the kinds of spaces she might inhabit, his brain felt like it did while drafting a new project. Unlike with adapting *The Proud and the Lost*, he didn't know the characters in her life, though she was starting to get to know his.

That reminded him. Ulla, now freed from her conversation with the saleswoman, had anchored herself near a shoe rack. She didn't seem surprised when Wes edged next to her. "What's up?"

"I hate it when you say 'What's up.'" He had inherited her peevishness, the kind they both got under stress. Her tone was clipped, the consonants exact, but he could tell she was not okay.

"What did you want to talk about?"

"Your father and I are planning on separating," she said simply, not looking up from the heels in her hand.

"What?"

She still couldn't look at him, and he couldn't stop looking at his mother not looking at him. "It might be permanent, it might not. I wanted to tell you before the media got ahold of it."

"You *are* the media."

She turned to meet his gaze, finally, and gestured with the heel. "Oh, you know that's not true. Although my SEO manager tells me that clicks are up ten percent, whatever that's worth."

She said it in a throwaway tone that made him think she knew exactly, in dollars and cents, how much that was worth, but he saw the glaze of tears in her eyes anyway.

He softened his tone. "Why . . . why are you separating?"

"The spark is gone," she said simply.

And he laughed. He couldn't help it. A couple who had been together for forty years. "Of course, the spark is gone," he said. "I mean, doesn't the spark just—*go* at a certain point and the marriage kind of, I don't know, maintains its momentum anyway?"

"We'll see," she said. "Absence makes the heart grow fonder, they say, and maybe that will work for us."

A crash in the background made them turn around. Mo seemed to be apologizing to a mannequin that she'd knocked over. It wasn't until he got closer that he noticed the woman behind the mannequin, who seemed also to have been knocked off her feet. "I'm so, so sorry. I found something I thought I might try on, but—"

"It is useful to take it off the mannequin first," Wes called across the shop, unable to stop himself.

Mo glared so hard that he saw the light at the end of the tunnel. The look only made her button nose crinkle in a way that was cute, though he doubted she'd appreciate being called that word. After a minute, bodies—plastic and real— were upright again and Maureen headed into a dressing room with the dress in question.

He took advantage of the relative privacy again. "So is he living at home still, or—"

"He'll be staying at our home in Tahoe. He's got his cars loaded on a trailer to head down there now. And the cat."

"Harold will hate that." Harold was a ragged old tabby that had been adopted at a Broadway Barks event a few years ago and only taken to his father.

She nodded her agreement. "It's for the best. This way we don't have to pay a keeper to watch that property over the summer anyway."

"Silver linings," Wes managed, though inside he was devastated. He hadn't seen his parents be affectionate with each other in years, but he assumed that was just a habit, the cool monied distance between an older couple. Marble countertops and polished rims on your car and not touching each other: that was older couplehood, wasn't it? And then he thought about the blush in Gary's cheeks last night in the hallway and couldn't stop his frown. Passion wasn't time-stamped, and he supposed he wanted his mother to have . . .

privacy. He wanted his mother to have privacy and the space to figure it out herself. If the story didn't get out to the press, she'd be able to do that. Most outlets were too busy interrogating the love lives of twenty-year-old celebrities to worry about media moguls in their early seventies.

Maureen stepped out of the dressing room and turned toward a three-way mirror. The dress she had put on was stunning but simple: a cap-sleeved floral silk number that cut off at the knees. He probably shouldn't have noticed the way it nipped in at her waist in the right places, accentuating her hips. He definitely shouldn't have noticed the way it curved around her breasts, the front of the dress high necked so they were fully covered but somehow still emphasized. It was almost like writing subtext. Hemingway's iceberg principle of a book, except with breasts and hips and . . .

He cleared his throat. "That's beautiful."

She turned, seeming surprised that he and his mother were watching. "It's on sale," she said. "I mean, *really* on sale."

"You must be from the Midwest," Ulla said. "I had a roommate in college who always had to make that disclaimer about something nice. She was from Indiana."

"Iowa." Mo blushed, the little bit of her chest that was showing turning pink as a sunburn. She ran a self-conscious hand down the front of the dress. "I don't really need it."

"We barely *need* anything in this life," Ulla countered. "But sometimes I think about beautiful things as helping me to understand the next life. Just a little flavor."

That made Mo laugh. "You think heaven has tailored pleats like this?"

"Oh, I don't doubt it." Ulla laughed.

"Your sister is getting married, right? There's always a need for something fantastic for weddings," Wes said. He couldn't imagine anyone else in that dress, and he had a good imagination. So good it was having trouble not imagining her out of it as well.

She seemed surprised he remembered. "You're right. Okay." Wes caught her glance down at the price tag, then out the window.

"Let me get it," Ulla said.

"No," Maureen said, her voice suddenly solid. The blush crept higher up her chest into her cheeks. "I mean, no thank you."

Ulla paused. "As a gift for putting up with Wes this weekend," she said, making her voice light.

Maureen's finger twisted in the hem of the dress. "How about this," she said, "I will pay you back once I get my book advance for the adaptation."

"That's presumptuous," Wes said.

Ulla clapped. "Perfect," she said, and placed the dress gently on top of the pile.

Mo walked out of the store with a dress bag over her arm. Ulla kissed her son's cheek and gave Maureen a pat on the arm as they walked toward their respective cars. Her social schedule called her away to a boat party. "It's awfully early in the season to be out on the water," she said, "but needs must."

Again with the idea of needs, thrown about so carelessly. What did anyone need, really, besides the basics? But Wes couldn't imagine his mother without the lifestyle she lived, the smell of her perfume and the way her clothes were perfectly pressed. He couldn't imagine his mother without his father, perhaps the ultimate accessory—a seventy-year-old version of Ken, with a tennis racket and sports car. Mo and Wes watched Ulla drive away and turned to one another, their two-ness suddenly more intimate after being observed by a parent. He had never been a teen under his parents' roof for any stretch of time, what with boarding school and summer camp every year from ten to eighteen, but he had noticed his mother watching him watching Maureen, though. Embarrassing. He hoped Maureen hadn't noticed.

They walked for a while longer, comparing the window displays at the various stores. Downtown Greenwich had a collaged feel—a mixture of upscale brands and local boutiques, antique stores, and restaurants. A gardener watered a basket of just-blossoming flowers hanging from a hook on the streetlight. Greenwich was careful and curated, like arranged flowers that depended on daily watering. Maureen reminded him of wildflowers. He scarcely had time to wonder where that thought had come from before he almost smacked into her back. She had stopped in front of an expansive glass window.

It was a gelato place that Wes had overindulged at on more than one occasion. "What's your favorite gelato?" he asked.

Mo scrunched her nose again, even more evident under the overlarge sunglasses she had pulled from her purse. The morning sun had risen higher in the sky. "I hate the texture of gelato. I just like ice cream."

"Heathen."

"But for ice cream flavors, I like pistachio."

He shook his head, hard. "No, pistachio gelato is much better. That's my choice. Always." Her pace quickened, though he didn't think she noticed that it had. He hustled to keep up. "Gelato has less fat in it."

"I don't worry about fat when I'm eating ice cream," she shot back. "Do I need to?"

God, she did not need to. He had schooled himself into thinking about it for years in the cookbook business—low-fat everything had been the trend for so long. He also knew he wasn't skinny, and never had been. He was fine with his body, and he was more than fine with hers, not that hers was his business. He leaned toward full flavor and full fat when he cooked for himself and loved dating people who did the same.

Not that he was thinking about dates. "Because gelato is served a little warmer, it numbs your tongue less."

"I like cold ice cream. That's literally the point of ice cream."

"The point is that because your tongue is not numb, you can taste everything. All the pistachio deliciousness. It's all there. And listen, it's okay for you to be wrong sometimes, Mo." He had meant the last statement as a friendly barb but realized the moment it was out of his mouth that he'd made a mistake.

She stopped then and turned around. "How did you know my nickname?"

A couple that had been walking behind them veered around her stopped position. Wes steered Mo to the edge of the sidewalk, in front of Diane's Books. He realized it was the first time he had said "Mo" aloud and not Maureen. He didn't want her to suspect he knew anything about her. God, especially not about him having a Google alert on her name.

"Lucky guess. I had a friend named Maureen that I called Mo."

"Uh-huh," she said, looking more closely at him. She bit her lip, a lip she had obviously already been gnawing on because it looked pink and plump. *Don't look at her lips, Wes. Rule one.* "You've read my stuff." Her tone was certain.

"What?"

"You laughed at me for following you on LinkedIn, but you've read my short stories! I sometimes publish under the name Mo Denton. You've read my work."

He absolutely had. He had, in fact, read through all the ones he could find last night in bed when he couldn't sleep. She had a short story in *Alaska Quarterly* last year, and one in *Ploughshares*. She had an achingly perfect flash fiction in *Split Lip*'s print edition, and she had posted on Threads about a close call with *The New Yorker*. With her talent, and a little luck, she would be in it someday, he was sure. "I liked what you read this morning. Where have you been published?"

She raised an eyebrow and kept walking. "Fine. Never mind. But realize that I won't be bulldozed over about my ice cream opinions."

"Why do I feel like challenging someone from the Midwest on their dairy choices is a battle I can't win," he mused aloud.

"Get used to losing, Wesley Spencer. I intend to pay your mother back for that dress."

With that jab, their route circled back to the car, and having wasted all the time they could that morning, they headed back to the Hill. Lunch loomed, then dinner with more of the family, and he would have to pretend he hadn't seen Mo in the dress she carried over her arm. He had to pretend because if he didn't, he wouldn't be able to scrounge up the competitive spirit to fight for his book articulately. *Get used to losing,* she had said. Seeing her in the dress, seeing her expression soften this morning as they shared a joke, made him want to roll over on his back and expose his soft parts to her like any beta male in a wolf pack. She could go for his throat if he thought about those lips too hard. God, he wanted her to go for his throat.

He needed to get back on his game.

CHAPTER NINE

Mo

Maureen thought about texting her friends an honest play-by-play of the weekend, including the private performance of her book, getting too high to function in front of her rival, meeting a media bigwig with her own brand of dish soap, then trash-talking that bigwig's son constantly, mostly to his too-attractive face. Her body had stopped making cortisone hours ago, maxed out. Maybe that was why the reading over lunch had gone so well. Instead of mentioning any of this, she texted them a simple *Hi, I love you both. Please send Perkins pix* as she lay on her bed, digesting both her lunch and the weekend so far.

Mo had thought she would nap, but instead she stared at the ceiling. Wes's second reading had been good. Really good. They hadn't coordinated their readings from the middle of the book, but both had selected their interpretations of the dinner party scene from near the center point of the novel. Wes finally hit on that latent sexual tension between Clive and Perkins that he'd talked about in the car, and Mo could see what he meant about the undertones in the book. The way he wrote about Clive looking at his longtime friend and knowing he wanted him was electrifying. The whole setup, this artifice of adulthood when the main characters were only in their early twenties. And still—they were adults. They had been through war and parenthood, but the longing, awkward and almost adolescent, remained. It was a potent scene, and Mo wanted to flip ahead to the next chapter after he finished. She could picture him reading that selection on a stage in three years, accepting some major literary prize.

She knew he looked good in a tux.

During the reading, she'd focused on his fingers, watching them curl around his paper, and wanted to ask what instrument he played growing up. She was certain, after meeting Ulla for only an hour, that he had been forced to play something. To distract herself from his body, she had made mental guesses—maybe violin from a young age, Suzuki method. Mo bet he'd been sat down with a bow at age two and performed for guests at the mansion. He came from such a different universe. Mo had played the kazoo from the cereal box, the recorder in fourth grade, and a miserable rental clarinet through middle school. Mo could tell her parents really loved her because they recorded those god-awful concerts and would probably show them off as proudly as Ulla had shown her a picture of Wes in his boarding school uniform (he had a plaid tie!).

Mo's reading was the same party but spun forward eighty years. An upscale patio barbecue—polo shirts for the men and wrap dresses for the women. There was wine, and the characters were just old enough to have the right kind of matching glassware. Mo's Eliza—Liza—was restless, her dress itchy and her period late. In the scene, Liza sipped her wine and thought about ultrasounds, the way they revealed things you only suspected.

Mo couldn't look at Wes after finishing her chapter. She hated that her first impulse was to check his face or ask him what he thought. She thought about the way he described gelato and ice cream, how ice cream was served so cold it numbed the flavor out, and she wondered if prose could do that too—be too cold and emotionally distant to let the flavor and feeling come through. She wanted to ask him, *Could you taste it? Could you taste my scene?* Instead, she complained of a headache, thanked Estelle for lunch, and retreated to lie down. Soon, though, the rest of the family would arrive, and Mo would have to be on her best behavior again.

She draped an arm over her eyes, wishing she could nap. She rolled to her side, then heard the tap on the door. "Who is it?" she called.

"It's Wes."

She sat up and smoothed down her hair. He didn't deserve to see her ruffled. She refused to give him the satisfaction of flyaways. "Come in. It's unlocked."

He opened the door and stood in the hallway. Instead of entering, he lingered near the door and stared at her. The look wasn't full of antipathy or calculation but instead, unless she misread it, confusion. Confusion, as if he hadn't been the one to knock on her door. After a few seconds of silence, the air between them was thick enough to slather with jam and take a bite of.

"Hi," he said. "How's your head?"

"Better when someone isn't asking me how it is," she said honestly. "But it's okay. Thanks."

"I was taking a self-tour of the house and thought you might want to come too. You said you hadn't been here before."

The offer was nice, too nice to turn down. She had considered wandering around by herself. She stuffed her phone in her back pocket and nodded.

The started on the ground floor and wound through the empty rooms from one wing to the other. Drawing room, morning room, guest room—the spaces blurred together as they walked from one to another. As they walked, Maureen couldn't help but show off her knowledge of the Hill, and of Morgan, finding comfort in his rebuttals with his own tidbits. "These bas-reliefs were originally Morgan's sketches, some of them self-portraits," Wes said, to which Maureen could reply, "And the materials came from local quarries."

As they passed a tapestry in an alcove, Wes paused and pointed to the intricate threadwork. "That's E. J.," he said, gesturing up at the woman stitched there. Her eyes were light brown, the same color as her hair, and her hands were folded in her lap on top of a notebook.

"Hello, E. J.," she said softly, running her fingers over the coarse material.

"I love tapestries," he said, still gazing up.

"I'm not rich enough to have an opinion on them," she jabbed back, her tone light.

"No, look," he said, glancing in both directions before flipping the corner of the art over. "Look at this chaos."

The threads collided, woven in knots and bundles that barely reflected the order on the other side. There was beauty in the chaos, but also, she couldn't help but feel too seen by the disorder. Her brain felt like that, competing for her life against someone she found intriguing while attempting to look respectable.

Suddenly, she heard a noise down the corridor, and Wes stepped back from the tapestry, dropping its corner. He gave her a guilty look and waved a hand to encourage her to follow him. They walked down another hallway until they came to the entry to the library. In the doorway, Mo held her breath. The space looked exactly as Morgan must have experienced it.

"No tapestries here. No paintings. I'm a little surprised," Maureen said.

"The story goes that Morgan believed that libraries should have books as their primary decoration. Books inspired by other books, I guess," Wes said.

Maureen turned, unable to stop her smile. "Sounds familiar."

Wes turned back to the floor-to-ceiling oak bookshelves while Mo continued to explore the room. A plaque above a rather ordinary desk near the window marked it as *her* desk. Before reading it, she knew its importance. At this desk, history was made. Mo felt the warmth of the wood and took in the scratch marks on its surface. In a house of opulence, Morgan's desk was simple. When she turned around, she noticed Wes watching her. "We can move on," she said, blushing.

"When you're ready."

She took another deep breath and gave the desk one more thankful pat, grateful that Wes had returned to his perusal.

They climbed the stairs into the wing opposite from their rooms. They passed closed door after closed door. "I wonder whose rooms these were when E. J. lived here," Mo said to break the silence. "Servants?"

"Probably. Or guests."

"This whole place is so empty. It would make a great haunted house," Mo said, without really meaning it. Though it was mostly empty, Estelle was so generous and open that it didn't feel isolating. It must be awkward to live in a house with plaques on the walls, ready for public consumption.

"I like it," he said. "But it's fun to imagine it in its heyday. I can't imagine going to one of E. J.'s parties, can you?"

They entered a ballroom that marked the halfway point between the wings. Soaring ceilings with a great dome above, crowned in stained glass. The midsummer sun struck everything in pinks and greens. Maureen could visualize this room in the late evening of a summer in the 1920s. After sunset, with the stained glass dimmed, breezes from the open window would dance with fingertips of candlelight from holders lining the wall. "I think I could imagine it, actually. She was famously extravagant. A modern, female Gatsby, except married. I bet Estelle has some stories." The Great Depression wasn't even a consideration at that point, not even an imagining on the bright spot that was the time after WWI and the flu pandemic of 1919. People ran wild, tossing their inhibitions to the wind in a way that wouldn't be mirrored until the seventies.

Wes kicked a foot against the marble floor. "A little slippery. It would be hard to dance." He ran a hand through his hair, and Mo watched its path a little too closely. She realized her attention and turned to watch her shadow on the wall, which also turned its head. She liked seeing Wes's shadow next to hers, though they looked even closer together in shadow form.

Wes kept speaking, his tone musing. "I think she settled down after motherhood. It's always amazing to me that she wrote *The Proud and the Lost* before having Estelle. She said it was mainly based on—"

"Her fears of what would happen to her after motherhood," Mo finished. She turned away, moving her shadow farther from his and examining the inset tapestries of flowers and trees on the wall as they talked. "I know. I read about it in college."

"The fertility angle is interesting. I noticed that in your reading today. I hadn't really thought about how she probably was pregnant at that party, timing-wise. Not that I have mapped out a literary character's menstrual cycles or anything."

"Oh, I did," Mo said, then realized how weird it sounded. "It was for a paper for that class. A women's studies/English crossover class where we talked about periods in literature. Uh, not like thematic interrelated years of writing, but actual menstrual periods." She tried to catch his expression. She wasn't trying to unsettle him purposely, but if that was a side effect, she'd take it.

His face gave away nothing, maddeningly. "That's cool," he said, sounding genuine. It annoyed her when men were put off by the existence of periods, as if women weren't much more inconvenienced for six days a month, plus all the hormonal turmoil on either side of that. Maybe his interest was part of the agent persona. In her experience, an agent was good at selling a lot of things, including a feeling they wanted you to have about yourself. In this case, making her feel uncomfortable didn't work into whatever four-dimensional chess he was playing.

"What novels did you read in the class?" As Wes asked, he sat on a bench on the far end of the ballroom. His body language invited her to join him, and after a second, she did.

"A lot of the classics. *Little Women. Middlemarch. Pride and Prejudice.*"

"It's been a few years since I've read any of those, but I don't actually remember any mention of periods."

Mo laughed. "I know. The class focused on the erasure of natural body processes—periods, pregnancy, menopause—even in these texts heavily read by women. Sometimes these older books were so much about the mind of the woman, but they didn't mention her body. At least not the normal mechanics of it."

"It wasn't considered genteel to talk about," Wes said. She could smell him from his position, a citrusy, piney smell that could only be from cologne. Unless he naturally smelled that good, which would be royally unfair.

"Kind of like masturbation," he added, jarring her from her thoughts, which had veered too close to his body anyway.

She choked on a laugh. "I mean, yes. Absolutely."

"Tell me Ahab wouldn't have been wanking off every day, Moby Dick or no Moby Dick. I mean, a dude at sea?"

"Jane Eyre would totally have been rubbing one out on the regular," Mo said. "Young woman with a tough job and a hot boss? That's—"

"Only natural," he finished. He stood, breaking eye contact, and rubbing his hands on his jeans.

"Stress does that to some people," Mo said to his back. She could still sense the warmth of his body, just a foot away.

His eyebrow quirked. "Does *what* to some people?"

It was her turn to stand. She wanted to see if he would step back from her, but he held his ground. "You know . . ."

"No, tell me."

"Makes them horny," Mo said, not seeing a point to avoiding the word.

"Oh, see, I thought stress made people OD on edibles. My mistake," he deadpanned.

She shoved him lightly. The hardness of his chest under her hand made her stomach go liquid. He must have seen something in her face, because his laughter stopped. His glance snagged hers, eyes brown and flinty.

Once, on vacation in Colorado with friends, she'd seen a wildcat up the hill, hidden by the trees, all except those gleaming eyes. Instead of feeling hunted now, his changed expression made something in her predatory. Her heart race-horsed in her chest. She wanted to feel the full weight of him, take the measure of this man who was trying to beat her. He was her better by so many common standards—educationally and financially and socially. But here, this weekend, in this ballroom, they were equals. She was staring at his mouth. As she forced her gaze back up to meet his, she noticed that he too had been eyeing her lips.

Without knowing who leaned first, leaning happened. Mutual leaning, though Mo would never admit to leaning more than Wes did. Once their lips met, the kiss deepened instantly. A magnetic tug so deep she felt it through her core. She was so dialed in to his lips that when his fingertips whispered over the back of her neck, she froze. It was her fault for focusing on the kiss so completely. Or maybe his fault for having the power to do that, directing her whole being through a sieve until all her neuroticism and ridiculousness had been processed into a thin sandy mixture that he let fall through his fingers. Until those fingers touched her.

He must have felt her back go taut. He drew back like she'd bitten him. "Sorry," he said. The light shifted above them as a cloud passed over the sun, the yellows and greens and pinks going dark, the spell of the last few minutes broken. "I don't know what came over me."

"No, I wanted—"

"Okay, good, because—"

"Stress." She interrupted his interruption. "Too much stress."

He smiled wanly. "Something like that. I wouldn't figure you for the reckless type. You seem too—I don't know. Type A?"

She scoffed, then took a breath. "Type A? I'm a perfect AB mixture, thank you very much." If he wanted to pretend the kiss didn't happen, she could do that. She couldn't forget what she'd felt pressing against her leg, even through his expensive jeans. It made her curious and yes, deeply and enragingly horny. But midwestern girls were good at many things, and hiding behind a smile and joke when all you wanted to do was scream or punch or kiss someone was one of those skills. "We should continue the tour."

"We should," he said, but as they walked down the hallway he said, "You have a really good mouth. It's—pert."

She took the chance to appreciate the ceiling before responding. They entered yet another room, this one a gallery with plenty of distractions from his exasperating eyes and the way he kept trying to knock her off-balance. If she didn't keep moving, she might accidentally kiss him again. "Pert mouth? That makes it sound like I wash it out with cheap shampoo."

His eyebrows pulled together. "Is that a shampoo?"

"Oh, I bet you were bathed in the finest of argan oils with sheepskin washcloths or something."

"Sample size, but sure. Something like that. Let's say that my mom has always gotten a lot of free products. Expensive and nice-smelling ones, and I've taken my share of them. I got my pick of the men's ones."

"But you had to share them with your dad, right?"

"Ha, not anymore." His back was toward her as he looked at an impressionist painting of a shepherd and lamb, but she could tell his manner had changed. Something in him completely shut down, as if the room had cooled forty degrees, but only on his half. She had no idea what the problem was. Did his dad get sick or something? Was that what all the frantic whispering was about at the dress store? She had pretended not to notice, focusing on her dress, but she could tell something was wrong.

"You didn't hear that," he said after a moment. "Sorry. I'm—not on today."

"Not on?"

"Don't you ever have to be *on* at work? Or with friends? I feel like that's all I'm ever asked to be."

"I mean, I'm friendly at work, or professional. It's not a struggle for me, but I guess our jobs are different."

"And you . . ." He left the space open for her to fill. She realized she hadn't told him she was the cliché small-town-girl-in-NYC-doing-the-food-service-thing-to-make-rent. It was a cliché because the formula worked. "I work in catering."

He considered that. They gave up any pretense of looking at art and sat on wooden chairs stationed near the front of the gallery. "Not writing?"

"No," she said simply. "I had some friends who worked writing gigs—copywriting for companies, editing for textbooks, freelancing listicles and essays. It all seemed like so many words, draining the well before you even got to the writing you wanted to do. I'm not knocking it—money is money. Personally, I wouldn't have the creative stamina for that lifestyle, and sadly, I don't have the family money to just write."

She didn't mean it as a jab, but he obviously took it that way from the way his spine straightened. "I work. I work hard."

"I'm sure you do."

He ran a hand through his hair and stood. "I didn't get into agenting with my parents' help. I applied with a fake name for my first internship, actually. When I got it, when I started working, I had to come clean, but I wanted to start on my own terms. The literary world is its own beast, luckily or unluckily. One that my mother hasn't tamed. I always wanted to be the person to help books be discovered, to scream about the ones I loved into the universe. It takes a lot of my time. It's a lot of laptop time. Writing and agenting is—"

"A lot?"

"A lot, yeah. Sometimes all I get are my morning pages. Usually a morning page, singular."

"I do that too. They're mostly shit, but it's good to get it out of my head."

"I can't imagine anything you—" He stopped himself. "It's useful. The lack of filter."

"It's nice to be unfiltered sometimes," she said. "And thank you for complimenting my lips."

He laughed. "Honesty is hardly a compliment."

"You have nice lips too," she said. She didn't add that she liked talking to him, and that her prose made her breathless. "I ruined the mood."

His mouth quirked. "Moods have a way of reappearing, at least in Victorian lit."

"So you're saying this was foreshadowing?"

"As long as there are no exes in the attic, ready to set fires."

"At least none that we've seen on the tour so far." She refused to smile at him again. If she did, she was worried she wouldn't stop. "I need to get my head on straight for tonight. It's obviously not right now."

"Fair enough." He rose and brushed the nonexistent wrinkles out of his shirt. "But while I walk you back to your room, I have to ask: Did you talk about madness in your class? I hated when I saw it in literature as a symptom connected to feminine childbearing or lack of children."

And of course he had been thinking about that class all along. She laughed, and as they walked, she recited as much of the syllabus as she could remember from almost ten years ago as if she weren't picturing him naked.

Which was just as well, since Gary stepped into their path just before they got to her room. He seemed surprised to see them walking together, and she was suddenly extremely grateful they were not caught doing anything else. "Estelle's daughters have arrived," he said. "Cocktails in fifteen."

Mo glanced at her phone and saw that it was almost four—later than she had expected. No delaying the inevitable. She was going to meet the people who would control the trust if for some reason Estelle . . . well, she didn't want to think about that, especially since she liked Estelle. She also thought Estelle really liked her and her book. She was ready to make a second and third first impression on Estelle's kids, but she hoped she could still rouse some fighting instinct when her mouth felt bruised from Wes's kiss. Her kiss too, she guessed, though she'd never thought about how a kiss really belongs to two people at once. It always felt like she was kissing someone, or she was being kissed, never that two magnetic forces were meeting.

She needed to get her head out of Wes's mouth and back into her work. Wes gave a wave over his shoulder as he left. "Door open or closed?" he asked.

"Closed." She had fifteen minutes, and she needed to either climax or cool down, and honestly, it could go either way. Plus reapply her mascara. She needed all the time she could get.

CHAPTER TEN

Wes

Wes came downstairs first, despite needing a few minutes to lie on his bed and stare at the ceiling. He imagined lifting Maureen's shirt over her head and rumpling her hair. He pictured the softness of her skin under his fingertips and what her low, sweet voice would sound like moaning into his ear. The curse of being a creative. He had more than enough imagination to play the whole scene out to its frustratingly satisfying conclusion.

He needed to stop thinking about her, though, or he wouldn't make it down the stairs without getting another erection. Attraction or not, this was still a competition. His best skill was charm, and he hoped to introduce himself to Estelle's daughters before Mo. He hadn't gone on a tour with Maureen to seduce her, but if that had somehow thrown her off the game, then all the better. Boxing had taught him to get in a jab when the opportunity allowed—but that wasn't why he'd wanted to see Maureen. In all honesty, he was lonely and unsettled after the news about his parents. Seeing Mo, walking and talking to her—and eventually kissing her—had been such a shock to the system that it almost made him feel balanced again.

Gary greeted him at the bottom of the steps. His mustache bloomed around his mouth, fuzzy and gray. Wes wondered if Estelle liked it. He had never been much for facial hair, but then again, everyone's tastes were different. Gary was a good-looking older man, especially in his knit green vest. Gary glanced behind Wes as if waiting for Maureen. "She's on her way," Wes said. "Probably soon."

"You're attached at the hip, from what it looks like to me," Gary said, smiling.

At least she's not my boss, Wes wanted to say, but he refrained. "Lucky for me that the competition turned out to be so interesting."

He could see Gary wanted to ask something, but Wes didn't want to answer anything. Instead, Wes asked, "What do you think of our chapters so far?"

"Very distinct. To be honest, I never much liked *The Proud and the Lost*. Not really my kind of book. I like mysteries. Detectives in English countryside, bodies turning up at the county fair and the vicar is involved. That kind of thing."

Wes was gobsmacked. "How in the world did you end up working for the Morgan estate?"

"Estelle gave a lecture at my college many, many years ago."

"Oh, about books?"

"No, accountancy. She worked as an accountant for years. Anyway, we clicked. I was more interested in her than in her mother's work, and that seemed like what she was looking for.

I will say that her late husband was a big fan of her mother's, and it made it boring overhearing them. Not that I was spying, but working for her for so long—I think even Estelle got bored of thinking about her mother's legacy at times."

Wes could understand the notion of being bored of hearing about a famous parent. He stood at the French doors into the drawing room while Gary plowed forward. The room hadn't changed much in an hour, but the atmosphere sure had. Four figures were silhouetted by the large windows. One was Estelle, of course, and he knew two others. Estelle's children were notorious via gossip and photographs. Neither the gossip nor the photographs had been especially flattering, but Wes was willing to give them the benefit of the doubt. He knew how the tabloids could be.

Back when Wes was little, Ulla had begun her upward climb to celebrity and Wes became an infrequent feature of that attention. He sometimes disliked being sent to boarding school, but at least behind its walls, he had a foot of brick and ivy to cover him.

Rather than dodging the limelight, Estelle's children had done their best to stay in it. Her older daughter, Flor (short, Wes assumed, for Florence or Flora?) was a celebrity Realtor around the Hamptons. She had an overworked nose that smelled of too much surgery. That nose appeared all over billboards that said things like "Trust Flor" and "Flor's the Door to New Homeownership" (which Wes read in a kind of off-rhyme, like 'FLOR is the DOOR to new HOMEownerSHIP'—probably giving her family's history in literature too much credit).

The younger daughter, who was in her late forties, was Talia. Talia was a curvaceous brunette whose default expression seemed to be *something smells bad*. She had starred in a range of lifestyle reality TV shows called *Rich Wives of Manhattan*. She was most likely the reason the whole family had gotten dragged in and out of the tabloids in the first place. From what Wes had seen, Estelle had never participated in the *Rich Wives* franchise. As the literary agent to the estate, Wes had enough contact with her lawyer to know that the word *gauche* was thrown around frequently in terms of how her younger daughter had made a name for herself. Talia's husband, Gus, was an entrepreneur of some kind, which was never made explicit in the show and was even less explicit in the wording of the company. He "managed logistics" for a "transportation firm," the kind of transportation never being exactly obvious. It all felt mafia-y to Wes, but he would never mention that to Gus, who was even taller in person than he had been on TV.

Seeing Flor and Talia in the flesh was jarring, but Wes took a deep breath and followed Gary inside. There were light-green cocktails in tall glasses sweating slightly on a silver platter on top of the coffee table in the middle of the room. Delicate butter cookies filled a second, smaller silver platter, with a stack of white napkins set next to it. He grabbed a drink but ignored the cookies. Suddenly his stomach wasn't up to it. The glass cooled his too-warm hands, and he took a sip. Mint and lime mixed in Wes's mouth, along with something slightly sparkly—distinct. Distinct in a terrible way. Wes made a noise that made Gus turn around. The noise might have sounded like trying to spit something out. He swallowed instead and studied Gus's square face. "Surprising taste. What's the mixer?"

"Mountain Dew. We call this the Mountain Mama. Feels appropriate for the Hill."

It wasn't. Wes would need to find a convenient window ledge to forget it on, but the only candidate for that had Talia leaning out of it.

"It's a favorite of mine," Gus said, "though Tally says it's responsible for all my dental bills." He offered a hand to shake, not smiling. "Gus. You must be Wes, the agent-turned-novelist."

"Still an agent too," Wes said. As he shook Gus's hand. he thought about the email wasteland that waited in his inbox. He had purposefully left his laptop behind and unsynced the work email from his phone for the weekend. He had, however, answered two client texts about nerves and revision questions. It was hard to say *Hi, give me a tiny break. I'm a writer and need my creative space and time to be nervous, too.*

Flor turned from the sofa and gave a demure wave. "I don't shake since the virus. I can't believe we all shook hands for so long; my God, what barbarians we all were. Even my clients get used to the wave these days. When I close deals, I sometimes will shake, but you know how the pressure of that deal moment feels, don't you?"

Wes nodded, trying to manage a response that didn't bring COVID back up again, and settled on turning his attention to Talia. She, it turned out, stayed near the window as well, but only to allow her cigarette smoke to drift out of it. "Hi," she said, voice deep and throaty and familiar. "I'd shake your hand—I'm not a kook—but Mom says smoke goes outside or I do, so . . ."

Wes waved, cut off at the knees here with only his little shell-less snail of a creative self to offer. They were about to hear the ending of his book, the little tender work of his heart, without hearing any of the preceding chapters. Suddenly he had a better idea, one that came from his agent-mind, not his writer one. "I'll make some copies of my full manuscript to leave with all of you in case my final chapter makes you curious about the rest."

"Oh, Gary could do that, couldn't you, Gary?" Flor asked lazily.

Wes saw Gary's back straighten. "I could."

"Make a copy of the one that Mom has. We'll have a sister book club. Won't that be fun?" Talia asked, blowing a final puff of smoke out the window.

"What about having full copies of both manuscripts?" Flor asked. He could tell from the change in the room that Mo was behind him. He wasn't trying to sneak one past her or get a leg up by offering his full book, but he was embarrassed that it might look that way. He took a sip of the awful drink, resisting the urge to look over his shoulder at her.

When he did, he saw she was wearing the dress she'd gotten that afternoon. His heart beat faster at the sight of her pale arms crossed in front of her. She shouldn't be allowed to drive him to distraction when he was the one that had driven them to the Hill.

Talia glanced at Maureen. "Yes, both books. Or, Mom, what about the one you told us about too? The horror movie one? Clive goes on a killing spree? You said it was very *The Shining*. We could see all three."

Estelle's expression clouded over. "No. We're not considering that one."

Flor turned to Gary with the air of someone in a drive-through. "We'll each take a copy of these two, then, Gary."

Gary put his plate down and rubbed his hands on his gray slacks. "I'll go get those printed."

Poor Gary. Were there print shops open in this town on a Saturday afternoon after five? Did people do business here? They must, sometime between golf rounds. A lot of business was done on the links, right? Not in Wes's business, but in somebody's. Maybe in transportation logistics.

When Wes rejoined the sisters, they were deep in discussion, both holding fresh drinks. Mo and Wes must be at least two drinks behind at this point, but how anyone could drink Mountain Dew in a room with West Elm wallpaper and original plaster sculptures, he could never figure. Now that the windowsill was abandoned, he left his sweating, neon drink there. The family seemed to have forgotten the authors in the room, except for Estelle. She smiled at him, and Wes swore he saw an eye roll in that smile before she turned back to her daughters. He should try to join their conversation, but there was something deliciously naughty about standing next to Mo in a room full of people who didn't know they had been making out. Well, not making out, but kissing at least. A kiss. A kiss he wished he could repeat.

Wes edged closer to the wall, and Mo followed. He wondered if her brain had played out a million scenes that could have been. She smelled delicious, like apricots. "You showered," he said.

"I did. No Pert though."

He couldn't back down now. "Thought it might wash some of the dirty thoughts from your head?"

She didn't look at him, but he saw her smirking into her glass. She took a long sip, then winced. "It didn't."

He grinned, not looking at her. She could be trying to off-balance him, but he didn't care. The buzz in his blood was completely unrelated to alcohol.

"I heard you're giving a copy of your book to the daughters," Mo said.

"Yours too," Wes said.

She reached discreetly behind him. From their position, it wouldn't be obvious to anyone else that she momentarily rested her hand on the curve of his ass. When she squeezed it, like testing a piece of fruit, he suddenly wished he worked in produce or that he was produce, more accurately. That he was one of the apricots that got to make up the body wash she'd rubbed all over herself minutes ago.

"You're trying to throw me off."

"Wouldn't even dream of it. But"—as she said the word, she lightly pinched his right cheek—"the competition ends after the reading. After dinner."

"Officially."

"At least our part of it," she said, removing her hand and looking him in the eye now. Her expression was suddenly serious. "If this competition isn't fair, Wes, then dirty thoughts or not, you're getting nowhere with me."

"It's fair. I promise it will all be fair."

She nodded, as if to herself. "So, do you have plans for tonight?"

His mouth went dry. He could make some, he was certain. He wanted them to involve more of that delicious pressure.

Luckily, the dinner menu featured no pork products. For a few of the guests, it seemed to include almost nothing at all. Flor was a vegetarian and Talia was doing a fourteen-hour fast. Talia refused to even acknowledge there was food on the table. Drinks had been changed to something less fluorescent for dinner, a Riesling to pair with the meal. Gus flushed as he drank, cheeks glowing under the chandelier's light.

"Aren't you fasting?" Flor asked her sister.

"Clear liquids only," Talia said, gazing through the wine glass at Flor, then winking.

Instead of eating, they were talking about New York real estate. Wes could fake this conversation in his sleep, but it obviously baffled Mo. Flor turned to Mo after five interrupted minutes of monologuing. "And where do you live, darling?"

Mo stumbled through a response, but once she got her cross streets out, Flor raised her eyebrows and changed the topic.

Wes picked at the asparagus and goat cheese tartlets, his thigh pressing against Mo's under the table. He wanted to be alone with her, to be past the final chapter. He was too nervous to eat or drink.

Dessert was raspberries and fresh whipped cream. As the bowls were being set on the table, Gary walked in. He glanced at the cold tartlet at his place setting and grimaced. "Can I have two desserts instead?" Wes heard him whisper to Angie.

Angie patted his shoulder and brought a second serving.

"These are delicious," Mo said, trying to draw Gary into the conversation. Wes noticed that Flor and Talia hadn't even said hello or thank-you to him since he reentered.

Gary finished his first bowl, then moved on to the second. "The raspberries were locally sourced."

Mo looked shocked. "In April?"

Wes had no idea when raspberries were in season but was more than happy to continue a conversation that both Gary and Mo seemed interested in. "How do they manage that?"

Gary smiled. "It's an indoor greenhouse for berries across the harbor. It's an ingenious setup."

Mo had a gift for putting people at ease, and Wes loved that she was interested in so many things that had nothing to do with things he understood. Gary looked happier by the end of the conversation, and Estelle did too. Flor and Talia looked either like the alcohol was finally hitting them or bored to pieces by the time Gary and Mo had discussed the pollination strategy, plus the couple that ran the place. Flor's head rested heavily on her palm as she stared out the window, while Talia kept stirring her uneaten dessert, pushing the cream side to side like a tidal wave.

After the plates were cleared away, Estelle clapped her hands together. "Shall we get into the main event?"

The entire group adjourned to the library, and Wes got to see Maureen's expression soften, her gaze catch on the desk by the window. In the center of the room were several large, plush couches. The hardwood floor was softened by a gray-and-white plaid rug.

Seltzer fizzed in the background—Gus was using one of those old-fashioned seltzer bottles to make after-dinner cocktails in the corner of the room. Talia opened a window along the far wall to smoke, and the breeze unsettled some of the dust on the bookshelves so that it caught in the light. Gary settled himself in a stand-alone wooden chair next to Estelle's side. Wes sat next to Maureen on the love seat closest to the door. It was hard to tell who was more likely to bolt. Mo tapped her fingers lightly on the manuscript on her lap. Her red nail polish had chipped in spots to reveal the pale natural nails underneath. How hadn't he looked at her long, tapered fingers yet? He had been probably too busy looking at her other attributes, but now he wanted nothing more than to snag her hand off her book to keep it from shaking like it was now.

They were going to read the ending of the adaptations, by far the most problematic and often discussed part of the original book. In the original, Eliza died in a car crash, but critics had debated for almost a hundred years whether that crash was an accident or suicide. Any adaptation would have to take a stand on that.

"So, do we flip to see who goes first?" Wes asked once Talia had a chance to finish her cigarette and close the window.

"You can do the honors," Mo said.

He didn't really want to, but those shaking hands shook him too. Maybe it would help her feel better. Wes took a deep breath and dove in.

In his version, Wes ruled it an accident. In Morgan's novel, Eliza opened the door to the study of their large mansion and saw something, something unexplored, and drove off into the night. In Wes's version, Eliza walked in on the lieutenant and Clive holding hands by the fire, the closest Clive ever came to physical intimacy with Perkins. Eliza had barely come to grips with accepting the lack of connection of her life when she walked in on this. She could put up with a loveless marriage if both parties weren't finding love. In Wes's adaptation—though it wasn't explored in the original—Clive drove after Eliza in Perkins's car. It was snowing. It was late. If he had let her go, she might have lived, and thus was the ultimate new horror of it, and something that brought Wes's book from a retelling to a true adaptation.

When he finished the chapter, he sat back on the couch, heart beating fast. He should have stood through the reading. He should have slowed down a bit. He was nervous to look up at Estelle, her children, even Gary. He was more nervous to catch Mo's expression next to him. In graduate school, he had taken creative writing courses. He remembered the angst of sitting in a workshop with the rule of not being able to defend your work. Criticism came from all sides: Why did the character do this? What was their motivation? What if it started in a different place? What if you crumpled this whole draft and started fresh with the echo of it in your head? He was keenly aware, even more so than before, how he had been the only person to read this book. He was a good reader, an even better editor, but suddenly he felt completely cut off at the knees about this tender project. Finally, he faced the room.

Gus was smiling broadly at Wes. "So, Clive is *gay*, huh." He said it like the word *gay* could be substituted with *drunk*.

"Uh, bisexual was my interpretation."

"Is that actually a thing?" Gus asked, eyebrows raised. "You can't sit half on a horse."

Wes felt his blood pressure spike. "Well, as a bisexual male, I'd have to say that horses haven't come into my sex life at all. Can't speak for you, though."

Gus's face screwed up, but he decided to laugh rather than be offended.

"So the love story with Eliza is fake?" Flor asked.

"I don't think that his attraction to Eliza is fake, but I think he—"

"Spicy," said Talia. The word made Wes crinkle his nose. "I liked him watching her crash. I could see the scene in the movie."

"We haven't talked about movie rights," Estelle cut in. She wasn't speaking loudly, but the strength of her words redirected the conversation.

"I thought it was well written," Flor said judiciously, but didn't expand on that to say what made her come to this conclusion other than the dollar signs that her sister had shot into the room.

Wes was nervous how Mo's version might end, even having heard less than a third of it. He remembered her old manuscript from the slush pile at the old agency and the keen way she used sparse prose to put in a knife and twist it before you'd even known you'd been stabbed. Heartbreak with four words. He wasn't a good actor, not really, and he worried how he would react to her Eliza, this Liza of 2005, dragged from independence into a prison of expectations and then brought to her death. He didn't want to cry on the couch.

"Anyone need a fresh drink before Maureen begins?" Gary asked.

Talia shook her glass, though Gus and Flor covered theirs. "Are you expecting your hubby dearest to drive you?" Gus asked, his tone wry.

"Well, I can always take a horse if he doesn't," Talia laughed, shoving him with a hip. "Oh, someone will. Gary would, I'm sure. You know I have a tarot-reading birthday party after this and I don't want to drink on camera right now."

If she thought she would sober up before her drive to Manhattan, she must have a different metabolism. Like a hummingbird, but with chardonnay.

"Mo, do you need anything?" Wes asked.

She shot him a look, and he realized he'd called her the nickname. It was like his brain had a trading card with her photo and the name *Mo* underneath it. He hated that when he pictured this image, with full stats and facts on the other side, the *o* in *Mo* was a tiny heart.

"I'm good," she said.

She began and shattered any chance that he might win this thing.

CHAPTER ELEVEN

Mo

Eliza had gotten a raw deal, and Mo wanted to correct it. Liza got away in Mo's version—her drive went awry, but only mildly. She skidded off the road, where she caught her breath and waited for Clive to come chasing her. Liza waited. She waited and he didn't come, and it was the sign she needed not to give it another chance. When he didn't, she pulled back onto the road, slower, and drove toward the sunrise.

Was the story less dramatic because a woman had a chance to leave and not die? Maybe, but Eliza deserved better, and so did modern readers. Honestly, after reading the original novel a million times, Mo had internally fanfic-ed even brighter versions of Eliza's story. She had written Eliza into the arms of a pizza boy who stole her away. She had written her into a spaceship (*The Martian* had just come out, so she had an excuse). This adaptation allowed for a redemptive ending that wasn't too sappy but let Eliza live. It shouldn't be a stretch that a woman got to leave and make more mistakes. Eliza deserved to live long enough to experience good sex. She deserved to make her own joy and to let someone love her like she needed to be loved.

Not that Mo was trying to wish-fulfill through her.

Maybe a little.

Mo read clearly and straight through, without looking up. When she came to the end of the final paragraph, she cleared her throat.

There was silence. Gary stared at her, then clapped softly. Estelle joined, but her daughters didn't.

"Did I miss it?" Talia asked, gesturing with her empty glass. "Does she drive further down the road and hit a tree or something?"

"No, she doesn't die."

Gus laughed without humor. "How can it be an adaptation without having the same ending?"

"Well, I wrote it. I say it's an adaptation. What else do you need?"

"Honey, we're just saying that without the original ending, it's a different book." Flor sounded so condescending that Mo wanted to throw her manuscript at the wall.

Mo let herself look at Estelle's face. She smiled slightly, a real smile. The kind where the tips of her eyelids rose. Being from the Midwest meant that Mo was used to dissecting the language of smiles, picking out the false from the real. "Well, good for Liza," Estelle finally said, when she realized Mo was focused on her.

"Mom, it's a different book with that ending. Don't you think readers will hate it?" Flor spoke as if Maureen weren't even there. "It could have been written by someone who only read the Wikipedia article about the book and decided to do her own thing."

"You seemed perfectly willing to read the horror movie abomination version," Estelle noted. "I didn't hear any complaining when an ax murderer entered the adaptation."

"Mom," Talia said. "You're being silly. Everyone would read the horror version. No one would read that." She gestured with a hand dismissively in Mo's direction.

Mo felt like she'd been slapped. She couldn't stop herself from jumping back in. "I love your grandmother's original book. Love it and respect it. I tried to do honor to her characters while also making the story fresh for modern readers."

"Modern readers seem to find nothing wrong with the original book," Flor said, tone cold. "As we've seen year over year in the royalty statements."

"No need to argue," Estelle said. "Especially since I've been reading the entire novels and will be making my determination without external input."

"Then why even invite us?" Talia said, swaying. "What's the point?"

"I thought you wanted to see what I've been doing lately," Estelle said. "Plus it's been a little while since you've come over for dinner." Talia seemed ready to interrupt. "Without trying to shove a makeup crew in here and put me on television."

"That was one time," Talia protested.

Gary raised his eyebrows, and Mo knew those were stories she wanted to hear—she'd probably have to start watching that *Rich Wives* show. Mo felt better that Estelle didn't seem to hate the ending. She felt sure that once she read the whole novel, Estelle would come to see the ending not as a cop-out but as a reinvention worthy of Morgan's name.

No one had stormed out, but the discussion was clearly over. Gary told Wes and Mo that the family wanted to chat alone, and moments later, Wes caught her arm and led her gently out of the room.

"Well, that could have gone better," Mo said. All the confidence she had managed had drained. Despite the deflating feeling in her stomach, she couldn't help but laugh. "For me, at least. It went well for you." His reading *had* gone well. She had barely breathed while he spoke. His ending felt natural but hurt her heart. The twist was expected but unexpected at the same time.

"Only Estelle's opinion matters." Wes led Mo outside, and the front door closed behind them. The sisters' cars were parked in the long front drive. The two cars together cost more than her parents' house in Iowa, she was sure. The cool air brushed against Mo's cheeks. She hadn't realized how warm she had gotten inside, even without drinking much. After the embarrassment last night, she had been determined to stay in control. Instead, she'd ended up fighting with the daughters of the woman she came to impress. She pictured what her face looked like when she got angry. When she blushed, it looked pink and childlike. As if she needed another reason to lower her credibility. It was too late now to do damage control, except in her own thoughts.

"I thought you might want to take a walk," he said. The sun had set, and as they strolled around the edge of the house, they could see into the front room they'd left behind. The window was slightly open, Flor smoking out of it, and raised voices came through the crack. "If I wanted to really know what they thought, I'd go listen," Mo said.

"Let me appeal to your better angels and say you shouldn't give a damn what they say."

"Angels don't know much about damnation," Mo said, but she looked away from the window, trying to tune out the chorus. It was bad when you assumed people were saying mean things about you. It was worse knowing for sure that was happening. As they walked farther, though, it was less obvious that other people were even inside the house. Aside from the scattered outdoor lighting, the yard was shadowy. Mo could imagine fireflies darting in the back grass in a few months, how lively things would be with the pool full. Splashing grandchildren. Ugh, splashing grandchildren with camera crews circling for reality TV.

By the time they got to the large cement patio overlooking the pool, her legs felt alive after sitting for so long. "Can you ever see the stars out here?" Mo was used to the long, gray sky at night in the city but didn't know if they were far enough outside of it to see the stars again. She saw none tonight, but a thin veil of cloud clothed the moon like a scarf.

"Sometimes," Wes said, then he paused. "I don't usually look, to be honest. My mom would know."

"Your mom would know because it's her job to know everything that might be interesting to anyone."

"For a price."

"Nice work if you can get it," Mo said, without really knowing what she meant by it. She wanted to fight someone who could fight back. She was in a bad mood and tried to focus on the scenery—the darkening lawn and the cool breeze that blew suddenly around them. She felt the skin on her legs prickle. "It's cooler than I thought it was."

"Like me," Wes said.

She didn't want to laugh, but she did. She loved how everything seemed to come so easy to him. She hated how everything came so easily to him.

"Want to dip your feet in the hot tub?" Wes said.

The patio was illuminated only by subtle in-ground lighting. The back of the house was dark. The kitchen staff were done with cleanup from dinner and drinks and had gone home for the night. The pool house, which probably sometimes hosted guests, was similarly dark, so that she felt momentarily peaceful. "Sure."

The area was walled off behind a slatted privacy fence, obviously not on the tour route. Wes edged off the cover of the in-ground hot tub, undoing the sides and sliding it up and placing it near the ADA lift next to the basin. He dipped a hand in the top of the water, then leaned over to adjust something on a box nearby. She knew as much about hot tubs as she did about Maseratis—she could probably handle one if she needed to but wanted someone else to do the servicing. After a second, more bubbles hit the surface.

Wes sat on the cool concrete beside the hot tub. He took off his calf-length socks, then rolled the cuffs of his pants. He patted the ledge next to him. She left her flats on the pool deck away from the water. She paused momentarily, worried about the dress that Ulla had bought her, but ultimately, life was short and she sat down next to him. Mo placed her feet in the bubbles next to his and leaned back. The sides of their hands touched, not that she meant to do that, but she didn't move them away either.

It was strange: They were still competing, technically, but the active part in the competition was over. She remembered hearing about all the sex that went on in Olympic villages—the thousands of condoms handed out to prevent superathletic post-Olympic offspring (or more likely, international transmission of STIs). The air was magnetically charged so close to someone at your level. Sure, she'd gone out with other writers, but they had acted dismissive about her work. It was clear that Wes respected her as they went head-to-head. He listened. She wondered what he would have thought of her first book, the one that never sold. She had also poured a part of her soul into that book, and she wanted to share it with him in a way that she rarely had since that project failed to sell.

The warm jets pulsed against the backs of her thighs, massaging the tension she hadn't even known she held there. She must have moaned, because Wes bumped his shoulder into hers. "That good, huh?"

"I was more tense than I thought."

"What kind of tense?" His voice was light, teasing.

"Oh, the sexual kind, for sure," she said, matching his tone.

He smiled, then began to unbutton his shirt. He slid it over his head while she pretended not to notice. Then, glancing behind them at the dark house, he undid his pants and lowered them. The privacy fence mostly walled in the hot tub so that it felt like being in a room—a room without a ceiling. She thanked the landscapers for the fencing so that she could enjoy the view of his body in private. He wore plain blue boxer briefs tight against his thick thighs. Above them was a soft fold of stomach, a dark line of hair tracing enticingly down. He caught her looking. "It's basically a swimsuit," he said.

He did a perfect box fold on the clothing and laid it in a pile next to the hot tub.

"I do not know why you're folding your clothes when you're going to get them wet," she teased.

"Wet is just fine with me," he said. "Can I help you release some tension?"

Her dress suddenly felt too tight across her chest, or maybe she wasn't breathing enough. "By doing what?"

"Nothing you don't agree to. I was thinking of helping those jets," he said, stepping into the water. The hot tub interior lights certainly did justice to his body—solid, with more than a suggestion at the muscle definition in his abs and arms. His shoulders, those shoulders that had hefted her up last night, looked sturdier bare and in shadow than they did under his polo shirts and button-downs. It wasn't that she didn't usually go for preppy guys—okay, maybe she didn't usually go for preppy guys. But his prep had an edge of self-deprecation to it that she appreciated.

She had gone out on a few dates since Aaron, and some of them had gone further than kissing. Nothing had made her feel the way Wes did as he held her calf in his hands and began to rub.

He looked up at her from the water, one leg in each of his hands, and asked, "Is this all right?"

Mo moaned as his thumbs applied pressure up and down her calf. Knots began to untangle. "This was always my favorite part of a pedicure," she said.

He smiled at her. "Me too, honestly, though some women might think it's weird that I have an opinion on them."

"You like nice things," she said.

"Yes," he agreed, his hands moving farther up her leg, "I do."

She let him sink his thumbs into the front of her lower thighs, pressing and moving his fingers in a steady rhythm. "Tell me if this tickles," he said, "because that's not my goal."

Those hands worked for a minute, set to make her legs into jelly, before creeping ever so slightly upward. They brushed under the edge of her dress hem, the hem she had lifted to her upper thighs to avoid getting it wet. Looking at her lap, Mo couldn't see his hands underneath the fabric, but she could see him, wet and mostly covered by bubbles near her knees. "What is your goal?" Mo asked.

Suddenly his hands shot from under her hem to grab her around the waist. He pulled her into the hot tub with him. She blinked, the warm water fizzing and bubbling all around her. "To get you wet."

She pushed herself off his chest, the sopping fabric of the dress flowing upward in the bubbles. "You asshole," Mo said, laughing.

"I'll pay for dry cleaning," he said.

After a glance at the dark sky and reminding herself of the solidness of the privacy fence, Mo pulled the dress over her head and let it flop on the deck of the hot tub. "There. Are you happy?"

"Extremely."

Her bra and panties were still on—like a swimsuit, as he said. Just not as water resistant. The fabric of her pale-pink bra had turned translucent, but she didn't know if he could tell from his place across the hot tub. In a few seconds, that question was irrelevant because she had rocket-pushed off the side of the tub to get closer. Now, with her already pulled into his arena, he was acting composed, cool. Like this was a hotel and they were two guests meeting for the first time. His eyes closed, head drifting back, and his arms draped along the cement tiles. She sat next to him on the ledge of the tub inside the crook of his arms. After all, this was no closer than they'd been this afternoon when they'd kissed. It was, in truth, less close than she'd wanted to be from the second they'd stopped—which was directly on top of him. Her hips on his hips.

Even thinking about him made her core hot, or it might have been the water.

His arm fell from the ledge around her shoulders. His middle finger caught the edge of her bra strap and ran the length of the skin underneath it—up and down. Okay, it wasn't just the water.

He caught her glance, trying to read her like he'd read his manuscript. The same controlled ease, the sense of confidence, of ownership. It made her mouth water.

"This okay?" he asked.

She wanted to nod. Still, a worrying thought broke through the sensation of his fingers on her skin. "What if there are cameras?"

He paused his attention for an instant, then glanced around over her shoulder and up at the building. He nestled her under his arm, then murmured in her hair, "There might be, but if we stay under the water, they can't see anything." He slid his hand just to the edge of the strap, then under. "Can I touch you?" His voice was husky, low, hard to hear against the sound of the jets.

Her head tried to interrupt her heart—which was telling her *please, please, please yes*. Her head won out. "Is this a bad idea?"

He didn't exactly growl, but he made a noise that almost broke her. "Probably."

"But maybe we need to get it out of our systems."

"I vote for that," Wes said. His hand drifted under the current of the hot tub and rubbed her calves again. "I've been staring at you all weekend like something out of reach."

She thought about the midwestern way no one ever took the last slice of cake at family gatherings, that constant deferral of pleasure even when they were hungry for it. She'd never thought of herself as reckless, but she kept imagining the story. The possibilities. *Sure, my book never got picked up, but let me tell you about that weekend. Making out with a celebrity in a hot tub. Kissing a rival under the stars.* The story wasn't that, exactly, especially since she couldn't imagine telling it to anyone but herself. No, the story she needed was one of letting go.

His touch traced from her knee upward, and she didn't stop him. She did, in fact, reach a hand to his stomach, feel the soft muscle there and the edge of his waistband. "This isn't part of the game, right?"

He huffed a laugh. "I mean, how do you even draw those boundaries?"

"But we'd need to. This is just for fun. And just for tonight."

"Agreed," he said. His voice was ragged, wrecked. The tone made her bite her lip, and she was grateful to be curled into his shoulder in the dark so he couldn't see her weakness.

"No angle. No games."

"Yes," he said. A single word, making it sound so easy. She wanted to believe him.

"Do you have condoms upstairs?" she asked, hoping her voice didn't betray how hard her breath felt to reach for.

He paused, then swore. "I don't." His hand caught hers in midstroke.

That made her laugh, come back to herself a little. "Why does that mean I have to stop touching you?"

"I should have bought some. I mean, I should always have some."

"We don't have to have that kind of fun," she said. "But we should probably go inside."

CHAPTER TWELVE

Wes

"Mind if I shower?" Mo asked. They'd spent hours tangled up together. Her hair was mussed in the particular way that only rolling around on a bed could muss someone's hair.

"No, feel free," Wes said.

She rolled off the bed, her naked body disappearing into the en suite bathroom. She could have gone down the hall to her own, but he was grateful for this moment to watch her. She peeked her head out from the doorframe. "Would you mind grabbing my pj's from my room?"

"Sure." He wrapped himself with a robe and padded down the hall. Her room was messy—concealer and blush containers open on the table and suitcase gaping wide. He picked up her pajamas. He didn't mean to hold them close to his face, but he did. They smelled like her, undiluted by the chlorine water scent that he'd been breathing in the past few hours.

When he got back into his room, she was finished showering and the clock on the nightstand said eleven thirty. They had been as quiet as they could, quiet to match the quiet house they had entered after their hot tub time. They dripped water on the hardwood floor while he mentally made apologies to historical preservationists everywhere. They wore soaking clothes upstairs, treading softly on the rugs and ignoring the stair squeaks. The door to Estelle's room had been firmly closed, with no light shining underneath.

This moment felt stolen and precious. He tapped on the bathroom door. "Clothing delivery."

She reached a bare arm out to snag them, and he slipped on his own pajamas. He hoped he had gotten her out of his system, but he would make sure of that by spending every second with her until they left. Tomorrow, real life resumed. In less than twelve hours, he would be driving her back to the city and to their normal lives and routines. Maybe their lives would change after this weekend.

Because of Estelle, not because of each other.

He was under no assumptions that a convenient weekend hookup would lead to something more, and honestly, he wasn't really looking for a relationship. He was too busy. Two of his clients were set to go on submission this week to publishing houses. He was finalizing contracts for another two and in the process of wooing one more from the slush pile. And there was Ulla—as much as she had her own people, she called him frequently to talk, and that would only become more essential with the separation.

He thought back to a conversation with one of his clients who had just had a baby plus had a toddler at home. She told Wes that by the end of the day, she was "touched out." She simply wanted no one to be setting a finger on her. He felt that way with his public face, with a set smile and firm handshake and industry know-how. He was *on* so much of the time that his home was an oasis from anyone needing him. He hadn't enjoyed relationships for the past few years or pursued them because he hadn't wanted the complication. He'd had some great hookups with nice people, but he didn't need more than that. His social needs were fulfilled by a zillion different interactions daily, online and on the phone and—

Mo slid a hand up and down his arm. "Did you come around to my view of ice cream yet?" she asked in his ear. She nestled into him, spooning his body from behind. She was a little shorter than him, but being held felt good.

"Was that your goal here? Anti-gelato warfare?"

"I wasn't trying hard enough," she said.

Unsaid: *this* time. Unsaid: if there was a next time.

In the breath before he flipped over and spooned her instead, he could almost hear her thinking about tomorrow too. He flicked off the light. "You staying?"

"Well, the walk back to my room is pretty dangerous."

"I almost got eaten by a lion in the hallway getting your pajamas."

"Right, Gary's pet lion," she murmured. She wiggled to move his arms lower on her torso. Suddenly, their bodies clicked. He closed his eyes. As he was starting to doze off, she said, "Can I ask something?"

"Sure."

"Do you seduce men and women differently?"

He laughed. "I don't know if I've really *thought* about seducing anyone. It just kind of happens."

"Come on, the whole hot tub thing was such a move," she said.

"So you're saying my moves work."

She laughed. If he were being honest, he would tell her that he would have done anything to make her happy tonight. That he could see her tension radiate through her body from that last reading, felt like he had sensors tuned in to her alone. When they had gotten back upstairs, there'd been no seduction required. They worked together—him on her, her on him. Mouths and hands moving, both focused on each other. He didn't think of himself as some lothario. "I'm good at knowing my audience."

"When did you know you liked both men and women?" she asked. "My roommate Sloan is bi, and she told me that she knew in high school."

He paused momentarily, squeezing her hips to tug her in closer. "I didn't really know until college. I went to an all-boys boarding school growing up and always knew that attraction was there." He was used to talking about this, with clients and on social media. He thought being open about sexuality was the least he could do as a gatekeeper in the publishing process, showing people who might still be closeted that there was a place for them. But it was different talking about this with someone he'd been intimate with and who wasn't seeing him as an authority on anything except himself. "When I went to college, like a lot of people, I did some exploration and realized that I was also very much attracted to women."

"Sorry if that was too personal. I think you're the first man I've been with who has slept with men too."

"That you know of," he had to add.

"Oh, that's true. It's naïve, I know. I'm not really a country rube, I promise."

"No, I don't think that." He rubbed a hand across her torso. "But writing my book was important to me, working through the themes of closet culture, especially back in the Roaring Twenties. It's not like gay people were invented in the 1970s or something. I've tried to actively search out projects that talk about gay history in literature, and I hoped my novel—sorry, I'm not trying to sell you on my book."

She was quiet for a minute, long enough that he thought she might be asleep. "Is it weird that I really want to read the rest of it?"

Wes didn't tell her that Gary had made a copy of her manuscript for him and that it was waiting in the bottom of his suitcase. Unlike her, his room was meticulously put together so she wouldn't find out that secret. It seemed only fair that she should get a chance to read his as well, but he selfishly wanted to watch her reactions, know what she thought of it, even as he was hoping to read hers in the privacy of his room so he could take her in at his own pace. "No, that's not weird."

She paused again. He pictured her biting her lip, those perfect pink lips he'd bruised by kissing so ferociously. "I had a thought. What if we continued our readings? When we're back in the city, but for us."

He wanted her. He didn't need to tell her that, and he never would. He'd gotten a night with her, and now he could just appreciate her work. Totally normal, friends with literary benefits. "I would like that. I mean, you have my number."

"Right, from Friday when you picked me up," she said.

"Well, text me and we can figure out when to do some more readings when we're back."

They fell asleep after that. It had been a long time since he had stayed to cuddle with someone, but she had almost taken that as an assumed right, and he loved that from her. They were bound to be under the same roof tonight anyway, so they might as well be in the same bed. It was just natural. It was easier to let two magnets attract. *Why not?* he asked himself, drifting to sleep.

Around four in the morning, they both woke with a start to the whir of sirens outside the window.

PART TWO
The Lost

"To have the lights of the city dare to shine in this torrential rain—well, that must be a sign, mustn't it," Eliza said. Clive raised her delicate hand to his lips.
—E. J. Morgan, *The Proud and the Lost*

"Oh, heartbreak. If my heart could be a truly broken thing, I could replace it. I could patch it and find another like it," Eliza said. "As it is, I am broken, too."
—E. J. Morgan, *The Proud and the Lost*

CHAPTER THIRTEEN

Wes

Breakfast was somber and rushed, the staff trying to serve Wes and Mo the best they could with Gary and Estelle gone. After breakfast, they had no one else to say goodbyes to before packing into Wes's Civic. In the middle of the night, they had watched a stretcher take Estelle away, Gary climbing in with her, a folded wheelchair and packed bag in tow. Wes wondered if the choreography of an emergency was one Gary knew well, if this wasn't the first ambulance ride Estelle had taken lately.

Wes received a text from Gary as they were loading their suitcases. "Heart attack," he told Mo. "She's not doing so well."

Unspoken: how lucky that Gary had been there. It hadn't really been luck, it had been love, or something like it. Gary, Estelle's assistant and lover, had been with her. In a different version of this life, in a different version without their affair, the staff would have found her lifeless in the morning. Wes didn't even want to think about it, but he couldn't help picturing Estelle in the same pale crepe pants she'd worn at dinner, paired with her cashmere sweater, stiff on top of a mattress.

Wes and Mo didn't talk much on the drive. Even after all they had said—and done—to each other last night, he didn't know how to begin a conversation after they'd watched an ambulance pull away from the estate together, holding hands as the sirens whirred down the long driveway. It wasn't even like they knew Estelle very well, but there was no code of conduct for what to say after a tragedy.

Wes pulled into the fire lane in front of Mo's building. They both hesitated as she reached for the door handle. She settled on leaning over to give Wes an awkward peck on the cheek. He'd smelled her soap the whole ride, and with her mouth on his cheek, the scent was intoxicating. Did women know how good they could smell? It seemed illegal. "Want me to get your bag from the trunk?"

"No, I got it."

"Say hi to Perkins for me," he said.

After dropping Mo off, Wes drove to New York-Presbyterian Hospital. Sunday traffic wasn't as bad as weekday traffic, but an accident near the Washington Bridge caused him to stop and process for a few minutes, which he didn't want to do. Instead, he rolled down his window, hit random on his music app, and turned up the car stereo. It was a game he'd played since he was a teen. Hit random, and whatever song came on was your song of the day. He believed in it more than horoscopes. When "Total Eclipse of the Heart" came on, though, he decided he got one veto. The next song was "SexyBack," which made him think of Mo slightly less. The car next to him had their window rolled down too, and a fiftysomething man with graying hair bopped his head along to Timberlake's singing, mouthing the *uh-huh*s.

You couldn't beat this city.

NewYork-Presbyterian was a huge metal-and-glass structure overlooking the river that could have passed as a fancy hotel. Wes didn't think he'd be allowed in to see her, nor did he really want to. Wes was uneasy around hospitals—the smells, the sounds—it all got to him, even at this hospital, which was admittedly the nicest one he had ever been in. He purchased a card-and-flower arrangement from the gift shop and took the elevator up to the designated floor.

He wrote the card in the elevator, using the wall as a desk. *Estelle,* he wrote. *Wishing you improved health and grateful for you. All the best from Wes.*

As he walked down the hall on the correct floor, there was Flor, sitting in the waiting room. She wore a sweater as green as Wes felt. He took a seat next to her, and she glanced up from her phone. "Oh hi, Wes," she said, as coolly as if she'd expected him there ten minutes ago.

"I'm so sorry about your mother's condition. I came to check in and see how she is."

Flor's lips pursed. "Well, if we could all be in there at once, they would be going marvelously, but as it is now, we can go in pairs only. And of course that means that only one of her children can really be there at a time because of Gary." At Gary's name, Flor rolled her eyes, and Wes could picture her as a teen. Maybe she even sold real estate back then. *The finest locker this side of seventh-period geometry.* "Anyway, such a shock. I mean, not a complete shock at her age, but still."

Wes nodded, unsure if Flor wanted him to agree that it was a shock or not a shock, or if she wanted any input at all. "Well, I'm here if you need anything."

"Even a kidney?" she asked.

He must have gaped, because she laughed. "Oh, Wes, kidding. It's her heart, her too-big heart in every sense, that's got her in trouble. No kidney needed. But I am glad you stopped by." She glanced around, as if the nurses were spying on them. After a second, she turned to him again, voice lowered conspiratorially. "I chatted with Talia, and of course we're on the same page about *P&L*. We are absolutely rooting for your project."

Wes hadn't come to talk about the book, but now he could see how it looked that way. It didn't seem like the time or place, and there was no way anyone could have read the entire novel since yesterday. He truly had come to check in on Estelle as, if not a friend, then a longtime associate.

"Well, the way we see it, your adaptation could sell very well, especially with the gay angle." She said the words quickly, and it came out *gangle*, which sounded even worse.

"I wouldn't call it an *angle*—"

"But of course Mother said we needed to read both projects, but I don't know. I don't know about that other one."

"Maureen Denton's book."

"Right. I mean, if people wanted a happy ending, they'd read a different kind of book. Happy books don't sell."

Wes was about to correct her, explaining that romance novels actually made up a large part of the book market and sold the idea of a happy ending to millions of people a year. He was annoyed about someone trying to tell him how his industry did or didn't work, but he was interrupted by a nurse calling Flor back.

"Anyway," Flor said, standing and pulling her purse over a bony shoulder, "if Mom's health tanks, it will be me you hear from next. I don't think it will. God knows I don't. But if it does, I'll be in touch. You can count on it."

Wes left the card and flowers with the attending nurse before Talia came into the lobby, unsure he could handle another round of guilt and hope and horror, all stirred together. After a second thought, he untucked the flap of the card and added more to his message, signing, *All the best from Wes and Maureen.*

CHAPTER FOURTEEN
Mo

When Mo reentered the apartment after the weekend, the smell of home hit her: the hot, ever-lingering scent from the furnace (even in the summer) and lemon Pledge. Like any lazy Sunday, Sloan was painting her nails on the couch. The routine view of it, Sloan with old magazines under her feet to protect the thirdhand sofa and Mackenzie with the second book in her favorite series open on her lap, pinged as coming home in her chest. They had turned the Christmas lights on, which hung from bookshelf to bookshelf, crisscrossing the room that served as the kitchen, den, and dining room.

Maureen slipped her flats off and leaned against the wall near the door. "Me next?" she asked. Her bag slumped beside her. She'd unpack that baggage later, but she was desperate to talk to someone. She was worried about Estelle, she was horrified that she'd messed around with Wes, and her toes did look terrible.

Sloan sighed and finished the swipes of color on her pinkie toes. "Okay, but you do need to clean the kitchen."

"I know, I know."

"We saw no rats while you were gone. Maybe the mayor actually is cleaning up the city," Mackenzie said.

"Do they have them in Greenwich?" Sloan asked.

"If they did, I bet they'd each be assigned *Breakfast at Tiffany's* pearls with a black dress or a tiny, rat-sized golf cart or something."

"Am I wrong, or are you back early?" Mackenzie asked.

"Early and for the worst reason. Ms. Morgan-Perry had a heart attack. We left this morning," Maureen said. "I feel so powerless that I can't do anything to help her."

"I'm sure she's getting the best care available," Mackenzie said. "Sit and fill us in on the rest of the weekend."

Maureen sat heavily on the couch next to Sloan and placed her toes on the stack of magazines. Sloan focused on Maureen's big toes first, alternating back and forth between her feet. Swipes of neon pink lit up her nails like liquid fireworks. "Did you bring back the rest of my gummies?"

Mo snorted. "Yes, and two was too many, you were right."

Sloan tsk-tsked. "I told you, lightweight. I hope you didn't make some viral Instagram while you were high."

"Because it would hurt my reputation?"

"No, because I didn't see it yet, and that means my algorithm is all messed up."

Mo laughed, finally. The release felt unnatural. It felt good to pretend the past twelve hours hadn't happened, at least while she could keep up the facade. "You're wearing makeup?" she asked Mackenzie.

Sloan finished the middle toes, smirking but not looking up. "She had a date." Sloan sang the last word, stretching it out like taffy.

"You slept over?" This was news. Mackenzie hadn't had a steady boyfriend during the entire time they had been roommates, and she had never been one to sleep over with randos.

Mackenzie shook her head. "No, it was a breakfast stroll in the park."

Mo wrinkled her nose. "That seems illegal on a Sunday morning."

"Right? It should be punishable by law to be up before nine and have to look good." Mackenzie sighed. "He took me to church, which was cute and awkward. I had to tell him I hadn't really been inside a holy place in a dozen years."

"I'm guessing he didn't count the library?"

"No, he didn't." Mackenzie chewed on her lip. "And the vibe was off, even without the praise band music. Which, again, not super romantic. I was happy to attend his service, but on our walk, I mention my interests—"

"Your favorite romantasy series," Sloan interrupted.

"My favorite romantasy series," Mackenzie agreed, gesturing to the book in her lap, "and he couldn't comprehend the term *fae daddy*. I think he might be more interested in saving me than in wooing me."

Mo laughed. "Yeah, when people talk about soulmates, it's usually not because they're only interested in saving your everlasting soul."

"A special kind of catfishing? Maybe loaves and the fishing?" Sloan asked.

Mackenzie was blowing her fingernails dry, shaking them so that the bright-red nails made slashes in the air. "Enough about me. You were pretty radio silent this weekend. I'm sorry about what happened with Ms. Morgan-Perry, but you have to fill us in. How was Mr. Famous in person? Sloan told me about her research."

Mr. Famous. If only her attraction were just that instead of this complicated mix of competition and horniness and the blooming sense that there was more to Wes than met the very public eye he was often in. How likely was it that you happened to meet your new favorite author at what was basically a job interview, and also find him magnetically attractive? His brown eyes, lightly curling hair, and broad chest—oof, she hadn't known she wanted a thicker guy until she felt how good his arms felt around her in that hot tub, anchoring her to him. He wasn't much taller than she was, but he was solid, and that solidity was just what she wanted now when she felt so adrift. When the ambulance had pulled away, they had gone back to their separate beds until morning—spell broken. She slept horribly, and she missed his body heat, the comforting cocoon of his arms.

She felt the threads of something bigger weaving inside of her, and it scared her. For now, this thing between Wes and her felt like early book projects always did—something she created, nurtured, could revel in inside her skull, but felt worried about sharing for fear of hearing feedback that she didn't like. Still, if anything would help her process, it was her two best friends.

"Uh, Earth to Maureen." Sloan waved a hand in front of Mo's face. "I was asking how your weekend went?"

"You look like something happened and you're waiting for a reason to tell us about it," Mackenzie added.

Mo chewed her lip. "That obvious?"

Mackenzie laughed, that full bright bubble of a laugh that couldn't help but relax Mo. "Look, if I had gotten some action this weekend, it would have also been obvious. Details, please."

Sloan sat up and clapped twice. "You owe me for the gummies! Details!"

Mo spilled everything. There were times when being used to thinking up concrete and interesting descriptions came in handy.

* * *

A year ago, during a lunch catering shift, Aaron had barged into the kitchen and proposed to Maureen. It was a running joke now, every time Mo worked afternoon shifts with Amy, her boss, that some dude was on his way with a ring. With the distance of time, it'd become even funnier. As they stood in the kitchen, waiting to bus the dinner plates, Amy nudged Mo. "Is he coming before, during dessert service, or after?"

Mo folded a stack of napkins into bishop's hats. "Listen, the whole *running through the airport* trope from our childhood rom-com favorites had to go by the wayside because of security, so we're workshopping replacements. *Propose during an inopportune moment at work* could be acceptable. From the right person."

"Which he was not," Amy said.

"Absolutely correct. What about you, Amy? If Rebekka were to propose again, would you want it now, when you have downtime, or do you prefer the spectacle of interrupting the toasts?"

Rebekka was Amy's partner in both business and life. The two had met at Howard, falling in love with each other and with event planning at the same time. Amy pressed her lips together with serious consideration. "Oh, she would have never. She knows me too well. If we did this whole thing again, hot-air balloon proposal or I'd stay single."

"I respect that," Mo said. As emotionally exhausted as she was from the weekend, she was glad to have the Sunday shift to get her mind off things. If she had been stuck home all day, the temptation to Google news articles about Estelle's health or text Wes would overwhelm her self-control. At work, she had timelines to balance, as well as glassware. It was a point of pride for her that she hadn't broken any glasses here. Back at the barbecue restaurant she'd worked at in college, people used to shout "Opa" sarcastically when someone dropped a plate or dish. She had been that someone twice. Judging from the stodgy blue and black suits in the room, Maureen couldn't imagine that the retirement dinner they were serving would have many of the type liable to yodel out a caustic remark at the staff, but you never knew.

The dinner was small enough that she and Amy were the only staff. Besides asking for a lot of decaf coffee, it wasn't a challenging service. Mo was spared from further rumination when Amy brought out the layouts and prep sheets for the upcoming week. Mo took notes on the spreadsheet of the various contacts, allergies, and special situations they needed to follow up on. Amy ran a finger down her copy of the paper and pointed at the different arrangements of tables—six ten-spots, four eights—while Mo followed along, definitely not thinking about Wes's artful tongue and the multiple places it had marked her body last night.

On the subway back to the apartment, she noticed that her hands had pruned from dishwashing. She rubbed her wrists and stretched her raisiny fingers, watching the dark walls of the tunnel pass her by. She liked riding on Sunday nights—it was quieter. A nurse dozed against the window in the seat next to Mo. Across the aisle, an elderly man in a sweatsuit thumbed through a *TIME Magazine*. She hadn't even known they still printed paper editions of *TIME*.

Maureen bet people felt that way about books too. Sloan and Mackenzie read, but so many people Mo knew didn't. It was so strange to dedicate your life in pursuit of something that would not matter to 99.99 percent of the world, even if your book was a relative success. Anna read romance novels with Mo, which she appreciated, but her sister had refused on principle to read *The Proud and the Lost*, even in high school when it was assigned. "When there is a CliffsNotes of something," Anna had said, "that is a sign that God doesn't want you to waste your time."

Mo's rejoinder was always that nowhere in the Bible did it say that God's name was Cliff, but whatever.

Maybe it was talking about Aaron with Amy, or maybe it was being fresh from her first good orgasm with another person post-relationship, but she let herself think about Aaron's proposal for the first time in a long time. He had burst into the kitchen during a dinner service, proposed while she was still in her apron. Could any action be romantic if someone was thinking about table settings during it?

So she'd said no. He'd asked, and she hadn't been prepared. Of course he'd been hurt, but he slung words at her that dug so deep she wondered how long he'd been thinking them. "You work too much. You want too much. Like, when you're not at your job, you're writing. I thought I could show you how much I love you. How much I want to spend my life with you. I thought I could shock you out of your routine."

If she could've thought of anything to say, if she could rewind to that moment, she would tell him that her routine *was* her life. She didn't know what else to say beyond that. He had liked her in their quiet, domestic moments, and he had liked the moments he could show her around to his friends. He didn't like the hours she needed to herself, space to think and write and exist without him being the center of her day. The warning signs were there, had she paid attention. Sure, he hadn't overly celebrated the short stories she had published in the year they had been together. She thought it wouldn't bother her to have a boyfriend who "didn't read." In the past, if a guy could understand the space she needed to make for her writing, then they could make it work, but something had changed inside her as she'd been working on the adaptation. Why was ambition a dirty word for women? Why was it so bad that she worked hard?

If the weekend with Wes had done nothing else, it had shown her that she wanted a partner who was as excited about her work as they were about her body. Her creative life was a part of her personality. It was such a big part of her, and she needed someone who could not only tolerate but embrace and support that.

If only they weren't her direct competition.

CHAPTER FIFTEEN

Wes

Being a workaholic came in handy when Wes was trying to distract himself from having any feelings at all—good, bad, ambivalent, stressed—but it was less useful when dealing with constant sexual thoughts. Not that there weren't other feelings, confusing ones, wrapped up in his thoughts about Mo, but he could pretend not to feel them while he proofread recipes for crepes and formatted the submission for one of his fantasy authors. His email, which he had ignored all weekend, created a ten-foot-tall digital barricade to hide behind by Monday morning. He had at least thirty emails that needed responses approximately yesterday, preferably last week, and a hundred he would cull through before EOD.

By noon, he'd dug through a third of the most urgent issues and drunk three cups of coffee. He took a thirty-minute lunch break to clear his head and walk around the park, hoping to also free himself from the constant urge to text Mo. He walked down the front steps, protein shake in hand, mentally bargaining with himself. *Suppose you get all your work done by five. Maybe you could text her then.*

The birds were flirting with each other on the sidewalk, which didn't help things. Pigeons chased each other like horny assholes, and sparrows made aerial passes at one another. He thought about what Mo had said about pheromones. Maybe those were to blame. She'd left some kind of chemical marker on him, which despite a silent ride home and visiting the hospital yesterday had set him up last night for some of the hottest dreams he'd ever had.

Not that if he texted to say hi, she would come over. And definitely not that if she came over, they would have sex, preferably in his large-enough-for-two-people-shower, the one he'd never taken full advantage of since moving in.

He didn't realize how hard he was squeezing the shake until it splashed all over his shirt. He detoured, taking a shortcut back to the door of his condo, and used the rest of the lunch break to wash up, change, and pretreat the laundry. Wes worked from his couch, in his brownstone, which wasn't technically *his* brownstone but his parents'. It was a late-nineteenth-century, dun-colored three-bedroom in Fort Greene. His living room and upstairs office were lined with bookshelves, including books he had sold for his clients. He loved the brownstone: the wide windows facing the park; the open kitchen; the eclectic art on the walls.

He would love this brownstone even more if he could show it to Mo. He finished work by four thirty and held off texting until five so he didn't seem desperate.

Hi, it's your personal driver.
Kidding, hi. It's me.

Hi, me. It's me, too.
Good to hear from you, me.
Hi? Still there?

> *Sorry just trying to figure out if I should say*
> *it's good to hear from me, too or from you, too, me*
> *This is getting kind of confusing.*

And you say you're a writer

> *About that, did you want to keep reading?*
> *Our books, that is?*

Yes
!
Sorry, meant to put those together. Yes!

> *Cool. Here's my address. Free tonight?*

Yes

> *No exclamation point this time?*

I don't want you getting the idea that I like
you that much.

> *!*

Wes's place was always clean, so he didn't have to do much tidying before Maureen arrived at eight. When his phone rang at 7:50, he assumed she'd gotten there early and was waiting to be let up, but the caller ID said something different.

Wes cleared his throat before picking up. "Hi, Dad."

"Ulla said she told you this weekend? About everything?" His dad always cut out the general niceties at the beginning of a conversation. Despite years of living in the States, he still had a slight Irish brogue and a definite Irish lack of appreciation for bullshit conversations. His dad knew that if he asked how Wes was, Wes would lie and always say fine. Wes knew if he asked his dad how he was, he would always tell the truth and include every sore joint he had, so they had come to this agreed spot in the middle.

"How's Tahoe?" Wes asked by way of an answer.

"Oh, fine, fine. I drove the 'vette out here. Long ride for the little bugger, but I think it enjoyed stretching its legs. Everything else is coming in a pod later. Have you seen those pods? They put them in the yard, and you pack everything in."

"*You* packed everything in?"

"Well, I had some people pack things in. Then the truck came, and it met me here. The person that invented that must be rich."

"You're rich," Wes said. The clock on the microwave said 7:55. "Listen, Dad, I have a friend coming over soon. Did you need something?"

A smile came into his dad's voice. "A friend? A boyfriend or a girlfriend?"

"A girl friend, with a space between *girl* and *friend*," Wes said. "Friend that is a girl."

"Always so literal. I wanted to make sure you're all right. I know that it's a change, but we both love you very much. I'm still here for you. Just—"

"Just in Tahoe."

"Right, just in Tahoe. But a phone call away."

"Or I can pack you up in one of those pods and send you back here, huh?"

His dad laughed again, but then turned serious. "Listen, I remember when my parents divorced—"

Wes interrupted him. "Ulla said it was a separation?"

A pause. A throat clearing. "Well, she has her own ways of phrasing things. Marketing them, as she does."

"Oh," Wes said. His knees felt weak suddenly. "I didn't know it was final."

"I won't interrupt your time with your friend." Wes's father put a slight emphasis on the word but softened it in the next sentence. "But we're still a family, and I love you, son. I don't get to tell you enough."

Wes hung up, disconcerted. He wasn't thrown by his dad's affectionate tone—his father had always been a hugger, a feelings sharer, whereas his mother had the buttoned-up manner of someone too used to being burned by people's uncareful words. His dad was worried that Wes might be worried, which in turn made Wes feel even worse. He leaned into Ulla's worldview in most things, uncertain how to emote in the same open way his father did, but now Wes wanted to call him back and ask *Whose idea was it?*

The doorbell rang, shaking Wes out of his mental spiral. He threw a last look around the living room, lit a candle on the fireplace, and walked down the stairs to the entryway.

Mo had a bottle of wine in one hand and her manuscript in the other. Wes didn't bother telling her he had both wine and her book here. He'd managed to hold off reading it so far, waiting for her. His own personal audiobook narrator.

Who Wes had kissed and done much more to. Whose taste he knew. Whose breasts looked really good under her yellow linen jumpsuit.

She handed Wes her pink coat, and he hung it on one of the hooks leading from the stairs up to the main floor. Wes saw her glancing around and tried to take in the place from an outsider's perspective. Hardwood floors and high ceilings. Mismatched art on the wall he'd collected from flea markets and friends' art shows. In his main room, a mural of Winnie the Pooh smoking a hookah with Piglet dominated the wall. She gestured at it. "And I'm the one who got in trouble for edibles last weekend?"

"Hookah is only flavored tobacco," Wes said, hands up in defense. "My friend Ajay made it. They have a show quarterly. This was one of the less risqué pieces in their collection."

"Oh no—hopefully not sexy?"

"No, no. But children's book characters and drug use was the theme of the show, and some of them got dark. Something about the toll of criminalizing drug abuse? It got a write-up in the *Times*."

She sat on the couch, nestling an orange throw pillow under her elbow to prop herself up. "I don't have much reason to be in this area often."

"Well, I don't have much reason to invite people over, so thanks for coming."

"Are you sure you're not midwestern?" she laughed. "That definitely felt like a deferential neighbor about to bring out a casserole."

"I have absolutely never made a casserole."

"As a person of Iowan origin, I'm not sure this will work," she said, then blushed. "Like, by *this* I mean being critique partners. My MFA cohort has mostly fallen out of touch, and most of my writing friends in the city are poets."

"Well, I can't promise to critique your book," Wes said. He didn't want to critique her book. It was one of the things that had made him consider leaving Yuri's agency before circumstances forced him to. He found that he had been unable to find much to criticize in Maureen's first novel. Yuri told Wes then that he didn't have the editorial eye needed to work in this business, and though he'd proved her wrong time and again, he couldn't help wondering whether, if he had allowed himself more emotional distance from Mo's first book, found some sort of flaw that no one else could see, she could have whipped it into the kind of shape to be sold. Wes didn't tell her this, though. He couldn't tell her that this wasn't his first time falling in love with one of her projects. Revealing that detail would reveal too much about who he'd been while Yuri's intern. And what he'd done.

Instead, he took a deep breath and said, "I think this is a mutual-admiration society. Or at least that's how I see it. For books, that is. I really like hearing yours."

"Like an old-school literary salon," she said, standing again. The jumpsuit shifted, pressing against her hips. He watched her move as she walked into the kitchen. Observation was an important skill in a writer. "Wineglasses and corkscrew in here?"

"Yes," Wes called. When she didn't immediately return, he roused himself and followed. He found her standing in front of the open fridge.

She wheeled around, wine bottle in one hand and a block of cheese in the other. It was a three-year aged cheddar he'd bought a few days ago. "I hope you don't mind," she said. "If you didn't have plans for this, it would pair really well."

"I mean, I was going to shred it for a casserole," he said, straight faced.

And then she threw the block of cheese at him.

CHAPTER SIXTEEN

Mo

Once Wes and Mo got settled on the couch—wine poured and cheese sliced thinly with one of those wire cheese cutters—they started reading from the chapters of their books, alternating back and forth. Mo liked the way he edged to the other side of the couch and watched while she read, not interrupting until she'd gotten to the end of a chapter. She was less patient, interrupting him to ask where he'd drawn material from and trying to peer into his brain, the brain under the curling brown hair he had that she knew from experience was fun to comb through with her fingers.

Was it surreal to sit across the couch from someone she'd had very good orgasms with and not be touching them? Yes. But after the weirdness of how things ended on Sunday, it was a relief to pretend it had never happened. Almost. Still, he didn't kiss her cheek when she got to his house. Even in the kitchen, after she threw the cheese—not *at* his head, as he had accusingly stated, but *near* his head—he hadn't touched her. No playful shoving.

It wasn't like the electricity was gone between them, but something was off. She hadn't gone over to his place with any unstated hope that they would pick back up where they left off Saturday night. Or maybe she had hoped that but was adult enough to understand that flings happened. Normal people could be friends afterward. It just hadn't happened to her yet, this fling-then-friend thing that she guessed they were walking into. Or, more accurately, this LinkedIn-connection-then-rival-fling-now-friend thing.

She finally allowed him to finish his second chapter, and he refilled her wineglass. As she nibbled on the cheese, she held a hand below her chin to catch the crumbs. "I do have plates," he said, looking amused. "As long as you promise not to throw those at me too."

She reached out, intending to wiggle her cheesy fingers in his direction, but he caught her hand in his and held her palm up for inspection.

"What?" she asked.

He wiped her palm, then smiled and released it. "Getting the crumbs off."

"I thought you were going to lick them off or something." She meant the tone to be joking, but her breath caught when she imagined his perfect tongue and what it had done between her thighs.

He lay the manuscript down on the table and inched closer on the couch. His gaze tracked her expression. "You're a good distraction, you know that? And I am not easily distracted."

His tone, almost sad, surprised her. A glass of wine in, stomach buffered comfortably with good cheddar and thirty pages further in his book, Mo felt happier than she had been an hour ago. But he didn't look similarly content. "What do you need distracting from?"

He lay his head back and rubbed his chin gently. She tried not to remember how nice that scruff had felt scraping against her belly as he kissed down her body. He must use oil to keep it soft. No, she would focus on the moment, on this man who obviously had something on his mind. After a second, he said, "My parents are splitting up."

"Oh. I'm sorry."

"You didn't do it."

"No, I know. Is that what your mom was talking to you about this weekend?" Mo felt even worse for tagging along to what had probably become an intense family moment.

"Sort of. She told me they were separating, but I guess they are filing for divorce. Ulla: queen of the understatement. She said, meeting Beyoncé in the late nineties, that she thought she would 'do well for herself.'"

Mo laughed at that. "She wasn't wrong."

He refilled the wineglasses, then took a sip. "I know it's dumb to think this has anything to do with me. I don't live at home, and it's not like I won't see them. Ultimately, they're adults and they have to live their own lives, not the life I wish they could live."

"Which would have them stay together?" she asked.

"Right, which would have them stay together. I guess I always found hope in their marriage lasting so long, despite her getting famous and him barely tolerating the limelight. I loved being able to point to them as an example of very different people making a relationship work."

"Ha, well, my parents are a good example of that, if you still want hope," Mo said. "My mom was a farm kid–turned–

Democratic organizer and fell in love with a construction worker who'd never traveled. They met in high school, dated, then before they settled down and had kids, they went around the world together. I think they've brought that love of exploration to everything they've done since. Even when it's owning pigs."

"That's pretty cool," he said.

"They're going on thirty-eight years. I'll get to celebrate with them when I go home next weekend for my sister's wedding shower."

"What are her colors?"

"Daffodil and gray. I'm not used to having a guy friend ask, to be honest."

"Ha, I've sat in on enough of the layout and editorial meetings for *Ulla*. If I get married someday, I'd have opinions."

"I think grooms *should*."

"Anyone involved in a marriage should have an opinion about a wedding. I helped Ulla realize that she was missing a lot of engaged couples who might not have seen themselves covered before," Wes said, visibly relaxing as they steered further from the topic of his parents. "A few years ago, my friends Ajay and Loris got married, and she covered it for the magazine. Not only do they have style and a sense of humor—Ajay is the painter who made that Winnie the Pooh painting—but Ajay was a broom; they're nonbinary and loved that term. Representation is important in the media. When magazines only talk about brides and grooms and ignore the brooms, marriers, and partners, you miss out on a whole chunk of people trying to celebrate their love."

They each finished a second glass of wine, and Mo was halfway through a third when she said, "I turned down a wedding proposal last year."

He put his glass down on the table and raised his eyebrow at her. "Really?"

"For someone who should be great at reading, I totally misread the whole situation, and he thought it was more serious than it was. I mean, he hadn't even met my family yet."

"See, I always make all my friends meet my family at random coffee shops and used-clothing stores with no preparation," Wes said.

Mo laughed. "Definitely preferable to the alternative. Plus, he surprised me at work. It was not a good surprise."

"He probably didn't even bring the customary engagement casserole," Wes deadpanned.

"For your cultural edification, if I had been Minnesotan, it would be the Proposal Hotdish. Absolutely written into law." She was glad to joke rather than linger on one of the most embarrassing moments of her life. "No matter what state, a potato is essential. Tater Tots are customary."

"Do the Tater Tots go on top, or is it a mixed-through thing?"

"Oh, on top. There's also a multilayer cheese throughout, *then* on-top situation."

"Sounds pretty kinky," he said, then picked his glass up and noticed it was empty. "Wow, I've had enough to drink."

Mo snorted into hers. They had been so busy talking and laughing that she hadn't even thought about nestling under his arm. Now, more than tipsy, she didn't want to make a move. He seemed to see her hesitation as she drew her hand from the place between them on the couch. "Let me call you an Uber. It's late."

"Oh, sure," Mo said. "Thank you."

He held her gaze and said, "About my parents—we need to keep that between us."

How weird it must be to have your family's personal business of interest to the world. She was used to how fast rumors spread in a small town, but New York felt so huge that it was easy to be anonymous—unless you were rich and famous. "Of course."

Maureen gathered her manuscript and bag while he cleaned up the living room. He held the neck of his wineglasses between his fingers on one hand, then carried the cheese board and cutter with the other. She surveyed the room when he went into the kitchen, suddenly worried that she might not be back. She hadn't even seen his full book collection, and she imagined it was huge.

Even that adjective made her feel a little weak at the knees, remembering the weight of him on top of her, his broad back, the sensation of him between her hands under the sheets. She prayed he would chalk up any blushing to the wine and not her dirty brain. She didn't know what he wanted from her. They were still competitors, at least she assumed so. Estelle was hospitalized and Wes was stressed by this new separation. Timing wasn't great, but being so close to him and laughing like they had tonight made her realize she wanted more eventually. This friendship was great, but also, she wanted the kissing again. She wanted his body on hers.

"Ready?"

"Yeah, for sure."

He waited with her on the stoop until the Uber came, double-checking the car type against what was listed in the app. As she was about to get into the blue Focus with the driver, Abraham, Wes caught her hand. "Thanks for coming over. This was nice."

"I want to hear more," she said. Her voice came out more demure than she felt, weaving through the dark spring air to become something furtive. "More of your book, I mean. It's kind of a tease to leave me wanting more like this."

"I've never been called a tease before," he said. He ran a finger over her cheek, then stepped back over the threshold. "Thursday?"

They made plans, and she got into the back of the Focus with cheeks burning and a smile on her face. If Mo had worried that she had friend-zoned herself, that light touch, that gentle caress, told her everything she needed to know. She didn't need to worry—at least not about him wanting her. Everything else, including her feelings getting hurt, the chance at publishing the book of her dreams, and not ruining her sister's wedding somehow? Well, that was a different set of problems altogether.

CHAPTER SEVENTEEN

Wes

Wes started Thursday morning with cereal and a text from Mo. *Did you do your morning pages?*

He smiled at the phone. *Yes. And they are complete shit. You?*

Not sure if I should say they are worse shit or better. If we're competing.

I doubt they could be worse. Regardless of quality, he was grateful for the practice of typing every day. He liked thinking of it as typing, not writing, because it freed his brain to be terrible. He was more than surprised at the direction this work had taken the past few days, though. After the conversation in the hospital, he couldn't get the idea of selling trauma off his mind. He had never written something with a happy ending, not even in short story form, and was challenging himself to do just that. He was typing a romance novel that no one would ever see, and it was stretching every bit of his creative muscles.

He saw she had texted again. *Still on to exchange chapters tonight?*

Wes allowed a suitable number of breaths to pass before he typed back. He thought about her too much—the way her voice sounded when she read aloud, the thump of his heart when he saw her pink coat come into view. *Yeah, absolutely*, he texted.

My roommates are out at a show, if you want to come here, she offered.

Wes considered her noisy street, the compact apartment. The probably thin walls and nosy neighbors. He wasn't imagining doing anything that might necessitate privacy—but they could. As in, if they wanted to read extra loudly, it would be good to have no shared walls. If they did other things, he didn't want her to have to stifle herself like they had to at Estelle's. "My place is still fine, if you don't mind making the trip."

She texted back a thumbs-up, and Wes didn't imagine what her real thumb could do as it rubbed him, her hand enclosing . . . He couldn't do that, because he had work to do.

He worked diligently all day so that he could unplug that night and truly be present with Mo. The only break he took was to answer a call from Ajay.

"I need you there," Ajay said, their voice pleading. Their voice was always pleading this close to a gallery opening. It was less than two weeks away, prime worry time.

Wes pictured them on the other end of the phone, running their hands through curly black hair. Ajay had been so distraught before the opening of the Winnie the Pooh show that they made Wes come over for Jell-O shots beforehand, something they hadn't done since their dorm days at Penn. Wes could still taste the astringent mix of vodka and lime in his mouth. Alcohol shouldn't be chewy. "I will be there, Ajay. You know that."

It had only been chance at the admissions office that matched them together freshman year, but love and true fondness had kept them that way. The only real challenge to the friendship came when Ajay started dating Loris, a one-time fling of Wes's, during sophomore year, but that was ten years plus one wedding ring ago. Now Ajay, Loris, and their elderly puggle, Hubert, lived in a cute condo on the Upper West Side that was overstuffed with paintings and furniture with trendy stick legs and uncomfortable seats. They had framed pictures of their *Ulla* wedding coverage in their front hallway.

"What's the theme this time?"

"Theme?" Ajay puffed out a breath. "I prefer to call it the next extension of my oeuvre."

Wes laughed. "All right, so what is the extension this time? Care Bears Doing Lines of Coke?"

"No, it's called Power Rangers. I'm painting the richest people, the famous, the political underpinning of society, but with Power Rangers."

"As in *Mighty Morphin*?"

"It's a play on nostalgia, obviously."

"Obviously? I forgot Power Rangers were even a thing."

"Your loss."

Wes bit his cheek, afraid to ask. "You didn't paint my mom, did you?"

"Oh, honey, I can't tell you that. I'm not telling anyone ahead of time. I painted these in secret. Not even Hubie has peeked."

Wes thought about the imperative to protect his mother from the paparazzi right now. But honestly, it was unlikely that a mostly obscure modern artist would make waves big enough to drench them all. Even if it did, he had to support his friend. "Can't wait to see you," he said finally.

"Bringing anyone?" Their tone was as curious as it was needling. Loris and Ajay, like many long-settled couples, ruthlessly matched up single friends.

"Maybe."

"Not your mother! Not that I don't love her. Bring her, too, but bring *someone*, or I will be forced to Pygmalion you a partner one of these days."

"*My Fair Lady* version or actual statuary?"

"Both. Either. I will musical theater your life if you don't figure it out."

Wes laughed. "All right, yes, put me down for some guests."

He hung up without telling Ajay that the only person he wanted to see was on her way to his place and he'd been thinking about it all day.

He saw Maureen's book sitting dog-eared and marked up on the kitchen counter, where he'd left it after perusing it over his dinner tonight. The truth was this: He had already finished reading her book. Twice. He'd been interrupted from his second reading by Ajay's phone call and now had come dangerously close to Mo seeing it lying around. Wes took it to the bedroom and stuck the manuscript under his mattress like it was a dirty magazine.

Wes had to act surprised by whatever she read tonight. He practiced expressions in the mirror as he brushed his teeth, but they didn't look convincing to him. How to pretend he didn't know what was coming when he'd made tiny pencil marks in the margins of the copy Gary had made? Yes, he had delayed reading one of his client's books in the meantime, but he was only human. The rest of her novel had risen around him like a tide, carrying him into it. That was the sign of a good book: He thought about it when he put it down. It was hard not to analyze her project like Wes did with the authors querying him for representation. Unlike those projects, which he usually read on his e-reader, Wes had the paper copy in front of him. It was strangely personal to have the paper, slightly warm, under his fingers.

He couldn't stop thinking about having other warm things under his fingers.

A knock at the door. He needed to stop his dirty thoughts before he greeted Mo, or she would see something in his face. He would not think about sinking into her hair, her shoulder, him pressing—

He opened the door. At some point in the past two hours, it had started to rain without him realizing. Mo held a newspaper over her head, hair drenched like she had been saved from a ship. Wes ushered her inside, and she slipped off her shoes in the front hallway, shivering as Wes took her pink coat. "Sky opened while I was walking from the station. It came out of nowhere."

Like you, Wes thought. He took her arm gently as she walked barefoot into the living room. He was about to put her wet coat in the dryer when he realized that her dress was soaked too. "Do you want to get out of those wet things? I can put everything in the dryer while we hang out." She made a face, and Wes laughed. "And you can borrow clothes, of course."

"I was going to say—but yes, sure. If you have some gym clothes I could borrow or whatever."

"A robe?"

She nodded. "That'd be cozy."

Wes found his bathrobe, luckily laundered a few days ago and not used since. It was gray and soft and overly long. He liked to wear it in the mornings sometimes to remind himself why working from home was better than having an office.

And when she came out of the bathroom wearing only his robe, he reminded himself why being at his home was better than her place, for sure.

CHAPTER EIGHTEEN

Mo

When did handing someone a ball of sopping-wet clothes become such a fraught movement? Wes's hand grazed hers as Mo passed him the bundle—the dress she had picked out so carefully an hour ago, and even the underwear, which she'd chosen even more carefully. It wasn't silk or anything, but it was blue and lacy. She tucked it inside the dress so he didn't feel it on top. The robe cinched around her waist and fell to her knees, longer than the robe she had at home by at least three inches—which tracked, because he was about three inches taller than her.

She curled up on his couch, legs tucked under her. A fire roared in the fireplace across from them, reminding her of how lovely it could be to be safe out of the storm. Suddenly, she blanched. "My book. I'm sure—"

She jumped from the couch, ran to the front door, and dug into her soaked bag. Her copy, so carefully spiral bound last week for way too much money, twice as much as any book of hers would retail for on a shelf, was more than damp.

She nestled it in her arms and carried the limp pages back to the couch. "Well, there goes my project. Sorry the reading will be one-sided today. I don't think I can even separate the pages while they're this wet."

He pursed his lips, then took the soggy mess from her. "Let me put this in the kitchen."

"So we can bake with it? I heard you repped cookbooks, but I didn't know that was what you meant."

He stared at her for a moment, and she self-consciously ran a hand through her hair. It was damp and as ragged as the book had been. "What?" she asked when the silence had stretched between them a second too long.

"Do you trust me?"

It was a hard question to answer. She shouldn't, not with things as they were. He had reasons to look out for his own self-interest. Still, she answered honestly. "I want to."

That response made him look at her face for another moment, reading her expression like he'd read his own words at the Hill: carefully, with reverence. "Okay, I have a few things to explain. Follow me."

First, he detoured to the kitchen and put the lumpy book on the counter. It hadn't completely reverted to pulp, but its edges were curling up on the sides. He led her up the staircase that she had ignored on her first trip to his house. A place in New York with a second level was more telling than showing your bank account balance. There was another room down the hall farther that teased her—she had to guess it was his office, probably full of books she wanted to talk to him about. She wondered where he wrote his morning pages. There? In bed? On the couch? She didn't have much time to wonder as he led her to the lip of his bedroom and motioned for her to stop. She scanned the room from her spot at the door—the quarter-sawn oak furniture and the kind of careworn woven tan rug over the hardwood floor that looked effortlessly thirty. The kind of *I'm thirty and I have things figured out* that Mo longed for but knew she was about three pay grades away from attaining.

He leaned over the opposite side of the queen bed and pulled out a spiral-bound manuscript from under the crisp white linen. "So—this is also your book. Technically. Just another copy of it."

Her heart beat against her ribs. "How . . . how did you get that?"

"Gary. When Talia and Flor came to the Hill, he made me a copy too."

She felt her eyebrows rise, then lower quickly, thinking about how complicated that day had been in the best and worst ways. She focused on the question at hand. "You had a copy of my book this whole week?"

Wes crossed the bedroom, expression sheepish. "Yes. But here—" He put the solid weight of the manuscript into her hands. Her copy had been bound in pink, but this one had standard black rings. The front page, and everything else, was the same. She flipped through it and noticed notation in the margins—underlines and stars, even a few question marks. The marks trailed all the way from the first page to the last. He hadn't only had her book, he'd read it. The whole thing. And judging from the multiple ink colors, he'd read it a few times. "You finished it? Since Sunday?"

"Twice."

She couldn't help but laugh, though her hands were shaking. "When I was sitting here reading and you'd already heard those chapters, knew everything coming up—"

"I read it between Monday and today. That wasn't fake. Plus I wouldn't have to act like I was enjoying you reading to me. It's hard to fake things around you."

"Except when you've got this major leg up on me!" Mo realized she wasn't feeling angry but jealous. Jealous that he'd had a chance to read through her full book when she desperately wanted to do that for his. She shook her manuscript, and the pages flapped. "I call for a détente. I demand a copy of yours."

"Mine?"

"Of course. I'm sure you have one around here, maybe stuck on the other side of your mattress. It's only fair."

He paused, blinked. A sheepish look crept over his face. "But then you don't have a reason to come back here."

"Of course I would, you jerk! First, you have the best robes in the city." She took a step closer to him, all sharp edges melting at the uncertainty in his expression. She had misjudged things, obviously. She had seen the differences between them with all the power on his side—his wealth, his position in publishing, his parents' connections—but she had somehow upset his balance, unsteadied him. She liked that, the ability to get into his head as much as he'd been messing with hers, to crawl into his life and arch her back to make herself take up more room, a pocket meant for her.

He hadn't been caught in the rain. He had been allowed to keep on whatever he'd chosen to see her in tonight, and she took in his choices for the first time. A pale-blue shirt, rolled at the elbows. His hair had product in it that made it look controlled but soft. She reached out and touched his hair, pushing a strand away from his face.

He reached his hand up to touch hers, then brought her fingers to his lips. "You taste like rain," he said.

"Wow, city rain is toxic bathwater, so apologies for that."

He laughed and pulled her hand up slightly, kissing up her wrists, letting the robe drape backward to her elbow. She shivered as his butterfly kisses moved up the inside of the middle of her arm. It wasn't ticklish, that was for sure, but she felt a stirring of something that made her feel the need to swallow a laugh. She had to stop her mouth before she ruined everything. She caught his jaw with two fingers and redirected his lips to meet hers.

He put his hand on the belt of her robe, but she moved it off. Mo knew they hadn't come upstairs to do this, but his bed was right here. It was all so close. She dropped the manuscript and shoved him lightly. He fell back on the bed, smiling up at her. "You are so beautiful," he said.

"Don't be corny," she said.

"Like Cornhuskers?"

"That's Nebraska," she chided, kissing his cheek. "Again with failing the Midwest cultural competencies, Wes."

He turned his head to catch her lips with his. The robe had parted slightly now that Mo straddled Wes's body. One of his hands ran down the back of the robe while the other sat patiently on her bare thigh. He glanced down at their bodies, which were suddenly tangled. "I didn't bring you up here to seduce you."

"Your moves are just too effective, I guess," she said.

He sat up slightly, forcing her to do the same with their position. His eyes scanned hers, as if trying to translate her thoughts. "We shouldn't. You came over here to read, right? We should read."

She pulled her robe closed, trying to understand what had changed in the last minute. "What's wrong?"

"I don't want you to hate me after this. Do you know what I mean?"

She sat across from him, removing her weight from on top of him. His expression was guarded, more guarded than it had been when admitting he'd had a secret copy of her book. "No. Tell me."

"I don't want to do this because you feel like you have to. With me. Or to make it feel like I expect it because of what we did the other night. We said once we got back from the Hill that, well, that we got things out of our system. Just friendly. I'm fine with being friends. I want to be friends with you."

"But that's it. Is that what you're saying?" She couldn't help but be offended.

It was only because she was watching him so closely that she saw the fear in his face. "No, I'm just saying we can slow down. We don't have to rush anything. I don't want you to regret . . ."

"Is this because you're sure you're going to win?"

His eyebrows knotted in frustration. "This has nothing to do with the contest. It's that when this, whatever this is, ends—"

She kissed him, stopping his mouth with hers. She felt his face relax, his hand moving up to her cheek. "I wouldn't be here if I didn't want to be. Don't worry about endings. This doesn't need to be outlined, okay? Just improv a little here."

He nodded against her lips and muttered, "Okay."

She needed to pull him out of his head, so she changed tactics. "Aren't you at all ashamed of keeping a secret from me?" she asked. "Reading me in private?"

"Oh, I should have been reading a dozen other things, but I couldn't stop."

"Praise me, then," Mo said, her tone light. She leaned back on an elbow, tried to look puckish and self-assured. He rolled her sideways so he could get on top, then he brushed the damp hair away from her face.

"I didn't want it to end," he said. His eyes met hers, but one of his hands traced the outside of her thigh gently. "It was one long tease—knowing how it ended but going mad trying to figure out how you got there."

She wriggled her hips underneath him, unable to keep still. She felt him react, tighten against her. Good. She wanted him here, present. "More," she said.

He laid a palm lightly on her stomach to hold her steady, resting it on top of the knot to the robe. "And your sentences," he said, his mouth close to her ear now and fingers working at the knot. His beard tickled her cheek. "Who taught you to write sentences like that?"

Her skin tingled as he pulled back the robe, exposing her body to the air. She was still wet from the rain, and her skin goose-bumped in the cool room. She didn't want to draw the robe around her, though, especially since Wes lowered his mouth on her neck, kissing a line from one end of her collarbone to the other. "And your metaphors—your extended metaphors were sublime."

She pushed up slightly, face close to his. "Oh really? What extended metaphor was that?"

He kissed the upper part of her chest, forcing her back down on the bed. Between kisses he said, "The car, the car that Clive gives her. The one she drives away in at the end."

Her brain was trying to split in two now, one part—the part tied into the nerves in her breasts—wanting to focus on what his tongue was doing. Gentle flicks, the scratch of his cheek against her sensitive skin. But that part of her brain wasn't the one controlling her mouth. "What did you"—here she couldn't help moaning as his teeth bit down softly—"see that as a metaphor for?"

He looked up from his work, eyebrow cocked. "Oh, the car was the American dream, or at least as far as capitalism can take you."

She laughed at that. "Sometimes a car is just a car."

He made a noise of disagreement, then pushed back the rest of her robe to fall slack on the bed. His face rose toward hers, brown eyes meeting her hazel ones. He paused there, one hand moving back to her waist.

The touch, lightly moving across her hips, made her analytical brain fizzle, almost refusing to come back online as a shot of warmth went through her core. Sex and pleasure were sometimes intertwined in her life—but more often, sex was another kind of emotional intimacy first and foremost. She had a little device in the top drawer for nights when she needed release. She had been brought to orgasm by men before, but it wasn't a given, not even with Aaron. Men didn't seem to always take the time, and she felt awkward telling them what she needed. If a guy needed a checklist to get there, it wasn't worth it to her. But with Wes, it was different. She'd never been so attuned to what was going on with her body, never had a lover this patient. Every inch of skin waited for him to make his next move. She felt each part of him separately, dividing her attention as best as she could as one of his hands continued to play with her breast and his mouth moved lower and lower until it rested between her thighs.

She heard herself gasping—not orgasming but enjoying the heightened pleasure of his conscientious attention. He heard it too, casting his eyes to hers. Those eyes, warm brown under a tangle of dark hair. She couldn't resist any more and moved her hands to plant into his curls. He raised himself up and placed her hands above her head. "I'm not in a rush, are you?"

How could she tell him that she was—that the longer he took, the better he made her feel before she came, the more time she had to picture this happening again? The longer the memory, the more potent, the less likely that she could go back to her room tonight and not wish she'd stayed over. Not wish this would become something more. She didn't want to complicate things, but they already had, hadn't they? He'd read her book, and he'd read her—both too well. Both in ways that she hadn't even read herself. "Not everything is a competition."

"Isn't it?" he asked. "Because I bet I get you first."

That was a bet he won. As she came down, head still spinning and made worse by how hot she felt, she whispered in his ear. "You got a head start. Not fair." She liked the uneven playing field, the way her pleasure seemed to give him pleasure.

She tugged on the collar of his shirt, which was still on. In a minute, he had evened the score. They were both naked, him lying next to her and the robe kicked completely off the bed. He pulled a condom from the top drawer of his dresser and rolled it on. After, she kissed him, tasting herself on his lips, and as the kiss deepened, she shifted her weight on top of him and held his hands above his head. She pressed down on them experimentally. "You said you like to lose control sometimes, don't you?"

He didn't exactly growl, but he didn't exactly not growl.

"Listen," she said, biting his earlobe, then releasing when he sighed. "When I write a metaphor, you will know it's a metaphor."

He chuckled, deep in his chest, and tried to move his hands. She kissed him harder, holding them. She knew he could break free if he wanted to, but the wicked smile on his face told Maureen he was enjoying this reversal as much as she had enjoyed his hands on her earlier. After a second, she reached behind her, letting his arms go, and pulled him close.

Sometimes sex was the destination, the moment of climax, but every time Wes had touched her, it was journey focused. He was locked in on her, her pleasure, and she couldn't look away from his face. Finally, he entered her, and it truly felt like that—all of him filling all of her up, core to chest to head. He took up space inside her brain every moment, and not just these ones when they were naked. This was dangerous. She knew she shouldn't fall for him, but when he was so eager to catch her—when his hands were holding her tight enough to let her feel safe falling—then how could she resist? That face he made, the way he bit his lip to hold on for her, did it, sent her spiraling over the cliff and into herself again.

They finished together and lay back panting. She realized she was, in every sense of the word, really and truly fucked. She'd told him not to think about endings. To improv with her. The truth was that she wanted him, all of him, and she would never be satisfied unless she could have him.

CHAPTER NINETEEN

Wes

Finally, finally, he could appreciate the benefits of this huge shower. By the time he had warmed the water, Mo had joined him in the bathroom, and together they lived up to its potential. Wes knelt before her, worshipping her under the jets until she fell back against the wall and landed next to his shampoos on the seat. He had never brought a partner in here before. There'd been a woman a few months ago, but that hadn't lasted long and the only connection she cared about was the ones Wes could make for her. Then he'd seen a guy for about three months about a year ago, but the guy broke it off when someone else came along. Wes hadn't even been heartbroken. He hadn't been ready to make a commitment anyway, and it felt like serendipity to let him go.

But gazing at Mo's face under the running water, soaping her as she sat on the seat afterward—gently, not sexually, from her toes to her thighs—made Wes realize that he couldn't not do this again. He needed her, needed to be able to explore every room of this brownstone with her, but also every corner of this city. He wanted her to meet Ajay and Loris. He wanted to ask her thoughts about bookstores—which ones did she go to, and which booksellers did she ask for recommendations from? He wanted to know her coffee order—it felt wrong that he didn't already, when he knew so much about her body and her book.

They toweled off—or rather, he wrapped a towel around himself so he could grab her one from the hallway. She stood at the doorway, completely naked, watching him fetch it for her. "So fancy and domestic. You even have a linen closet."

He handed her the towel, and she dried her face before wrapping it around her body like a dress. Her skin, the part that wasn't covered, had goose bumps up and down from the few seconds' delay, and he felt a twinge of guilt. "Are you . . . can you stay over?" he asked.

"I mean, it is pretty late."

It was only nine thirty. "And it could rain again at any moment."

"This feels more and more like 'Baby, It's Cold Outside.'"

He grimaced. "Oh, man, I'm sorry. That song is awful."

"I like it in a corny way. No, I'm here because I want to be. And yes, I would be happy to stay over. My first event isn't until ten tomorrow, but let me text my roommates so they don't worry. I'm betting at least one of them will text some crude emojis back."

"What odds are you putting on this?"

She grinned, settling a strand of loose hair back over her shoulder. "You don't even know them."

"I'm going to say they won't, and the loser makes breakfast."

"Deal."

She texted them and borrowed some more of his clothes. She slipped into an oversized T-shirt he'd gotten from a conference in Atlanta a few years ago that said *Good Books, Good Looks* with sunglasses made from the *o*'s in each word. He wanted to take a picture of her like that and go all wife guy—she was so beautiful. The way her hair hung in loose waves on her shoulder and her face was so fresh without makeup, skin looking soft and kissable. Instead, he tried to remember this moment, take it in. How content he felt, not anxious about anything. Just happy.

She slid beside him on the couch downstairs, and he made tea. The rain battered the windows. The wet streets echoed the noise differently, making the city feel like a sister of itself. All thought of their books had fallen away with their clothes, and for right now, it felt like they could be any two people anywhere else in the world, sitting next to each other and fighting over what show to stream. She had, it turned out, terrible taste in television and watched all the new shows that her social media friends rapidly binged and lampooned on her feeds. "I don't care if it's trash," she said. "Someone has to watch it, and I volunteer." On her suggestion, they watched a concept dating show where all the contestants were dressed in astronaut suits and had their voices autotuned. You couldn't tell what gender someone was, what they sounded like, or, obviously, what they looked like. The show was called *Space Dates*, and the winning compatible couple—determined by tests later or something—would get spots on a manned commercial space flight.

"I would totally do this," Mo said. She glanced at Wes, biting her lip. "Not for any reason except for getting to go to space."

His heart thudded, but he kept his face neutral. "Right, oh, totally. I wouldn't want to wear pull-ups, though. I really don't think I could do it. And here's something about me—I hate to fly."

She raised her eyebrows. "Really?"

"It's true."

She glanced down at the shirt she was wearing. "But you obviously have to travel for work."

"Highly medicated only. And yes, first class. Money and the right prescription can make the situation better, but it's still not ideal." Not ideal as in if the plane hit turbulence, he had panic attacks that would register on a seismograph.

Her phone buzzed, and she glanced at the screen. By the size of her triumphant smile, Wes knew he'd lost the bet. She didn't know he had wanted to. He was a good cook and hadn't had a chance to show her yet. "Savory breakfast person or sweet?"

"Savory," she said. "I could eat lasagna for breakfast if it was acceptable."

"I will make you a lasagna if you want."

She grinned. "No, but something with eggs would be great."

They finished the show, his hands resting on her thigh and her hand on top of his, lazily tracing his knuckles. He gestured his chin up at the painting above them on the couch. "My friend Ajay has a gallery opening next Friday night in Tribeca. Want to come with me?" He had aimed for a casual tone but was surprised by how hard his chest hurt in the seconds before she responded. Did he mean this to be a date? That felt like a lot of pressure. "As friends," he said, just as she said, "Sure." She seemed pulled up short by his clarification.

"Or not as friends?" he offered. He was not good at this. He was, in fact, terrible. He would be better off romancing a statue.

"As enemies, then," she said, her eyes glittering. "I was trying to remember if I had to work, but I have a day shift next Friday."

He felt like an idiot. It would have been a good time to say something sincere, but he played along. "Right, enemies. Enemies at the art gallery. Totally normal."

"Sounds like an Agatha Christie title."

By the time it was late enough to go to bed, the tea remained undrunk because they'd been talking too much. She'd insisted on poking around in his office to check his book collection and had selected two to tuck into her purse. "Once it dries out," she said, shaking her still-soggy bag.

It was amazing to think she'd got caught in the rain only a few hours before. It was amazing to think that he hadn't known her last week. He felt better, lighter, with her knowing about the manuscript that he had of hers.

They hadn't read anything together tonight—they had just been together and given in to the dangerous temptation of normalcy. As they left his office, he took a bound copy of his manuscript off the desk and handed it to her. "To even the playing field, you can take this with you. To add to your stack of borrowed books."

She accepted it with a smile, opening the cover to start reading as she walked down the hallway. She set the book gently by the bathroom door so she could brush her teeth. He was his mother's son, always keeping spare toiletries around for guests. He handed her a fresh toothbrush from the linen cupboard. "I do have mini-toothpaste too, if you don't want to share mine."

"I think we're past the cooties stage," she said with a grin. They brushed their teeth side by side, bumping hips as they went to spit in the sink at the same time. She turned to him after wiping her mouth and kissed him, their fresh breath mixing like a commercial for dental hygiene. It would have sold him anything, to be honest. After she pulled back from the kiss, she said, "Listen, I do enjoy hearing your book. I didn't come over here to get into your bed."

"I know," Wes said. He took a small breath, wondering how much to put out there. If he was going to come clean about the other thing, it should be now too. The thing where he'd been following her career for years. There had never been a right time to tell her, and maybe there wouldn't be one.

But he could hold it a little longer. There was no chance, when they were holding up the pretense of being enemies and rivals, that she would tell her agent about him. He didn't want the full weirdness of everything to come cascading out—how he'd found her book in the slush and gotten canned from the same agency.

Soon. He would tell her soon. He didn't want her to think he was stalking her or worry that seeing him in any capacity might damage her relationship with Yuri.

She stood looking out of his window toward the rainy street. He touched a hand to her back lightly, and she turned around. "I'm not sure which side of the bed I'm supposed to get into."

"I need to be near the door. If there's a fire," he said. He realized how strange this sounded and corrected himself. "This is probably neuroticism I picked up in first grade from a visit to a firehouse or something, but the fastest exit in a fire."

"If the door isn't hot. Then it's out the window, right?"

"Right. Touch your hand to the back of it. Not that I wouldn't save you in a fire. Or—" Here he paused, unsure of how they'd stumbled into such a weird conversation. It was too easy to be too honest with her. "Wouldn't let you save yourself? God, this got morbid. Sorry."

She laughed, relieved. "Morbid is fine, and I will be honest: I like sleeping away from the door. Robbers."

"The extra few seconds to grab something."

"Oh, definitely this lamp here," she said, gesturing to one of his solid-bronze table lamps.

"Different kinds of anxiety. I appreciate that." He slid onto the bed.

She got in next to him, folding the comforter around her legs like a fort. "I don't trust people who aren't anxious. I'm serious. If someone is too Zen, I assume they don't pay attention to things."

He wanted to fluff her pillow, and that wasn't even a euphemism for anything. God, he needed to stop it before he really did something that freaked her out. He wanted to take care of her, this damp-haired genius in his bed. He wanted to find out what kind of muffins and birthday cake she preferred. He wanted to know if she grew succulents in her apartment. He wondered what her library holds list looked like, if any of it overlapped with the ten thousand advance copies of novels he hadn't gotten around to reading lately. Part of him wanted to know about her ex, about what he had done that had made her know he wasn't a forever guy. He'd never had a partner who he felt nervous might hurt him, but she held all the cards without either of them knowing the full game they were playing.

He woke up with her still in his arms. They'd kicked off the comforter and lay wrapped in only the thin silk sheet. He could see in the morning light the outline of their legs tangled underneath it, the way you couldn't pick them apart if you tried, but he felt those limbs. He felt her heat against his back and could smell his shampoo in her hair. He slid out to make her breakfast, pressing a kiss to her hair before he left her in bed.

CHAPTER TWENTY

Wes

After dodging Ulla's calls for more than a week after her announcement, he agreed to have lunch with her in Cobble Hill at a place she'd "discovered" on Smith Street. Only Ulla could get away with claiming to discover something with over a thousand Yelp reviews in hipster central. He'd been talking about everything with Mo, who agreed that having a little time to himself was important for him to process, but she also encouraged him to text Ulla that needing space was his reason for radio silence. After five days, his mother had suggested this place when he reached out again.

The place, when Wes got there, made him think about Mo all over again. "Uptrend Midwest Cuisine" was the fare genre, and lo and behold, there were Tater Tots on the menu. They were artisanal, hand-sculpted potato knurls, but all the same, it made him ache. The wallpaper had the too-conscious kitschy feel of someone's great-aunt's kitchen—roosters and red-and-white checker wall borders. The tablecloths, too, were red-and-white checked, and a small wicker basket on each table had folded cloth napkins and mismatched flatware inside. The menu prices were the first thing to tip him off that if this was someone's aunt's kitchen, that aunt was paying Cobble Hill rent and not Cedar Rapids.

Ulla ordered the soup—an heirloom tomato bisque with a grilled cheese lid, and after a glance at the menu, Wes chose the Tater Tot casserole. He took a picture of it when it arrived, texting it to Mo when Ulla went to the ladies' room.

> *I ordered this and still no one has proposed to me yet?*

Did you wink when you ordered?

> *Ah, I must have done it wrong. What time does your plane leave again?*

7 am tomorrow. Still okay if I come to the show tonight?

His heart beat faster at the thought that he'd get to see her at the gallery. *Yes and bring a friend if you want.* Then he texted her the address.

She hearted the message, but then sent back a thumbs-up emoji. He wondered if mixed emoji messages were the standard text protocol for rivals that fucked.

The casserole was good—corn and carrots and ground bison in a light gravy sauce, all buried underneath a pillow of tots and shredded cheese. The dish came with a side of homemade ketchup (spelled *catsup* on the menu). He dipped a fork into the sauce, then scooped up a spoonful of meat and potatoes. Delicious, but not the tastiest thing from the Midwest that he'd had near his mouth lately.

Ulla reseated herself at the table and glanced at her soup, then the casserole. "I'm going to need a walk after this. Heavy food."

"That's fine," he said, not mentioning that the place had been her suggestion. "So, Dad called me the other night and told me the whole story."

"We're hardly the first couple to, well, you know." She didn't look around, but somewhere, someone in this city would have paid their left arm to get this story.

Wes understood the delicacy of the situation in the same way he knew that secrecy was untenable. Someone, somewhere, would slip and this news would get out. He thought about how he'd told Mo, and maybe he shouldn't have. "When are you making a public statement?"

"We're thinking sometime after the summer. You know summer is always a slow news season, and we don't need to be written about more than need be. I can handle whatever the tabloids spew, but your father—I'd like to keep him from the worst of it."

"Is there someone else?" He'd been thinking the question for the past week but finally had the courage to ask.

"Not on my side."

Wes, very conscientiously, did not raise his eyebrows. "And was that what did it? I mean, finally, was that what ended it?"

She sighed, then took a sip of her unsweetened iced tea. She had this way of using her straw, trying to bypass her whitened teeth to avoid all stains. "I could have made it work, but honestly, I think we had run our course. Don't think badly of your father. Truly, sometimes these things have expiration dates."

He thought about the rights for *Proud and the Lost*, how the expiration of the authorial rights had been extended and extended and how much work it had taken on Estelle's part to do so. That wasn't even marriage, where the other party could fight with you, ignore you, or cheat on you. Making anything last long meant fighting against the natural will of time to change things, and Wes didn't like it. "I never pictured you two apart."

"Well, you weren't around as much from age ten on, darling, so let's be honest. How much were you really watching?"

"Fair enough," Wes said. His casserole was too cold to enjoy. He put down his fork. "My book might become a published book. The one that adapts *Proud and the Lost*."

His mother smiled at him, then raised her glass to clink against his. "This year will be full of surprises, Wes. Not all of them bad."

He thought about Mo's fingers stretched on the couch next to him, the press of her lips against his. How he'd had to stop midchapter, unable to talk about a couple kissing without kissing her himself. He thought about the little heart in the text message and cleared his throat. "True," he said. "Too true."

Ulla looked out the window, and despite her careful presentation, he knew she was sad and lonely. He recognized the expression because he had worn it himself. He remembered Ajay's offer and realized that a night out might help her feel better. "Do you want to see Ajay's gallery opening with me in Tribeca tonight?"

She focused again on his face and smiled as if she could tell what he was doing. "How weird is it?"

* * *

On the way to the gallery, Wes considered the likelihood of his manuscript becoming a real book. He daydreamed as he went past the bookstores he'd browsed as a kid. He'd attended dozens of author events at the Strand and imagined his name in the marquee above its entrance. Wes Spencer, *Too Proud*. The name would probably change in edits, if they got to edits. It sounded like a Fast & Furious movie now that he thought about it. The sequel to Morgan's original novel: *Too Proud, Too Lost. Proudest and Lostest, Part III.* Those were the kinds of spin-offs that strong literary estates like Morgan's had been meant to avoid. Was his strong enough?

He felt a pang of guilt, thinking about his future before thinking about the woman who was the estate right now. He had a little time before he was supposed to meet Maureen and Ulla, so Wes ducked into a bodega and grabbed a coffee to counter the cold evening air. Cup in hand, he stepped out and called Gary.

"How's Estelle doing?" Wes asked after the hellos had been exchanged.

"Better." Gary sounded exhausted. "We think she's better. We'll be heading home tomorrow."

"Thank God for that," Wes said.

"I've been reading her your projects, little by little," he said.

"I thought you hated *The Proud and The Lost*," Wes said, his voice full of fake chiding. "You know, Maureen and I have been reading the projects to each other too."

Gary made a noise on the other end of the phone.

"What? What does that mean?"

"Someone is going to get hurt in all of this, Wes. Are you sure you're maintaining your professional distance in this situation?"

Wes actually laughed. He wasn't, but how could he? "I don't represent the estate anymore."

"But you're still an agent. You know the power you have, and you're not a disinterested party here."

Could he tell Gary that he was going out with Mo tonight on . . . well, it wasn't a date. His mom was coming and he'd told Mo she could bring a friend. But he was *out* with her. Plus all the other activities they'd been taking part in that had required definitely not being out in public. They weren't exactly fuck buddies. Was fuck rivals a thing? He wasn't going to defend himself to Gary, though, especially not after what he'd seen at the estate. "Come on, Gary. Talk about professional distance. How long have you and Estelle been lovers?"

"You don't know anything about Estelle and me," Gary huffed, sounding genuinely hurt.

Wes felt bad, conscious that the purely professional relationship he and Gary had shared five minutes ago had stretched into something uneven and strained. You couldn't really know a person until you saw them under real stress. This was stress, and Wes was being a defensive jerk in the face of it. Wes sighed. The right thing to say was definitely *I'm an asshole*, but he thought of a way to reframe it. "I'm sorry. Let her know I'm thinking of her."

"Thinking of what she can do for you?" Gary shot back. After a second, he added, "Thank you. We're all under a lot of stress right now."

Wes patched things up the best he could before hanging up, then tucked his phone back into his pocket. What had he expected: a blessing? Some kind of revelation? Estelle on the mend or not, the edge in Gary's voice made Wes think that hearts couldn't be cured as quickly as all that. He wasn't going to "just circle back" his way out of this situation like he usually could. He needed to take a deep breath, take a step back, and enjoy the fact that nothing was finalized yet. Not having one of their books selected meant more time in this delicious limbo. In grad school, a term they'd talked about a zillion times was *liminality*, the space between spaces. Not a bridge exactly, but a tension between two concepts. The space between him and Mo didn't feel liminal, it felt electric. He thought about that old Oscar Wilde line, "The suspense is terrible; I hope it will last."

That particular aphorism was fresh in his mind when he looked up to see Maureen coming down the street in the dress she had bought in Greenwich. The dress she had peeled off in the hot tub.

He didn't know if he mouthed "oh shit" or said it, but the sight of her sent blood rushing to his cheeks and other parts of his body. He had to stifle his reaction, though, because Ulla was walking in step with Mo. They must have run into each other up the block, and they were talking animatedly. As he got closer, he swore he heard the phrase "extensive, body-wide acne" pass his mother's lips and noticed Mo's glance trace him in an appraising way.

Why had he thought that this second Ulla/Mo crossover event was a good idea, when it was likely his worst idea ever?

When they stepped inside the gallery and ran directly into Yuri Eikura, this prophecy was proven true.

CHAPTER TWENTY-ONE

Mo

Maureen had run into Ulla on the sidewalk outside and grabbed her arm like an old friend, or a lifesaver. "I guess we're both looking for Wes," Mo said.

"Oh, I am here for the scene. Keeps you younger than Botox to go to an art show and not understand a second of it," Ulla responded.

They collected Wes outside and entered together. The art gallery had lofted ceilings, white walls, and pine flooring. The buzz of conversation wrapped them as they entered, but it was still quiet enough that Mo heard Yuri's heels clicking against the wood as she approached. "You came!" Mo said, leaning in for the hug her agent offered.

But suddenly Yuri went stiff in Mo's arms, despite being the one to reach out for her. Did Mo smell bad? She had sat next to someone eating a fish sandwich on the subway. She felt Yuri's breath near her ear. "We need to talk later. Find me. Alone," and then she pushed gently away from Mo and excused herself.

Mo glanced around to see if the exchange seemed weird to anyone else, but Ulla's attention was elsewhere, and Wes was making pointed eye contact with his shoes. His gaze was so intent that Mo looked down at them—light-brown suede chukkas that she had to admit were nice but didn't warrant that attention. "Hey, Earth to Wes," she said, waving a hand in front of his face.

He looked up, rubbing his scruff in a nervous way. She wanted to touch that beard too, pet it to calm him down, but she didn't think he'd appreciate being treated like a cat. He shouldn't be the nervous one here. She was with both his mom *and* his best friends, two major steps that if they hadn't been just friends with extremely good benefits, she should be nervous about.

And she should be glad about that, of course. After getting a text that Ulla was invited to the gallery opening too, Mo had felt the invitation shifting out of the possible date category into the "general hanging out" category. If they were casually hanging out, then Mo decided to use his offer to invite someone too. Having caught up with Yuri by email once or twice a month for the past year, she was overdue to see her in person and had invited her along on a whim. Yuri, it turned out, represented a client who had tried to get Ajay to do cover art for a book, so she was familiar with their work and said yes. There were millions of people in this city, but somehow you were supposed to be equally unsurprised if someone did or did not know someone else.

Which was exactly the kind of whiplash she suddenly had looking at Wes's face. Suddenly her brain clicked. "Do you know Yuri?" Mo asked.

He cleared his throat, then touched her arm. "Kind of." He seemed ready to say something else when a tall person in a white blouse emerged from a crowd of people near the center of the gallery. They had dark skin and loose, curly black hair resting above one of the most beautiful foreheads Mo had ever seen. She hadn't considered how nice a forehead could be before.

Wes looked relieved at the interruption, removing his hand from Mo to offer to his friend. "Ajay! You have gotten taller somehow."

"Shoe lifts. Loris found them."

"You are already over six feet. You don't need them."

"Maybe I'm modeling them for you," Ajay said, then, smiling, turned to Ulla and Mo. "Ulla, doll, it's amazing to see you as always. And you are . . . ?"

Mo shook their hand. "Maureen Denton. So nice to meet you."

Ajay smiled wider. "Are you and Wes something?"

Wes cleared his throat. "Friends."

Mo laughed. "Also enemies."

"I like that dynamic, and I insist on the full story later. For now, look around. Get some wine, if you drink alcohol, and some cheese if you aren't lactose intolerant."

"Cheese is my love language," Mo said.

A man in a black shirt with short-cropped blond hair popped over Ajay's shoulder and placed a kiss on the side of their neck. "I'm also offering free insights on the state of modern journalism. Hi," he said, offering Mo his hand and removing Ajay's delicately from her grip. "I'm Ajay's partner, Loris. I work at the *Post*."

"Though he did intern for me once," Ulla cut in, tucking her long silver hair behind her ears, then accepting Loris's cheek kiss. "Couldn't keep him, though. He didn't care much about the state of modern table settings."

"Wasn't my passion, Ulla. You know my heart isn't in flatware. Spoons don't have enough secrets." Loris's smile was wide and infectious, too big for his face by half. He wasn't handsome, and his foxy features—big mouth, too-clever eyes—made him look like he'd been designed to be a gossip reporter. Those ears that stuck out slightly on the side? *The better to hear you with, my dear.* Mo made a mental note to be careful with what she said around this very charming stranger.

Everyone paused conversation to look around, as if they'd been cued to do so. Even with her crack-of-dawn flight to Iowa tomorrow, Mo was glad for the distraction. She'd never been to this gallery and certainly never seen anything like this show before. Groups of people ambled up and down the ramped space. Oversized paintings of Power Rangers interacting with celebrities hung on the walls. In the closest painting, Tom Hanks stood at what seemed to be the helm of a giant robot, obviously painted as a good guy in this situation (every situation, though, right?). Other celebrities got less-rosy treatment—they were the ones slamming down buildings while the Power Rangers took them on.

It was more fun for Mo to watch the people looking at the paintings. Eyebrows rose as people pointed out cultural Easter eggs. "Is that Four Seasons Landscaping in this one?" Mo asked, pointing to one of a former political lawyer.

Ulla clucked appreciatively, pressing her hands down over her long white dress to smooth it. "Oh my. Can't wait to take in the whole collection. Lovely turnout as always, Ajay."

"Wes, I'm stealing you to show you my favorite," Ajay said. "You too, Ulla."

Wes glanced at Mo. She could feel the sudden weirdness of this not-date. "Mo, coming?"

Mo remembered Yuri wanted to catch her alone, then shook her head. "You know if there's cheese, then I am legally required to eat as much as I can handle."

Wes grinned and headed up the ramp. Mo, too, turned to find the cheese table as she'd promised. No reason not to follow through on the dairy before tracking down her agent, but she was surprised to see Loris still standing next to her.

"Hi," said Loris. "Thought I'd chat with you for a second."

His tone was guardedly friendly, but something in Mo's gut iced over in preparation for the worst. She steeled herself for a few conversations all at the same time. Was this the *feeling out if you're good enough for my friend* talk, or *digging up who you are, as someone with the personal and professional interest to want to know*, or the *I've got something serious to tell you, like I got a genetic test done and you're listed as my closest living relative* kind of talk? The last one was unlikely, but her writer brain did social anxiety well. "Sure. Hi."

"I dated Wes," Loris said simply, then rushed to say, "And we've been friends for, well, practically forever. But I wanted to tell you a little inside knowledge."

Mo knew enough reporters to wonder what she had to give in exchange for this free info. "Sure, but why?"

Loris laughed. "This isn't like me giving up his deepest secrets. You two seem like you have a nice repartee, and he's never—literally never—brought someone to hang out with us. You are not *just* friends." Loris said this with the simple certainty that came with lots of personal observation.

Mo didn't confirm or deny this, but she did see Yuri standing near a huge painting of a former top network executive, who was depicted pinching a Power Ranger's ass. "Fair assessment."

"A hint about Wes. He acts very go-with-the-flow, adaptable, but he is terrified about not being in control of situations. He doesn't know this about himself. He truly thinks he is easy, breezy."

"Beautiful CoverGirl," Mo finished automatically, then apologized.

"I set you up for it. Anyway, if you grew up with a mother whose entire life was magazine layouts and sprucing up a room and being the perfect host, you'd probably end up with some quirks too. He's a fabulous friend—will do anything for you, seriously—but he has trouble trusting people. He will try to handle everything, emotionally and logistically, without bothering anyone. He doesn't get that it's not bothering someone and that it's communication."

You can't handle the truth, echoed in Mo's head, though she couldn't even remember what movie it was from. There had to be a German word for quotes like that which grew so far beyond their original cultural relevance. And now she was distracting herself from an awkward conversation by trying to find specific vocabulary in a language she didn't even speak. She thought about Wes's reluctance to have sex the first night she stayed over, his worry about things changing. "I don't know what you want me to do with this information," Mo said honestly.

"I want you to be patient with him and tell him he's an idiot when he needs it. He's not one, so you won't have to tell him more than once. Or a few times. I don't think he lets himself make mistakes. I have this theory that everyone has trust issues, they're just different trust issues. His trust issue is that he doesn't trust someone to love him after he fucks up. Usually he gives up on a relationship before he has a chance to be not perfect."

The breakfast Wes made her could have been a magazine layout, complete with a tiny vase of posies from the corner flower stand. She remembered not just the food but the careful way he'd leaned across the table to brush a hair out of her eyes. Other times, too, in the past two weeks of their time together. His smile under his well-kept scruff. His warm and earnest eyes. The uncareful curl of his hair, and his voice as he read some of the best damn sentences she'd ever heard in her life out loud to her. He did seem perfect in some ways—most ways. "Thank you for the insight. I don't know what my friends would tell someone in some corner about me."

Loris pursed his lips. "Well, I'm not most friends. Figuring people out is kind of my job. Ajay and I adore Wes, but we are pushy in his life about two things: He needs a romantic partner to love, and he needs a dog. Then he'll be fine."

Loris excused himself after being called away by a short, bald person with a sleeve tattoo of Chappell Roan lyrics. Mo took a breath. It felt like someone had handed her a key, a big important user manual to Wes, and she didn't know what to do with that information. She had known him just two weeks, thought it felt like much longer. She thought about what Loris said: *Everyone has trust issues, they're just different ones.*

Not me, she thought.

Except maybe she did. She hadn't trusted Aaron to understand her and love all of her. She hadn't even trusted her family with the information that she was writing something she was proud of, because she didn't want to hear the follow-up questions.

This was too much self-analysis for a Friday night. She chose a few more cheese cubes and took in the crowd of people around her as she tried to track down Yuri again, but her phone chimed before she could find her. It was from Wes.

You throw any of that cheese at anyone?

Lol not yet

Need to show you something. You should have come with me.

Her impulse was to text back an eggplant. She hovered over the emoji, then decided to send it. He replied with the *ha ha* reaction. *No, not that—yet,* he texted back. He was the kind of guy to use an em dash in his texts. How was he so perfect?

The word popped into her subconscious before she could think of anything else, and she repressed it with another bite, this time into a Camembert.

Maureen felt a tap on her shoulder, which made her swallow her bite and wheel around. When she coughed slightly from choking down the dry mouthful, Yuri patted her back slightly. "You all right?"

Mo held up a finger. "Snack issue."

Yuri pursed her lips, trying not to smile. At least she looked less concerned than she had at their first greeting. "We need to talk about Wes," Yuri said. We Need to Talk About Wes seemed to be the actual theme of the evening, not Power Rangers.

"Sure, okay." There was something in Yuri's face that made Mo's stomach clench.

Yuri paused, looking at the ceiling for a second. "Since I can't break my NDA with Wes's family, I'll have to be circumspect."

"Uh . . ." Maureen said.

"Let's find a place to sit down."

CHAPTER TWENTY-TWO

Wes

Wes took a picture but considered whether he should send it to Gary or not. He had no idea what the manners guides would say about sharing a picture of Estelle, who had been hospitalized until very recently, in a painting surrounded by children's television characters from the nineties. It wasn't that Estelle was portrayed in an unflattering way—the opposite, in fact. She was a superhero. In Ajay's painting, she wore a pink Power Rangers costume, and her wheelchair was painted in the same cheery pink with black stripes. Though her money had originally come from her mother, she was famous in her own right as a woman in the finance industry and an advocate for many causes. She was portrayed near one of the playgrounds that she had paid for, one of the first barrier-free playgrounds in the city. Wes decided that Estelle might at least find it funny, and at most see it as the compliment it was.

He thought he would probably send it, but not before he got Mo's opinion. Only because they had a similar frame of reference on the issue. And because he trusted her judgment. And because he wanted to see how she reacted. Not because they were a couple or something.

He checked his phone on impulse, but she hadn't replied since she sent the eggplant emoji. He hadn't been trying to imagine which dark corner he could sneak her into to kiss her. Not at all. He definitely hadn't noted that the corner with the burned-out lightbulb near the fire exit was perfect. He turned to Ulla. "I'll be back. Need to get a drink."

"Tell the drink I said hi," Ulla said, not buying his excuse.

He walked down the ramp back to the lower gallery space, his eyes casting left and right to catch Mo in that floral dress. It wasn't hard to find her; she looked like she was standing as still as a mannequin near the wall, and Yuri was hugging her. Wes felt his shoulders tighten in preparation to make more awkward small talk, but Yuri had left by the time he reached Mo.

During his one-minute walk, he tried to assemble a cogent way to explain the secrets he had kept from her. None of it was damning, exactly, but it was awkward. It was messy, and he didn't do well with showing other people his mess. He should have figured the truth would out before he had a chance to out it. The book world, encompassing many huge conglomerates and small presses and genres, acted as a small town, and gossip traveled accordingly.

Sensing his approach, Mo turned, her mouth set in a straight, pink line. "Have your ears been burning?"

He stared above her head and said, "So, yes. You might have learned that I used to work with Yuri, back when I was first starting out."

"She couldn't tell me much. Something about an NDA your mother made her sign."

Wes puffed out a breath. "Yeah, well—"

"She did warn me that you are ambitious."

"You knew that." *You are too* he wanted to add, but didn't.

"And Loris told me that you have trouble telling the truth."

Wes felt like he'd been slapped. "Loris said that?"

Mo's expression softened by half. "He didn't say it in so many words. He said you have a hard time when you're not in control of the narrative. And I'm honestly a little confused about the narrative at this point. Can you set me straight?"

Wes took a deep breath. The ambient noise of the gallery—its conversations and footfalls and laughter—was throwing him off. "Could we get out of here?"

They set off down Warren Street in the general direction of River Terrace. In Wes's head, he could keep her talking and walking long enough to get to the river, to look at it together. In his head, he could keep her from turning up Chambers to get onto the subway. The air was temperate outside, calm and still, and the sidewalks were somewhat empty. This was the closest thing to privacy he was going to get.

"I worked with Yuri for about a year. This was my first internship, the one I didn't use my name to get."

"Lying hasn't ever been hard for you," she said, not breaking stride. Before he could respond, she continued. "Why did you leave?"

"Uh, I was asked to leave. This is where the NDA comes into play, if you'll bear with me."

"I always picture an actual bear when someone says that," Mo mused. "Like Paddington getting in on the conversation."

"Pooh with a hookah," he said, grateful for a topic deflection.

She wasn't so easily, or permanently, diverted. "Fill me in more about the reason you left Yuri."

The gentle slope of the road pulled them toward the river. Wes took a breath before beginning. "There was an author represented by Yuri's agency. I'm not naming names, but he's the biggest asshole I've ever met. He'd been with the agency for years and had a habit of coming into the office and throwing his weight around. So one day, while I was there, he said some horrible things to Yuri's other intern. She was a Black woman. Is a Black woman. She's still with Yuri's agency, I think. Anyway, I won't repeat what he said, but it was the kind of stuff that people like him get away with all the time in those private spaces where they have too much power."

"You have power too," she said.

"I mean, I was only an intern, but yes. Social capital. White, cis, male privilege. And yes, I should have probably considered how to better use my power rather than punching the guy in the middle of the office."

She halted in the middle off the sidewalk. "Really? You punched someone?"

He stopped too, unable to meet her eyes. He stared directly into a streetlamp and let the light burst behind his eyelids when he closed them. "Yeah, I did. I knew better. It was stupid, but I couldn't control my reaction and I snapped. I boxed all the way through college, though you couldn't tell to look at me now." He knew he was softer than he used to be, but his broadness had always helped in the ring.

"Did you seriously hurt him?"

It was his turn to snort, and he started walking again. She kept pace beside him, not trying to overtake him for once. "No, no. One good thing about boxing is that it teaches you how to punch purposefully. I didn't cause internal bleeding or anything, just a broken nose." He considered, then added, "I mean, not *just*—he filed a report against me, deservedly. I shouldn't have done it. And of course the agency had to let me go after that. Loris heard that someone was sniffing around the story and let us know. My mother's clout was enough to hush-hush the whole thing by buying off the story from the tabloids and paying for the 'emotional distress' and medical bills of the guy. Not that he needed my money. Well, Ulla's money."

"You realize how weird that is, right? To have the ability to pay someone to rewind a bad decision?" They had reached the park and changed their course as other couples meandered on the paths ahead of them.

Her question, which wasn't really a question, needled him. "I was lucky to have access to Ulla's money," he said.

"No, you were privileged to have access to Ulla's money." Her voice didn't sound angry so much as tired. Green trees waved slightly in the darkness, their branches made into waving arms off the shadowy boulevard. "You know I'm dying to know who it is. Would I recognize the name?"

Oh, she would. "Yes. I don't think he's Yuri's client anymore, and I know that agencies aren't the moral gatekeepers of the opinions of the clients."

"Still."

"Yeah, I don't regret punching him. And when I moved on to my current agency, I fessed up, even with the NDA. They thought it was a good story and said I wasn't a danger, since I was in the New York area and the main office is in LA. It's unlikely I'll be breaking bones long-distance."

He waited for her to say something, but she didn't. In the dark, it was hard to read her expression.

"But the other thing, the thing I didn't know if Yuri mentioned . . ." He paused to see if she would give any indication that she knew. He didn't know if he preferred her to already know or not. When she looked blankly at him, he realized that yes, he would have preferred if Yuri had said something, because now he would be forced to see the full weirdness of it all settle onto her for the first time. "Can we sit?"

They sat on a bench, Maureen a hand's width away from him. "The period when I worked with Yuri, well, it was while you were querying *At the Counter*." He knew mentioning the name of her old book would signal that this wasn't a coincidental topic switch. Her spine stiffened. "And I actually was the one reading her slush pile—her queries and submissions—when it came through."

"And you hated it."

He huffed out a laugh. "Oh, absolutely not. Uh, in fact, I fought for it. It was the first project I advocated hard for to Yuri. It stuck with me, the messiness of the relationship of the servers. The ambivalence to buying in to what society was trying to sell to the main character, to—" Here he scrambled for the name.

"June," she supplied, sounding tentative.

"Right, June. So, yes. I was there for Yuri signing you as a client, but I left shortly after that. Because of the punching thing."

"You read *At the Counter*. You—you helped me get to Yuri." She truly seemed to not know how to digest this information. "I mean, do you expect me to thank you, or . . ."

Everything was going wrong. "Maureen, no. Not at all. I believe you would have landed with Yuri, with or without me.

Or an agent of similar caliber. If anyone didn't see the potential in that project, then that's their fault."

"Obviously, a lot of people didn't see potential in that project, because it didn't sell."

"Yet. It didn't sell *yet*," he said, then cringed. It was hard to sell a project that had already made the rounds to editors, but who knew? Maybe if she had a book out already—but if that happened, he knew what that would mean for his book.

"I don't really know how to feel about all of this," she said. "This is—a lot. This is a lot to take in." Her voice had the same carefulness as walking on a frozen-over lake, afraid that one wrong step will crack everything.

But it was Wes who felt like he was cracking apart. Too many tangled threads. Too much honesty. He should have guessed. He could have shared that he knew her work earlier. He could have tried to disclose the Yuri connection somehow. The fact that she was sitting with him at all after round after round of complicating revelations was a miracle. She was here. Even after Loris unloaded what seemed like a dumpster full of his faults in front of her, she was here. She was here, sitting and talking through stuff that would have had any person he had dated in the past four years scrambling for an exit and realizing *whatever connections this guy has, he's not worth the baggage.* Yes, all his baggage might be Gucci, but it was still battered as hell.

And maybe that was what was going on in her head, but if he didn't say something now, he would regret it forever. "Those things happened before I met you," he said carefully. "I didn't know how to tell you about them, especially about knowing your first book. How could I have told you I was a fan of your work when . . ."

"I barely have work to be a fan of," she finished. The corner of her mouth tipped up. "I haven't read your book yet."

"I didn't want to ask."

She rubbed her hands on her legs and stared at the starless sky above them. "I think I should head home."

He nodded. "Right. Okay. One more thing, all right? I know that was a lot, but I was serious when I said that I want even footing with what we have. Fair."

She laughed, but it wasn't bitter. "Wes, there is no such thing as even footing, but okay. I believe you. I just need a little time, okay?"

"Want me to walk you back to the subway?" he asked, after the silence had stretched on between them. He wasn't going to ask her back to his place. Not after this. He'd fucked it up from the very beginning. From before he let her open the car door and take the long drive to Greenwich, he'd ruined it.

"Sure," she said. "Early flight tomorrow." They walked in silence back up the hill to the subway entrance. They didn't hug as they went their separate ways, but Mo turned as she went down the stairs. She moved to the side to allow a woman to pass her. He called out to her before she could get too far down.

"I know you need space, but maybe I'll see you when you get back?" The sound of an approaching train traveled up the staircase, muffling his words.

She glanced over her shoulder, then back to him. "Maybe. I do have to tell you what I thought of your work when I finish it."

"I barely have enough work to be a fan of," he said.

The smile that appeared on her perfect lips felt like aloe on a burn. She lifted a hand in farewell, and the floral dress disappeared into the concrete and metal below the city streets. She was already out of sight by the time he remembered she hadn't seen Estelle as a Power Ranger. He added the image to a text and sent it, hoping that by the time she came back into cell signal, she would be glad to see his name pop up on her screen.

He went back to the gallery, holding his breath, and was relieved when twenty-five minutes later he got a text back. *She should buy that for The Hill.*

He typed back. *Make all the rooms Power Ranger themed. None of this fox and flower bullshit.*

She *lol*-ed, and then the phone went silent. When he glanced back up, Loris and Ajay were giving him knowing looks.

"What?"

"You really like that girl," Ajay said.

"Well, she hates me, so thank you very much, Loris," Wes said.

Loris held up his hands in front of him. "Hey, if telling the truth is a crime, then arrest me."

Wes shook his head, which hurt. His heart hurt too. He didn't know if Mo would forgive him. "Are you familiar with the *If you can't say something nice, don't say it at all* school of journalism?"

"I missed that day of lecture," Loris said. He pressed a reassuring hand to Wes's back. "Most of it was nice. You are a wonderful man, but no one is perfect. Listen, she is digesting information. Let her digest. Give her some space."

Wes tried to scowl, but his heart was beating too fast, his brain already zooming forward to next week and maybe seeing Mo again.

CHAPTER TWENTY-THREE

Mo

Anna insisted on having the bridal shower at her acreage. They could have rented out a local church basement or the family restaurant in Walnut, but Maureen was grateful Anna wanted to host. It was an excuse to let Mo see the dogs, and while Mo loved her sister, she *adored* her sister's dogs.

By an hour before the shower, her dad and Kyle had cleared the premises. At the few showers Maureen had attended in the Bronx or Manhattan, it was a whole-couple affair. In Anna's case, their mom and aunts had circled the wagons and kept it female. Hogs and dogs excluded, anything with a penis within ten miles was gone for the afternoon. Which, on the plus side for Mo, meant more time with her sister without Kyle. And, again, more time with the puppies.

The shower was raucous—six of Mo's aunts, twelve cousins, every friend of her sister's that still lived in the state, plus lots of Kyle's family (the ones with boobs) came. There were over sixty women, and Mo was grateful for Anna's renovated barn space, the same space in which she was planning to hold the wedding ceremony. The wedding service would be out on the lawn under several large tents. It was hard to picture right now with the land mines of doggy poop, but Mo didn't doubt that her sister's vision of a candlelit, flower-strewn, outdoor June wedding would come to pass. Anna made magic like that.

Due primarily to her sister's good planning, the shower went fine. Their mom had made butter mints, which melted on Mo's tongue as she made a list of the gifts. Towels, plates, forks—Mo couldn't help but think of Ulla as she took notes, wondering which of these items had her stamp of approval. After Anna had kissed the cheek of the last great-aunt and their mother had folded the last gift bag to save for another shower down the line, Mo swept out the barn and her sister folded the chairs back into a closed-off area behind the stables, one of the hidey-holes she'd kept around during renovation.

As their mother and Anna chatted about final fittings and centerpieces, Mo wondered what it would be like to bring a guy home to Iowa. During her past visits home, she'd noticed Kyle and her dad laughing together like they were born to be family. Was Anna somehow the matchmaker in this situation, putting together the perfect father-son pair? But someone like—really, any guy Mo might have brought home— wouldn't click with her father in the same easy way. Mo didn't know how her parents would react, since she'd never really tried.

No, Mo didn't miss Aaron. And she also tried hard not to miss . . . well, anyone in the city, especially anyone who kept secrets from her. This weekend she needed to focus on her family. Later, Anna and Mo would drive to Des Moines for the bachelorette party. After staying in a hotel room tonight, Mo would shovel herself back on the plane back to New York in the early afternoon Sunday. But first, the family dinner—Kyle included.

Mo's mom had made cherry pie with cherries frozen from last summer's crop. She had a dozen cherry trees in the front yard that, when they didn't get attacked by birds, produced the world's best sour cherries. Mo wasn't biased; this was an unarguable fact. Their dad made pork ribs—of course—all day on his smoker, with cherrywood from one of the same trees that had gone into the wood chipper after getting felled by a big storm last year. The green beans were the only thing not farm fresh, but the way her dad prepared them with butter and lemon was just like Grandma used to, and the whole meal felt like home had taken up residence in her stomach.

She felt lucky. She *was* lucky. A hundred years ago, her mom's side had been working in factories in Chicago, living in a one-room tenement. Fifty years ago, her dad's side had lost half their land during the farm crisis. Now they had enough. More than enough, but they still remembered how hard things could be, and that was where Mo's passion came from. Over dinner, her mom discussed the political candidates on their ninety-nine-county tour of the state. Dad talked about gutters. The normalcy washed over her. This chance to see her family reset her—plus, again, the pie was *so* good.

After her mom and dad shared about the work they had been doing lately, her father turned to Mo. "Okay, city girl. What's the good word? Doing anything interesting out there that you couldn't tell us over the phone?"

The word *doing* sent her brain to completely inappropriate places. "No, just—you know, writing and working."

"Are you still with Andrew?"

"Oh, his name is Aaron. Was Aaron," Mo corrected.

Her mother put down her fork with a concerned look.

"No, no—he's not dead. He's just not with me anymore."

Her mom's concerned look deepened. "And that was . . ."

"My choice." Mo took an overly large bite of ribs, sure of the alcohol later to come in the evening.

She hadn't told them about the breakup for the same reason she hadn't told them about the finished book project: They'd overreacted about both in the past. In both cases, they'd told everyone and their brother before anything was certain, and once it was clear there was nothing to be serious about, they'd had to go and take it all back. That active "oh, actually" cleanup made Mo's achievements, like finishing a whole-ass book and getting agented to begin with, feel paltry. Unimportant.

Everyone has trust issues. Loris's voice rang in her head. For a guy she'd met one time, he'd certainly become a little too forceful in her thoughts. Maybe she hadn't trusted her family enough with who she was, or who she liked. To Mo, the act of finishing her book wasn't unimportant, and neither were those relationships. Just because the books hadn't been published and those relationships had ended didn't mean she hadn't learned from them. But this relationship *had* ended, so she needed to finally rip off the Band-Aid and tell them about it. The book? That could wait. "The truth is, Aaron proposed, and I said no."

Her dad choked a little and then put down his rib. "He *proposed.* He had never even come home with you?"

Mo was grateful for his reaction. "Exactly. Not that I want someone to ask your permission—"

"Not mine to give," her dad said, waving a hand. "Not that Kyle didn't come in and try something like that."

And of course, the conversation turned to Kyle. He smiled next to Anna, barbecue sauce lining his lips. "I would have been more sure of the answer if I'd asked you," Kyle said, grinning.

Gag. And now they were talking about Kyle and Anna again, which they did for the next twenty minutes until dinner ended. Mo hadn't spent much time with Kyle, and nothing she had learned about him in their time together had made her want to. It wasn't like Mo wanted to harp on how her romance had gone to shit, and it wasn't that she was thinking *You can be amazed by boring-basic-ass Kyle literally anytime*, but she was feeling left out.

* * *

On the drive to Des Moines, Mo and Anna passed billboards that hadn't changed in at least five years. The city skyline was a welcoming hand, waving her back in. She'd loved seeing it from the air yesterday, but she had arrived in the daytime. Now, lit up by lights like rows of white teeth, the whole city smiled at her. It only had one real skyscraper—Principal Tower, renamed 801 Grand—but the low height of the buildings let other landmarks shine. She could point out the botanical gardens on the road into the city, the capitol—it was a sensible city. She'd gone to Iowa State University for undergrad, and many college friends found Des Moines big enough, vibrant enough. It had some great indie bookstores and concert venues. Her mom constantly reminded her that Des

Moines hosted the magazine publisher Meredith, so there were jobs for people with Mo's kinds of skills. Mo rebutted that having never owned a home or garden, she had never written the kinds of articles that *Better Homes & Gardens* might want to put out. It hadn't been far enough for Mo, or her imagination. At least it hadn't been right after college. She had to admit to looking at Des Moines Zillow and ogling how much house she could get for even her share of the rent every month.

The party plan was karaoke, and Mo had delegated choosing a spot to the other bridesmaids, current locals who knew Anna's recent taste better than Mo did. Ask her what her sister would have wanted to do on a Saturday night when they lived together a few years ago? She'd have had no problem answering that: Watch *Labyrinth* for the eightieth time and order pizza. But even loving her sister as much as she did, she didn't know what Anna's definition of fun was anymore. The bridesmaids, Lainey and Tiff, had chosen a karaoke bar called AJs. The bar was off Court Ave and walking distance from the hotel.

"Is your Venmo ready?" Mo asked as they stepped inside the bar. Her one contribution to the party was a huge paper sign that read *Buy the Bride a Drink* to scan with a QR code. As they entered, even the ID checker at the door smiled and scanned the code. Mo was grateful the other bridesmaids hadn't opted for games or necklaces with pendants that looked like dildos, but they did try to convince the college-aged boy belting out "Girls, Girls, Girls" by Mötley Crüe to come over and give Anna a lap dance, which he did for ten dollars.

Mo had two beertinis before feeling solid enough to put her name on the list to sing. She never ordered beertinis in

New York, but back here, it felt right. It was a draft beer—in her case, Michelob Ultra—with a handful of green olives in it. Sounded gross, but it was basically an appetizer paired with a drink. Very efficient.

She put herself down for "Pink Pony Club." She finished her drink and ordered another, and before she knew it, she was at the microphone singing about Santa Monica and big dreams, only one of which she knew about.

Sweaty and laughing, Mo finished the song, but in a few minutes Anna dragged her back up to sing a duet of "Sisters" from *White Christmas*, one of their favorites growing up. By the time the duet finished, Tiff had bought everyone shots of some eggnog liquor that the bar *still* had on hand, even though it was May.

Maureen choked down her shot and watched as someone from a new group took on the Killers. She thought about that first car ride with Wes to the Hill, wishing they hadn't left things so weird last night. Or wishing they had started things weirder, with him explaining everything the moment he saw her. Luckily, the bar was too loud and she had had too much to drink to replay every mistake and missed opportunity. She'd been in constant movement since she woke up this morning, no time to think, and that was for the best.

"I need to eat something," Mo said. Her stomach lurched with the eggnog—and maybe a little with the thought of Wes's face, admitting he'd read her first book years ago.

Tiff had wandered into a corner with lap dance guy, where they were furiously making out. Lainey, Mo, and Anna ventured outside. Lainey paused for a cigarette ("I only smoke when I'm drinking"), but Mo's attention was on a Super Dog food truck parked down the street. She tugged on Anna's hand. "You need to eat too," Mo said.

The sisters stood in line, the cool air doing its work to sober them. The streetlamps, too, made it harder to feel drunk than the technicolor red and blue bar lights had. They each ordered a fully loaded hot dog—relish, onions, ketchup, mustard, and jalapeños. "Sorry if this is kind of a laid-back bachelorette party," Mo said, mouth full. She swallowed, the bun sticking in her throat. She wished she had a beer to wash it down but knew she didn't need another.

"I wanted you here to celebrate all this with me. And I thought seeing Kyle at dinner might help you know him better."

Mo must have made some sort of face, a face dramatic enough that Anna could see its expression in the light of the streetlamp.

"What?" her sister asked.

"I don't get Kyle." She paused and tried to reroute, but her mouth got away from her. "I know you love him and he loves you, but I feel like you deserve someone . . . He's just so— listen, I don't want to say something that will hurt your feelings."

Anna's lips pursed. "Then you should have stopped talking two minutes ago. I'm going to chalk this up to alcohol or moodiness. Can you be happy with me that I found a guy I can imagine making a life with? Is this because you're jealous?"

Mo snorted. "Of Kyle?"

"You don't even know him. You barely even know me anymore," Anna said, her voice tight and hard.

Maureen felt the gut punch of that statement. "Anna."

Her sister relented, turning toward Mo. "What?"

"I am sorry. I'm sorry for not being here as much the past few years. Hell, do you know how bad I felt when I didn't even have an idea for this party tonight? I didn't know you'd grown into having a whole karaoke song list."

Anna shrugged a shoulder. "You could have asked."

"I could have. And I could have asked more about Kyle too. I know. I will try harder. Look," she said, getting out her phone and opening Instagram. "I will follow him. I will make kind comments about his life and learn more, okay?"

Anna paused, seemed to relax a little. "Love takes effort. All kind of love. It's a verb, not a noun, right? I love him, and I appreciate that you'll put in some effort to get to know him too. But be warned: His Instagram is a mess, but sure. It's a start. Prepare for lots of Star Wars memes and woodworking pics."

"And you."

"Yes, and me. We should talk more."

"I agree. Love is a verb. I'll do better." Mo grabbed her hand. "And maybe I am jealous. Not of Kyle. I will give him a chance, I promise. But I'm jealous that you have it figured out. I'm the older sister, and I feel like I was such a leader to you. I had everything figured out when we were younger, and now?"

"Now?" Anna prompted.

Mo leaned against the building. It was an antiques store. Small, haunted-looking dolls glared out at them. If she hadn't been emotionally socked in the gut, it would have been funny. "Now I'm a mess."

Anna leaned next to Mo, her long sweep of blonde hair coming loose from her half pony to hang around her face. "You seem off. I mean, besides insulting the love of my life."

"Ugh, again, I'm sorry about that."

"You should be. But tell me what's up. Let me sibling you a little."

When Anna used *sibling* as a verb, it evoked their best days together. At Iowa State, Mo had a terrible first-year roommate randomly assigned to her who was obsessed with insects. Her second year, she lived with friends and they fought nonstop. Finally, junior year, her sister became a Cyclone too, and they lived together off campus. Nothing had ever felt more natural than those days, coming back to the apartment and laughing about the idiotic things they were obsessed with. They siblinged back then: knew each other to the core; teased and loved each other in equal parts. It was the same ease now Mo had with Sloan and Mackenzie, but she'd lost the knack of it with Anna. Mo took a deep breath. "I wrote another book, but I don't think it has a chance to get published."

"That's big," Anna said.

"It's an adaptation of *The Proud and the Lost*."

Anna made a face, scrunching her nose so that her freckles rearranged their constellation. "Ugh, that book we were supposed to read in Miss Tucci's class in eleventh grade? With the car crash?"

"I'd read it about a dozen times before that, but yes." And, after a deep breath, Mo told her about the time at the estate two weeks ago and about Estelle, including her heart attack. She edged around Wes's involvement, but she had to mention him to make the story understandable.

Because Anna had superpowers, she must have heard something in Mo's voice. "You like Wes." When Mo didn't deny it, Anna pushed on. "Is that why you and Aaron broke up? Not that I was a huge fan of Aaron, but—"

"I actually broke up with Aaron a year ago."

Anna took a bite of her hot dog, then swallowed. "A year is a long time to not tell your family about."

Mo slid down the wall, below the eyeline of the haunted dolls. The concrete was reassuringly cold and solid under her. "I know. I'm sorry. I think I have this thing about admitting mistakes to you. Since I moved out there, I mean."

"Or, you know, since forever." Her sister sat next to her.

"I just don't want you all to worry about me making the wrong choice. Or be ashamed of me."

"The only way we would be ashamed of you is if you lost yourself." Anna knocked her shoulder softly against Mo's. "And if this Wes guy makes you feel like you're not good enough, then I don't like him."

"No, definitely not. I feel—I feel like my silliest me. My best me." Mo didn't have a hot dog to distract her now. "And that's probably how Kyle makes you feel. I'm such a dumbass. I'm sorry."

"You *are* a dumbass, and I love you." Anna stood up and offered a hand to help Mo do the same. "So, are you seeing this guy?"

"We're reading our books to each other—the rest of our books. And I'm getting to know him better." *In bed,* she wanted to add, like they used to at the end of fortune cookies.

Anna's face broke into a smile. "Oh, Mo, that is so cute. Only you would fall in love via book club, I swear."

"It's not a book club," Mo said, irritated. She thought of the manuscript in her suitcase that she'd saved to read on the flight home, like the dessert at the end of a long meal. "And I'm not in love with him. It's all . . . very complicated."

"You love complicated. You love complicated things so much you will literally invent them. That's half of what being a writer is, right?" Anna made her voice go sultry. "It's a sexy-times book club. Wes and Mo and the sexy-times book club."

"With car crashes."

"Oh yeah, only the sexiest car crashes." Her sister glanced around the quiet street. A truck drove by, casting its headlights to illuminate the freaky dolls in the window even more clearly. "You should call him," Anna said.

"I am not going to call him. It's, like, three AM there."

"You could text him."

"I'm not going to text him!"

Anna grabbed the phone out of Mo's hand and scrolled through the contacts. "Oh, he's been texting you. And you're seeing him next week?"

"Maybe."

"For a date?"

"No." She didn't know for sure. She didn't tell her sister how much she wanted it to be but how weird they had left things. Wes was a nepo baby, a publishing insider. Wes was her rival. Wes had read her first book. Wes had punched an asshole and gotten himself fired. Wes didn't know how to let things not be perfect, but what if she couldn't be perfect? What if complication really was all she was set up for?

Before she could ruminate more, her sister pointed meaningfully at her phone. "You have him in here under his full name? Wesley Spencer? What is he, your insurance agent?" Anna tapped for a minute, then handed it back to Mo.

Mo glanced down, where Wes's name had been changed to *Lover Boy Hot Sex XXX*.

Mo tried to shove her but was laughing too hard. They walked back to the bar, which was closing, to scoop up the other two bridesmaids. The Killers singer gave them an enthusiastic goodbye outside the bar, with an impromptu toast to Anna better than any Mo had thought up so far. "May your love be an example to others, and an example to yourselves. Let your love today and on your wedding day change and grow, and be for others a beacon of charity, hope, and joy."

"He's better than my Unitarian minister," Tiff informed the group as they ambled to the hotel. Mo was sober enough to check them all in with the night clerk. Tiff and Lainey went to their double-occupancy room, and Anna and Mo went to theirs. It was, Mo mused, the first time they had shared a room since visiting their grandma at the pig farm all those years ago. As she fell asleep to the familiar snuffles from her sister across the room, Mo wished she were sharing the bed with someone else.

CHAPTER TWENTY-FOUR

Wes

The best days as an agent were days where Wes got to call a client and tell them that their book had an offer from a publishing house. An editor at a major imprint had offered mid-five-figures for a client's debut novel-in-verse, and they still had four submissions outstanding. The client was understandably freaking out in the best possible way. "I'll be in touch soon with more," Wes promised.

Wes sent nudge emails to each of the remaining editors, and he posted the news to Slack while his colleagues all celebrated remotely. They could talk shop in Slack, make bets about what editors might want to offer based on recent projects they had seen announced on Publishers Marketplace. Usually, even with a ticking clock for other editors to respond within the week, he wouldn't hear things for days. Midmorning, he finally calmed his nerves enough to get back to work, but then his phone rang. It was one of the remaining editors in the running, Elena Evans.

They made small talk for a minute or two, then she asked if Wes was free for lunch today. He was—even if he hadn't been, he would have made time to be. They made plans to meet at a restaurant halfway between their places. Wes posted the development to Slack, and his colleagues were atwitter about it. Elena had been promoted to senior editor at Wildman, an imprint specialized in emerging voices in literary fiction. It was a connection that, whether for this project or another, Wes was desperate to foster into a good relationship. These kinds of editorial chats could be an X-ray into the industry. Yes, the agency had contacts at every publishing house, but an editor who would sit down for fifty minutes to give insight into recent acquisition meetings? Priceless.

Wes arrived early at the restaurant, a Thai place he'd been to many times when in Midtown. Despite being early, Elena had already snagged them a table. As Wes got closer, it became more and more obvious that Elena was pregnant. Her stomach was rounded enough to bump up against the table, even with her scooted half a foot back from it. He sat across from her and kept his gaze level with her face.

But she had obviously noticed his glance. "Ha, elephant in the room: I am basically an elephant now."

"Congrats, Elena. When are you due?"

"End of August. It's my second—he'll be my second baby—so I'm showing a lot earlier this time." She sighed and laid a hand across her belly. "I've been craving Thai, so thanks for agreeing to this spot."

They ordered, then found their way to the business of the meeting. Over spring rolls, they discussed the client's book, and she revealed that she'd been prepared to make an offer identical to the one Wes had already received. "I don't know if we're prepared to go higher. I'll certainly be taking it back to the team, but as you can see, I wouldn't be the one primarily involved in its editing and production. The timing's kind of off on this."

"I understand," Wes said.

"But I wanted to meet today because the last four projects you've submitted to me have all been exactly to my taste. I'll be honest, it's only that we've been outbid and no one else was as passionate about the project as me that I haven't already bought one of your books."

"That's great to hear."

"And now that I've been promoted, well . . ." She brushed her long, wavy hair over her shoulder, then picked up her fork. After swallowing a bite of pad see ew, she smiled. "I'm hungry. Let's say that. So, what else do you have?"

The emphasis on *you* made Wes stop momentarily. He did have a book, a book that, honestly, she would be the perfect editor for. His book. And they had a certain back-and-forth, a budding friendship. What would it be like to dip his toe in the water for something that would be cautiously proceeding in a few months anyway? He knew he shouldn't, but he couldn't stop himself. He put down his fork and leaned across the table. "I could let you in on the ground floor of something, but it's still very hush-hush."

"I feel like you're about to offer me Bitcoin or drugs, and I'm not interested in either."

"What if I told you that I used to be the agency representative for the E. J. Morgan estate, and what if I could say with surety that the estate is vetting projects to adapt *The Proud and the Lost*?"

She almost spit out her lunch. "*Are* you telling me that? Is that a sure thing?"

Wes nodded. "It's not common knowledge, but I'm sure it will be in the next month or so. I'm giving you a heads-up, not because"—he gestured at her pregnant belly—"but also because I remember the piece you wrote about *P&L* in *The Atlantic* around the ninetieth anniversary."

"It was the foundational book for me as a teen. The way it made me think about class and growing up . . . and obviously about family. I mean, did you know my first child is named Eliza?"

"Really?"

"I mean, of course it's a bummer to name her after a character who offs herself, but you must admit she's one of the best heroines in twentieth-century literature. So." Elena put her elbows on the table and leaned closer. "Who are the authors? What are the adaptations like?"

"Funny you should ask," Wes said, and he took a long, slow drink of water before he began.

* * *

Wes returned from lunch to a flurry of Slack notifications, more than half of them prodding for details on what Elena was looking for currently. He would certainly share what he'd gleaned, but he wouldn't share the conversation they'd had about *P&L*, at least not yet. Wes's boss, Jacob, knew that holding on to Estelle as a client would pay off in the long run; Jacob didn't know in how short a time that run would begin. Before traveling to the Hill, Wes had given the portfolio over to Jacob to manage without explaining why. "Too much else on my plate right now," he'd said. Wes hadn't told him about his book being considered for adaptation. He wasn't ready to share the details until everything was perfect.

It was time for Wes to find his own representation, though. He didn't want to ask someone in his agency to rep him. A move like that would undermine his bargaining ability if they got to the bidding stage. He didn't want to query anyone at Yuri's agency either—he imagined how awkward that would be and shivered. He did know another agent from the time they'd both worked there who had moved on from that agency and respected the deals he had made lately. He glanced over the query he had typed up months ago with the barest hope of Estelle agreeing to consider his book and sent it before he could overthink it.

How the tables have turned, Wes thought. He spent the good part of the rest of the day refreshing his personal email and his professional email at the same time.

By the end of the day, two more editors had told Wes they would get in touch soon with a counteroffer for his client. *Looks like we're going to set up an auction,* Wes said on Slack. Confetti emojis from his colleagues. He couldn't imagine working as hard as he did with people he didn't like as much. His colleagues worked second jobs and late hours to be able to do the work of representing books they loved. This business rewarded you if you were already successful or powerful in some other way.

He was preparing to FedEx his manuscript over to Elena, nestling it into the comfortable big brown envelope, when he stopped. He was keeping the project in hard copy to avoid having it on the record for now. She'd asked to have a sneak peek before she went on leave. Project FOMO was a real thing. There was always the next thing in this business. Someday he might be the next thing, and that thought thrummed through him.

But the specter of being called out at the gallery hung over him. Coming clean to Mo had been one of the hardest conversations he'd ever had. It was physically painful to show her the behind-the-scenes of his last few years. It reminded him of looking at the flip side of a tapestry and the mess of threads compared to the art on the front. No one bought a tapestry for the process, but for the final, front-facing product.

No matter what happened with the estate, it would be one of their projects, and giving Elena time to have a look before she went on maternity leave felt like such a small stitch in the overall artwork unfolding now. Still, he imagined how it would look, how it would feel, to tell Maureen about passing only his manuscript along to an editor.

He paused in the act of stuffing his manuscript in the envelope and looked around. There, on the table, was Mo's old novel draft, the one that had gotten caught in the rain on the day she slept over for the first time. The pages were warped, accordioned in on themselves like ocean waves, but it was readable. Missing her this weekend, he had reread that first-kiss scene in the first chapter, thinking of her lips. He had mentioned Mo to Elena during their lunch, but he hadn't said he had a copy of her draft. He shouldn't send it over, since he wasn't Mo's agent. But also, he could imagine the betrayal if his project was selected and Elena bought it.

Maureen said that there was no future for them, whatever they were, if things weren't fair. Fair it would be.

Without thinking twice, he shoved Mo's manuscript in the same FedEx envelope. He printed a shipping label. His stomach was in knots, but that was probably because he was hungry, right? Wes made a quick salad and refreshed his emails again—personal and business—with a news podcast running in the background. He could multitask, and in fact, sometimes he only multitasked. He worried that he couldn't ever sit and focus on one thing. When he saw that the agent he'd emailed had responded, he single-tasked to free the salad from his throat. Choking required lots of concentration. The agent asked for a full copy of his manuscript. In the body of the email, he said, *Okay, I need the full story of how this magic might actually happen, but your sample pages were great. Not going to ask what magic lamp you rubbed or what HomeGoods you bought it from, but if the rest of the manuscript zings like the first fifty, you're signed.*

Wes smiled, attaching the manuscript to the reply with the note, *Here's hoping it zings. And no promises on its placement, but let's say it's got a 50/50 chance.*

The FedEx driver knocked on the door, and Wes handed him the package containing his and Mo's books. It was hard enough to imagine a future with Mo, and he hadn't allowed himself to think that far ahead. Feelings got hurt in relationships every day, but even bigger feelings got trampled on in publication. Comparison was the thief of joy, right? So how could they keep any amount of joy in their relationship when they had only met because they were in direct, constant comparison with each other's work?

The only thing he could do was level the playing field as much as possible, even if that meant keeping the fact that he was doing so to himself for the time being. Who knew what Estelle would even say? Maybe, ultimately, no one would get the go-ahead, and he would never have to mention this happened.

CHAPTER TWENTY-FIVE

Mo

Anna sent Maureen three ideas for wedding hair—for Mo, not for herself. For months, Anna had known that she wanted a chignon with loose curls woven in with daisies. Anna too had received bouquets of daisies from their father when she was a grumpy teenage girl, and now the simple white blooms would make up her bouquet, the definition of simplicity and country charm. Mo loved seeing Anna's ideas for the wedding come together, and now that she had realized what a horrible sister and maid of honor she had been, she went about course correcting. She was grateful for having worked so many weddings over the years. After all, coordinating caterers and DJs was part of her day job. Anna seemed so grateful that Mo had to remind her that making a spreadsheet was easier than checking dilation on a dog—at least the DJs spoke the same language as you, and at least you could tell the caterers when to arrive, unlike a puppy.

Mo skimmed through the wedding hair pictures, feeling for the first time that she was a set piece in the wedding. She was being forced to care about updos again for the first time since prom when part of her wanted to straighten it and let it be. She emailed her sister back. *Thanks! I'll take a look.*

The wedding was in two weeks, and she had a lot to do between now and then that had nothing to do with her sister's nuptial bliss. Wedding season was in full swing at work too, two each on Friday, Saturday, and Sunday, with cleaning and reorganization of the layout between each event. Sloan brought Mo takeout between the two weddings on Saturday when she realized she'd forgotten to eat anything, planting a quick kiss on Mo's cheek and staring around at the wreckage from the first event. It had been a relatively small affair—only a hundred people—but the bride had chosen an Alice in Wonderland theme and at one point the flower girls had tossed hundreds of cards (all hearts) around the entire space. They must have been formerly used in a casino and bought secondhand, because they all had hole punches through them. Mo wondered if anyone had considered that someone might have to collect hundreds of cards afterward. It was fifty-two-card pickup times fifty.

The burger helped, thankfully, and at least her blood sugar was level by the time she had to move the eight-tops and place the next set of silverware.

She got home around one in the morning on Sunday, the second wedding having moved on to the bars once the bride and groom left. No official theme for this wedding, just "wealth." Custom macarons in the wedding colors had been stacked nearly to the ceiling. The couple had hired a band she recognized from her college album collection, and during the dancing portion of the event, after clearing most of the tables, Amy and Mo mouthed the song lyrics back and forth, using serving spoons as microphones.

Those were the moments she liked the job—especially when it was only her and Amy, after dinner service was complete and before they had to clean up vomit in the bathrooms.

The apartment was quiet when she got back, and Mo tumbled into bed, exhausted. She hated that she had to have an alarm set for the next day—at the ungodly hour of eight—but she would survive.

She didn't even get to sleep until eight, though, because Mackenzie perched on the edge of her bed with pancakes the next morning. "You need a full and balanced breakfast today," she said. "I can sense it."

"You sense it?"

"Okay, Sloan did a tarot reading for you, and she said so."

Mo yawned and sat up. She took the tray from her roommate and cut a piece of pancake. She took a bite. It was homemade, not from the box. It wasn't as good as the savory crepe that Wes had made for her weeks ago, but it was sweet and fluffy. "Thank you for this."

Mackenzie smiled and patted Mo's legs. "We keep missing each other this week. No ratport or anything. You doing well?"

"It's busy. I'm busy. You're busy."

Mackenzie nodded emphatically. The head librarian at her branch had delegated some of the programming planning to her, and the planning and running of events had eaten into her supposed off-hours. "I love it, though. Do you love"—she smiled through pressed-together lips—"what you're doing in the evenings?"

Mo squinted at her. "I'm working."

"Oh, when you've been at Wesley Spencer's place, that's working *something*, I bet."

Maureen hoped the light wasn't bright enough in here to see her telltale blush. She could feel it, though, starting at her chest and moving up to her cheeks. "I haven't even seen him this week. And I don't know what's going on."

Mackenzie laughed at that and patted Mo's legs again. "Oh, sure, okay. I believe that. I noticed what his name was on your phone, by the way."

Mo hadn't changed it, true. She handed the phone to Mackenzie. "My sister did that. You can change it back to show you I don't care."

Mackenzie picked up Mo's phone, looking victorious. When her finger was obviously swiping up, Mo reached for the phone again. "Hey, hey, hey," she said. "No reading the texts!"

"I am not reading the texts; I am taking in the number of them. This is quantitative, not qualitative analysis."

"Stop with your master's-in-library-and-information-science-speak," Mo said.

"Fine." Mackenzie relinquished the phone again after a few more taps. "Here."

Mo glanced at her contact for Wes, which had a picture of him that had auto-populated when she'd added him—something he had saved on his phone that shared with her phone. She liked the picture, him smiling behind aviator sunglasses, his tangled mess of curls standing up. It made her want to reach through the phone and brush it with her hands. Then she glanced at the name Mackenzie had typed in.

"*King Sex God*?" Mo asked, laughing. She waved the fork at Mackenzie. "If you hadn't made me a delicious breakfast, this would not stand."

"I don't think you do much standing around him. Ouch!"

Mo had hit her with the backside of the fork this time. "Keep it up, and you'll get the tines."

Mackenzie scooted off and ran to the doorway. "I'm glad you're getting anything!"

Mo laughed, shoving the rest of the pancake in her mouth. She was tired after a night of dreams about getting all of *it* that she wanted, and the pancakes weren't filling the need she felt the most right now, but they were something. And something made with love, that was for sure.

* * *

On her walk from the subway to work, Mo checked her email. On a Sunday, she wasn't expecting anything too serious, but she was surprised to see a notification from her writing email account. That email was a sacred space—she didn't even give out that email to her mom. It was the place she got news from Yuri, and the place where so many years ago she'd gotten the ask for a phone call with her. Her writing email had received multiple *New Yorker* rejections, including one saying, *Keep submitting—this is promising, but not for us at this time.* It was the place where she had gotten acceptances and notifications of all the major moments of her writing life, and looking through the archived emails, you could almost sense her career's dips and rises.

So what would this new notification bring: a dip or a rise?

Mo opened it, surprised to see an email from Gary, Estelle's assistant. Maureen had looked for news about Estelle's condition, but she hadn't found anything. She was grateful to hear from him. She skimmed the message while walking, staying to the side of the walkway to avoid bumping into anyone. By the time she arrived at work, she felt like she'd left her stomach on the concrete behind her. Estelle was doing worse and had been checked into the hospital again. She'd had a chance to finish the book and loved it, but—Gary put it as kindly as he could—Flor and Talia had also "tried to read it" too.

Tried to? Mo wondered what had caught them off guard. Couldn't they see how their grandmother's original book needed a sharper critique on wealth distribution? How it begged to take on traditional narratives of the home, of the hierarchy of women's labor versus what men traditionally did? Mo could see them scrunching their noses, saying, "Oh, this is too *political* for the classics," as if *A Tale of Two Cities* weren't political. As if Shakespeare weren't political. As if Thoreau, for all his "mom is secretly doing his laundry while he's chilling at Walden Pond," weren't political. Their grandmother's work was political too, even to the act of it having to be published under her initials. A few years ago, there had been talk of rereleasing it under her full name, but critics put a stop to it. No, E. J. hadn't identified herself as Emma Jean while writing it, and modern readers should take it with that context in mind.

Mo couldn't respond to the email, mostly because her hands were shaking too badly. She knew Gary was writing this while stressed about Estelle's health, plus juggling Estelle's daughters. She felt deeply for him, this man who managed so many other people's lives. Mo hadn't gotten to know him well, but from what she could see from their limited interactions, he seemed like a lake of a man—placid on its surface, but teeming with life and activity underneath that she might not understand or be able to see. She would reply tomorrow morning after she'd gotten a full night of sleep, but for now she needed to focus not on the dreams that had brought her to New York but on the job that would keep her here.

As she began prep for the first wedding of the day, her phone chimed. "Sorry," she said to Amy. "I forgot to silence it."

Amy looked up from the saltshakers she was filling—the bride had bought them special for the occasion, not trusting the standard glass saltshakers to apply salt in a fancy enough manner. "It's fine. We still have half an hour before the rest of the staff arrives. Bridal party and guests aren't due for an hour."

Mo dug out her phone. A text from Wes, still listed as King Sex God. She bit her lip at the name, trying not to think about the oral sex he'd given after breakfast at his place, her in the kitchen chair and him on the floor below her. She couldn't get *that* off track. His text scrubbed dirty thoughts from her head. *Hey, I heard from Gary and wanted to let you know Estelle isn't doing so well.*

Mo knew this, but now she wondered not how the messages they'd gotten from Gary had been the same but how they differed. What words of praise or adoration had Flor and Talia asked Gary to communicate to Wes, or had he heard those from the women directly?

Of course, Mo had already finished reading his manuscript on the plane ride. She hadn't been back over to tell him that. She'd somehow refrained from texting him her favorite lines, but she had underlined three dozen of them. She didn't want him to know yet how much his book had moved her, and it didn't seem like the full weight of her love of the book could be sent through text. She thought of words that blurbs someday might use to describe the book—*sad, but lyrical and thought-provoking*—and yet those words alone didn't demonstrate how it moved her. His interpretation made Mo see the original text in a new way, even though it was set in the same time period and even though Eliza's character was, well, very normal. So normal that her flaws showed through in Clive's eyes, so normal that Mo realized how adept Wes was at noticing people's flaws. She didn't want to think about how many he might have noticed in her.

Mo considered a text back, starting and erasing one several times. She settled on the shortest message she could, one that kept her cards close to her chest. *Sorry to hear that. Thanks for letting me know.* She sent it, then read back how impersonal it looked. How office-speak, how default-response. She waited for a few seconds to see if he would respond with something else, but he didn't.

Maureen was too afraid of how he would take an honest statement from her now, a serious question. She was afraid he'd misread her tone or read too deeply—or too correctly—into how scared she was that this was her last chance to make a project work with Yuri, maybe even to be able to rationalize staying in the city. After all, she could fail much more cheaply from Iowa.

If he were there in person, all five foot ten inches of him, she could have told him. It was so easy to say anything when she looked him in the eye, but when it was words on a phone—impossible. And if that was the case for two writers, what chance did anyone else have? She would see him this week. She could get her thoughts together better after she'd slept more and eaten more than a pancake. When she wasn't wearing an apron or thinking about how to highlight tropical orchid displays at the head table, they would talk. They'd figure this out, one way or another, but for now, she had a wedding to attend to.

CHAPTER TWENTY-SIX

Wes

It was Tuesday night and Mo was coming over. Wes's relief at her decision to speak to him again was matched with his neurotic anxiety to ensure the meeting went perfectly. In preparation, Wes tried out one of the recipes from a cookbook he'd sold recently. The client worked as a chef in Ontario at a Michelin-starred restaurant, and while Wes's finished creation didn't look as good as the mocked-up picture they had subbed with the project, it smelled delicious. The stew was a traditional Provençal recipe that took two days to make—one day to make the broth and a second day for assembly. Wes planned to serve this soup with crusty sourdough bread and whipped butter from the co-op. For dessert, he'd made fresh lime-basil sorbet, which took up a majority of the freezer's top shelf.

He'd already made up his mind to make tonight awkward. He owed it to her to feed her a delicious dinner, then tell her the truth about everything that had been going on in the past few days: him signing with an agent, Gary's email, and sending the books to Elena Evans. He knew that Gary had emailed Mo too, but he hoped Gary hadn't shared Talia's and Flor's full, caustic impressions with Maureen. They had scarcely mentioned his book at all, at least in a way that didn't commodify it. No mention of the prose. No mention of the characters. No mention of the plot or themes. He believed in his book, but the email sat wrong with him, especially when they seemed to think so poorly of Maureen's book, which he did love. He didn't trust the opinions of a reality TV star and a real estate agent on the book she'd worked so hard on, even if they were the heirs of the heir of a literary mastermind. Certain things couldn't be passed down, like taste.

Elena had sent Wes a quick email early in the week to let him know that his manuscript was at the top of her to-read pile. He got emails like this all the time from editors, but knowing it was about his project distracted him beyond all reason. But Elena had already read Mo's book, probably marked it up as much or more than Mo had marked up his own book.

First, though, he would feed her. First, he would be present with her. Mo centered him, or more accurately, when he was around Mo, everything in him tried to center toward her. He felt like a sunflower tracking the daylight trying to read her body language and facial expressions. Making her smile was better than any acceptance he'd ever gotten.

"Come on in," he said.

He didn't know how to read the air between them when Maureen arrived at his place. He opened the door, and she smiled slightly, moving past him. With her came a breeze from the street. No rain this time, at least. At the door, she handed his manuscript back. Things between them felt charged, but not in a sexual way—in a way that echoed the vibes of that first night at Estelle's, a budding resentment set off by mutual admiration.

He received his book from her and tried to read her expression.

She took a moment to meet his eyes before she said, "I loved it."

It was just a word, a word he read in blurbs for books all the time. It was one word in the dictionary, a single entry of a million, but it pinged in him. He shouldn't read more into it, but she had read him. His words and his work and his late nights and the times that he felt like throwing his keyboard at the wall, all wrapped up in those ninety thousand words. "Thank you for reading it."

"Well, thank you for letting me. I marked it up, for your reviewing pleasure."

His heart kicked in his chest. He couldn't wait to go in and look through to see what had caught her eye or where she'd stopped and picked it up again. It would be like spending time with her to spend time with her commentary and notes, and he would take all the time with her he could.

He could still sense the lingering weirdness from last week in her body language, though. The tense set of her shoulders. He could unveil the tapestry later.

Her eyes glanced around, and her nose twitched as she slipped off her shoes near the front door. "What's for dinner?"

"Bouillabaisse and fresh bread." She trailed behind him into the kitchen and glanced at the pot, which he uncovered with a flourish. Scrubbed, early-season red potatoes floated with carrots, pieces of cod, and prawns. He had fresh parsley chopped on the nearby wood cutting board for sprinkling on top.

She turned back to Wes, her face slightly green. "I am so sorry, but I'm allergic to shellfish."

He didn't swear, but he sure wanted to. He was such an idiot to cook for someone and not ask if they had allergies. He had lucked out during their first homemade meal together in that shrimp wasn't a common breakfast food. "Don't apologize for being allergic," he said. "I'm sorry for being a dumbass."

"No, I'm sure the soup is amazing. It just would maybe kill me."

Wes flipped off the stove and covered the soup. While he opened a window to air out the kitchen, he considered alternatives for their meal and a place to home this stew. He certainly didn't want it to go to waste after two days of work. "Just a sec," he said, excusing himself from the kitchen. He called his neighbors, Lee and Ilsa. He hoped they hadn't eaten yet. Luckily, they had recently gotten home from their shifts at the hospital and hadn't figured out what they wanted. He convinced them, with very little effort, that what they truly wanted was fresh French fish soup fast—say that five times. They would be over in the next fifteen minutes to get it.

That problem solved, he reentered the kitchen to the sight of Mo waist deep in his refrigerator, bent over in such a way that accentuated her beautiful curves. He'd never thought that the refrigerator's lighting could do a person justice, but it flowed around her like water. She looked good enough to eat like that, and he had to stop himself from coming up behind her and—

Instead, he cleared his throat, and she slammed the door closed. "Sorry. I'm not being nosy. Or maybe I am, but I wanted to see what we could make."

"What we could make that wouldn't make you break out into anaphylactic shock."

"Right, unless you wanted that as the entertainment for the evening." Her expression softened, a smile creasing her lips. Maybe she had had a long day. Maybe she had had a bad subway ride. Maybe he could fix whatever was wrong, but not with what he had originally planned for dinner. Maybe they could make something very good together tonight.

In the kitchen. Make something in the kitchen, obviously.

One thing was certain, with conversation flowing, the air had thawed slightly between them, though the room itself was cooler from the fridge being open for so long.

After a quick assessment, they decided on grilled cheese made with some of the fresh sourdough. He used the softened butter to spread on the outsides of the bread while she sliced a variety of cheeses from the cheese drawer. "You're lucky that the cheesemonger knows me by name now. I've started to go there weekly."

"Are the only things that people can mong fear and cheese? *Monger* is underutilized."

"Completely agree. Did you know," he said, spreading the butter thinly, "some people use mayonnaise instead of butter on the outsides of their grilled cheese?"

"Sacrilege," she said. "I'm from the Midwest and firmly believe in the power of mayo, but it belongs inside a sandwich, not outside."

"It's not bad, but I think butter is better."

"Always." She finished slicing and created a sandwich to toss in the pan. As she nestled the first sandwich on the griddle, the doorbell rang.

"That's probably Ilsa," he said. He grabbed the huge soup pot with two potholders, snagging the other half of the loaf and placing it on the lid. Ilsa was still in her scrubs, fresh from her shift on the maternity floor. She thanked him and promised to return the pot in an hour.

"No rush," he said. "I'm not planning on making more soup tonight or anything."

"Well, if you did, you know we'd always accept it!" she tossed back, winking at him over her shoulder.

When Wes reentered the kitchen, toasted butter and melted cheese hit his nose, and he almost moaned from how good it smelled. Mo had found an apron to tie around her waist (it read *Dad Bod* and was a joke gift from a cousin). He had always loved that apron completely unironically, but watching it wrapped around her hips was a revelation. She used a spatula to flip the first of the sandwiches onto a plate and held it out to him.

He moved to the knife block, pausing momentarily after selecting one. "Diagonal or horizontal?"

"Diagonal, then diagonal again. Triangles make sandwiches delicious."

It was exactly how he ate his sandwiches too, but he didn't comment. Smiling, he cut the sandwich they'd made together, the flow of effortless teamwork they executed. It was just a sandwich. He knew it was just a sandwich, but it felt so good to be with someone who intuited how dark you wanted your grilled cheese, how you wanted the cheese all the way to the edges so that it dripped down and hit the griddle, getting little cheese chips along its edges.

When both sandwiches were done, he snagged a bag of salt-and-vinegar kettle chips from the cabinet, and she grabbed the ketchup from the fridge. She poured a huge dollop on her plate before offering the bottle to him.

"Absolutely not," Wes said. He was relieved they were different at least in a few ways. It would make it easier if/when this thing between them fizzled. If/when life intervened to make things awkward. If/when a decision was finally made on the project and one of them would achieve their dreams and the other one would . . .

She shook the kettle chip bag, which was mostly crumbs. "You must have demolished these earlier."

"I've got more in the cabinet. One minute."

"Even when I was a kid, my dad used to buy salt-and-vinegar chips because he thought that would keep me and Anna away from them, but it taught me to crave them more." She took the fresh bag from him and looked down at it. "I never meet people who love these as much as I do."

"I love how they're a little sour."

"It's a special kind of kick."

He took a bite, definitely not thinking about cravings. Not thinking about how much he'd been thinking about Mo since seeing her at the gallery. With the selection of one of their books feeling more and more like a palpable event, it was pointless to want to make what they had more than it was, but he had never met anyone like her before. Not just someone he wanted to kiss but someone whose brain was full of things he wanted to see and learn about. Whose jokes made him laugh, even—especially—the dumb ones. Who was definitely, one hundred percent more talented than him, and who he wanted to get better at his craft alongside? Not to compete with her, but to be her peer. He could picture their friendship, not to mention anything else they had, like a physical presence in the room with them. Whatever weirdness they'd had from texts this week or stress from Estelle's health issues, their connection was undeniable. He would catch her up on everything he'd been up to. He could do this, but for now, he wanted to enjoy the way they felt like any other couple making dinner together. He wanted that.

"You have ketchup on your cheek," he said, reaching across the dining room table to swipe at it with a thumb.

She took his hand and brought that thumb to her lips, her tongue lightly licking the ketchup off, then releasing his hand just as fast. *Stop it. Don't think about that tongue. Don't think about those lips. Finish your damn sandwich.*

But a second later, she scooted her chair closer and put his plate aside. It held mostly crusts anyway. She sat on the dining room table, leaning down for a deep kiss. She broke away. "This week has been weird."

"Yeah," he said, slightly breathless. "It has."

A few more minutes of pretending they were just two people, full of butter and cheese, who were really good at kissing one another.

He wanted more of the kissing. "Do you want to hang out in the living room?"

She nodded, sliding off the table. She collected her plate and his while he grabbed the condiments and water glasses. He watched her stack the dishwasher. Technically, it was the end of the workday in California, and he needed to check his email and Slack before he could focus on their conversation. "Do you mind if I do a little work?"

She shrugged agreeably and flicked on the television, pushing buttons on the remote until she found the closed-caption options and muted the TV. She was watching more of that astronaut dating show, and he appreciated not being forced to listen, even though he kept glancing up to catch snippets of the typed dialogue. "Out of this world," one contestant declared.

Wes unplugged his laptop from his office desk and brought it down to settle next to her. He put a cushion as a buffer between the hot computer and his legs, remembering a long-repeated warning from his dad that "computers will shrink your balls" or something like that, in less crude words and with more of an Irish lilt. He scrolled through Slack, trying not to be distracted by watching Mo watch TV. He had some administrative work to catch up on. He refreshed his email once more for good measure, but then the doorbell rang.

He slid the laptop off his lap and set it on the couch next to Mo. "That's probably Ilsa," he said. "And I'm almost done. Thanks for your patience."

She smiled and waved a hand. "Go rescue your pot."

The whole apartment felt different with Mo in it, lighter somehow. Besides Ajay and Loris, most of his friends had never been to his place or him to theirs. Many of them were located around the country and around the world. It was harder for them to ask for favors that way, which made it easier to let them into his life from afar. In the city, he went to parties, but sometimes it felt like he was being sold something at them. He wondered why people had invited him: for the connections in publishing or for his mom or really, truly for his personality. And the people who understood that compulsion toward wariness were children of politicians or titans of industry, often not accomplishing anything related to their famous parent's work. Often not accomplishing much that interested him at all, since it sometimes involved spending their famous parent's money. But he'd had one of the best grilled cheese sandwiches with one of the people he wanted to hang out with the most.

He rarely had people in his life he cared enough about to be honest with. He had to stop putting it off. He would tell her about everything when he got back to the couch—the agent, the editor, and most recently, Gary's email about Talia's and Flor's responses to Maureen's book. He was ready. He could tell his face looked strange when Ilsa frowned as she handed back the pot. "Are you okay?"

He said he was fine, and she gushed that the soup was more than fine—delicious. Her husband had washed the stainless steel pot before returning it. Ilsa caught him for a few minutes to talk about happenings in the neighborhood. Wes tried to track her conversation as he built a script in his head for the next few minutes. Both the pot against his hip and the conversation waiting for him on the couch felt heavy by the time Ilsa said goodbye.

He put the pot on the front table, unwilling to take any more trips to the kitchen or distractions from Maureen, but when he reentered the living room, Wes saw her with his laptop perched on her lap. He couldn't believe her disregard of his private space. He breathed deeply, willing his shoulders to relax before he said anything. Computers were more private than underwear drawers. Annoyance clenched his stomach.

"Hey, need something?" he asked, hand out to receive the laptop.

"The truth would be nice," she said, placing the computer on the coffee table and regarding him with a serious expression.

"About what?" Wes looked more carefully at her face and realized she was crying. He sat next to her on the couch. She pulled her hands away, moving them to brush the tears from her cheeks, and scooted farther toward the arm. Wes froze, not willing to move closer when it seemed like he'd done something horribly wrong.

"I saw the email," she said. "I shouldn't have looked. I know I wasn't supposed to see it, but—"

Shit. Wes had known that Gary's email was sitting right in his inbox, and of course she had clicked, because who wouldn't? She had probably also heard from him this week how Estelle's health had declined, and of course she would want to know what Gary, or the rest of the family, thought. "Look, Talia and Flor have no insight into this kind of thing. I bet neither of them reads more than a book a decade. It doesn't matter that they say your book is unmarketable—"

"Flor and Talia said my book is unmarketable?" Her face, if it was possible to fall further, had done that. It looked like a crumpled version of itself. He looked away from the wreckage of her expression only to glance at his laptop screen, which had a different email pulled up, one that had just arrived.

He scanned the email from Elena, which was about his book, with her thoughts. He wanted her praise to buoy his heart, to live in the current of her exclamation points and italicized flourishes, but he pulled back, focusing on Maureen. He was aware she was getting up from the couch while he'd been skimming.

"Hold on," he said, reaching toward her again. He needed to stop this, to explain the full situation. He had given an editor at Wildman his book, yes, but he had also given Elena *her* manuscript as well. He wasn't going to make the same mistake he had with Estelle early on. At the beginning of all of this, he'd thought that by not introducing Maureen into Estelle's life, he could save himself the trouble of ignoring her talent. He couldn't, professionally or personally, allow that to happen. As much as he wanted his book to land in front of an editor, he wanted Mo's to have the same chance. How could he want anything else? Her book was incredible. It had shifted tectonic plates inside him. The manuscript had been the weather-worn copy Mo had left at his place, since he had revealed his personal copy when she came over that night. And Elena had laughed at the state of it, emailed a picture of herself with an umbrella next to it and, in fact, read it first.

But how to explain? He had crafted a full monologue, but instead this was a debate. It was a fight. It was him angry at her betrayal of his privacy and her angry for, well, everything. He had planned to pull up the email from Elena in response to Mo's manuscript, the praise from someone who had read and understood her book like he had. The words of admiration and care, the probing consideration of what might be tugged and rearranged in the publication process. In short—Elena had fallen in love with Maureen's book, and he couldn't blame her. Wes had too.

And, unfortunately, with the author of that book, he realized.

"You don't understand," Wes said.

"What don't I understand?" She wheeled from the hallway where she had been leaning against the wall, putting her shoes on. "This isn't some simple misunderstanding like not knowing I'm allergic to something, Wes. This isn't a little white lie about your past with Yuri. This is you, using your connections. Using your power. Sending your book out to an editor at a major publishing house when you know that things aren't set yet."

She wouldn't look at Wes, directing her rage at the floor. Wes wanted to pull her face up to look in his eyes and see the good intention there. "If you hang on for a moment, I can tell you the whole thing."

"There shouldn't be a *whole thing*, Wes." She looked at him directly, tears still shining in her eyes but not falling. Her jaw was set, mirroring the line of her blunt bangs. "I shouldn't have read your email. Sorry for that. I am."

Wes nodded, unsure how to receive the apology when it was clear she had more to say.

And she did. She continued, hotly, as she made her way to the door. "I was stupid for thinking my project had any shot against yours. I know I was. I don't have a powerful family, and I don't have a million connections. I have student loans, for God's sake. Do you even comprehend what that feels like? I don't even know the names of people I'm supposed to rub elbows with, and even if I did, my elbows would never make their way into the rooms where those elbows were. I don't work in the publishing business, and I don't have the direct emails of the top editors in the country. My agent does, but she isn't off shooting a book that we can't sell to them yet." She paused by the front closet, taking a breath while removing her coat from a hanger. "I can't be here anymore. Thank you for the sandwich. And the chips."

"Mo, wait—"

She was already at the entry, her pink coat on. She glanced back as she turned the knob. "Good luck with the book. It's good, and I'm sure you deserve all the success in the world."

And then she was gone, the door slammed behind her.

Wes ran out to the front step, feet bare on the cold concrete. He would run after her, but he didn't want to waste time getting his shoes on. He reached into his pocket and grabbed his phone, shooting off a text to her. *Please come back. I need to explain.*

If she came back, Wes could tell her he was sorry. Yes, he had stepped beyond his normal bounds as estate representative, as a professional, and definitely as a friend, but he hadn't cheated her out of her opportunity. The way he'd gone about everything had been unprofessional, especially since he wasn't Mo's agent. Even though Wes had known Elena would love Maureen's book, it wasn't his job to pass off the manuscript—not without Yuri's okay, not without Mo's okay, and not without the estate's okay. But he'd known the way he would feel if Elena had only his book to read and consider. He'd known that the decision of which of their books got produced wouldn't be based on its likely reception by the editors at the big presses: it was in the hands of Estelle and her family alone.

Wes waited for Mo to text back, or for her soft knock on the door. He didn't want to sit on the couch, staring out the window like a dog for her, so he fell back on the couch and tried to watch the show that Mo had been watching. Astronaut lovers, unscrewing their bubble helmets to look in each other's faces for the first time. Their eyes meeting, the camera zooming in on their lips. The soft press of space suit against space suit as they came together for a passionate embrace.

The fucking fake astronauts were going to get laid for a reality show, and he couldn't even get a text back to explain and apologize correctly. He chanced a second text with more information, praying that it would be enough to get her to come back and talk. *I sent the editor your book, too.*

But the message went undelivered. She had blocked him.

He sighed, then scrolled through his contact information to find a number he'd hoped he wouldn't have to use. The phone rang, then clicked into the call. He took a deep breath. "Hi, Yuri. I've got some explaining to do."

CHAPTER TWENTY-SEVEN

Mo

"That fucking asshole!" Sloan said. She was painting Mo's nails again, this time for the rehearsal dinner. Mo had one more shift at work, then she would hop on the plane at JFK for a red-eye back to Des Moines. Maureen knew this was Sloan's way of showing her love, and she let her roommate take care of her as they sat on the couch, surrounded by junk food. None of them had to work before noon today, and Mo was grateful for their company.

The junk food acquisition was Mackenzie's love language, and Mo was grateful for her selection of every type of Twizzlers she could find—pull-and-peel, traditional, the whole range of flavors and artificial colors. Mo would bind her insides so full of waxy sugar that her body wouldn't fall apart over the next few days. Maybe if she had a big enough sugar high, Mo could pretend to believe in loving relationships and truly root for Anna to walk down the aisle with Kyle, who it turned out was actually a nice guy with a good sense of humor.

Who could have guessed. Not Maureen, because she did nothing but demonstrate what a horrible judge of character she was.

Whatever the combination of cuticle care and licorice Mo needed to feel halfway human, she had almost achieved it before her Thursday shift. She would have called in sick the past few days if she hadn't been taking the weekend off. She couldn't do that to Amy. Instead, Mo muddled through in a haze, not even wanting to check social media. She even blocked him on LinkedIn when she noticed he'd tried to message her there. Her entire body felt achy, like her broken heart had infected her with some terrible illness. Then, even worse news came down than the fact that Mo was a talentless failure: Yuri called to say that Estelle had died Tuesday night.

Mo tried not to think about how Estelle might have taken her last breaths while Mo was crying in Wes's apartment, feeling the ridiculous weight of striving for literary success crashing down on her. It was only a book, not her life, and she knew that. Still, she felt so emotionally wrung out, and it wasn't only because of the book or Estelle.

Mo had trusted Wes, even though she probably shouldn't have. Yuri explained that she'd connected with the editor at Wildman, and that she had a copy of Mo's book too and loved it. No harm done. It was all out of their hands at this point. All hypotheticals.

It didn't matter what anyone else said; Maureen felt stupid. Wes was a rival. It didn't matter that he had passed along her manuscript too, because he hadn't told her about it. How had she managed to trust her work, her body, and even her tender feelings with someone who was only out for himself? She'd felt like she'd grown so much in the past few years after moving out here. She'd developed a thick skin and a certain set of antennae to warn her away from assholes and the kind of people who could use her. Her number-one goal in moving was not to be taken as the country rube, but here she was, too trusting when she should have been more careful. She had been driving straight off the cliff, which happened to look like a curly-haired, scruffy nepo baby heir to a lifestyle brand, who happened to have written a book she couldn't stop thinking about.

It would be easy if it had just been a fling. Sex could be good in the moment, like ice cream, but there were few ice cream cones she stayed up at night thinking about. Wes was more than that cold sweetness, those licks of pleasure. That was awful imagery, and this was why she didn't write erotica. Still, she'd never met someone like him before who got her sense of humor, who effortlessly kept up with her mental lane shifts, and who cheered her onward toward her goals while teaching her something new along the way. He felt like a partner, until she realized he'd been running a different race all along.

Well, she hoped karma would fuck him, because she never would again.

Her bags for the wedding were packed and tucked in the kitchen, ready for a taxi after cleanup tonight. By the time she arrived, the caterers had already been hard at work for an hour. It wasn't a wedding this time—thank God, since she could not handle any more fake brides and grooms on top of too-sweet cakes. The event was some kind of retirement party. No DJ, no ridiculous rituals, fewer toasts, and fewer drunks. The flowers were tasteful bouquets of peonies and roses, and she thought, as she adjusted the vases in the center of the tables, of Estelle's upcoming funeral and the peonies that were certainly blooming on the Morgan estate by now. Maureen wouldn't be invited to the funeral—she had been in Estelle's life for only a single weekend—but still, Mo couldn't help but imagine the scene she would miss.

Maureen wasn't mad at Flor and Talia for what they'd said about her book. How could she be, with them mourning their mother? The fact that her book had next to no chance, though, deserved some kind of sorrow. Feeling sad about it made Mo feel like the most selfish person alive, mourning a career alongside, or more than, this full person and her complete life.

Before the event began, Mo pulled up the *New York Times* obit for Estelle. The first part of the article focused on her youth as the only daughter of a famous author. A paragraph snagged her attention. "Although *The Proud and The Lost* was written before E. J. Morgan had children, many have mistakenly assumed that after Estelle was born, E. J.'s creative spirit warped under the pressure of parenthood, like her famous heroine. Not true, the author's personal effects have shown. In fact, E. J. Morgan wrote letter after letter praising her daughter, full of admiration for her spunk and spirit, and rumors have flown for years that among the author's files are dozens, if not hundreds, of children's stories written by E. J. for her daughter."

Mo's vision went blurry with tears. Estelle had been so loved, not only because she was the daughter of someone famous but because she was herself. She would give anything to read those stories, maybe to her own daughter someday.

The rest of the obit focused on Estelle's life, not her mother's. First her education, then her unlikely career in finance. It wasn't unexpected because of her family's connection to literature, but because of her being a woman in an extremely male-dominated arena. For ten years, she had been a stockbroker on the floor of the New York Stock Exchange, her wheelchair given a particular location every day so she didn't have to fight in the melee. She had retired after adopting Flor, then Talia.

More than good investments in money, she had invested her time and effort into causes she cared about. In the nineties, she had personally overseen the construction of ADA accessible playgrounds all over New York City. Estelle had been a major philanthropist for the organization she'd adopted Flor and Talia from as well as donated to women's groups and LGBTQIA+ youth programs. She'd donated to literacy causes and for COVID vaccines in rural India.

Mo finished scrolling the obit, eyes more than misty by that point. Estelle had been a powerhouse of a woman. And though she had lived to be in her eighties and survived her husband, she still had so much to give. But Mo couldn't dwell on that, nor could she dwell on herself, or her poor sucker's heart. She had work to do.

Amy finished arranging canapés on a silver tray, each atop a perfect lacy doily, and smiled at her in a careful way, like she worried something might break inside Mo. Mo hadn't told her the whole story, but Amy knew something was up. "Heartburn," Mo had told her yesterday. Amy obviously hadn't bought the excuse but, after catching her expression, asked, "Heartburn?"

Mo nodded and stored the phone. Her aches, all of them, should be described as burning instead of breaking. Everything in her felt hot and unsettled, a kindled fire ready to consume her. She didn't want to do anything except eat more Twizzlers—maybe also some cheese, for protein—and watch *The Wizard of Oz* on TCM with Mackenzie. Mackenzie always sang all the parts, and it was always glorious, and not obnoxious, even with the Munchkins. Mo felt a bit like a house had fallen on her but prayed licorice would carry her through the rest of the shift. She could do this. She could make it.

Amy handed her a tray of wineglasses, and suddenly she had no choice.

* * *

The party was for fifty-five people, and Mo knew there was trouble immediately. The aura was familiar, the low chat, the eclectic dress. "Who is this for? What company?" Mo whispered to Amy. They were stationed near a potted fern near the entrance to the kitchens, waiting for people to congeal into small groups so she and Amy could circle them to offer appetizers.

"Hmm, some kind of media thing, I think."

Mo dreaded media events in general. She wanted to be the kind of person important enough to be invited; instead, she cleaned up spills. Mo had worked more than a few book launches and a gala for a major literary foundation, and every time it felt like having to watch a Broadway show from the lobby. Once, a journalist from CNN sabered a bottle of champagne in the middle of the room and Mo had to pick up shards of glass and clean up the spilled champagne, all for the sake of what became a viral Instagram. Glancing out the kitchen, Maureen appraised the room for any familiar faces. She didn't immediately see any famous or famous-adjacent people, until she noticed someone in the farthest corner of the room.

Ulla.

Ulla wouldn't recognize Mo in her catering uniform, right? After all, they had met only twice. Sure, in the meantime, Mo had been bonking her son, making grilled cheese with him, and storming out of his living room. Despite her anger at Wes, Maureen worried how Ulla was managing the divorce. Though Ulla was always svelte, she looked gaunt in her tiered black gown. Before that moment, Mo wouldn't have been able to explain the delineation between a dress and a gown. It was something in its vibe, and this dress said gown. It also, in the way it hung off Ulla, said *Help me*.

The party was obviously for an elderly man with a bow tie, who was glad-handing around the room. Amy's intel was that the man had been a photographer for publications all over the city, and Mo overheard conversations about his shoots in Papua New Guinea, Appalachia, Kathmandu, and Queens as she circled with appetizers. Mo handed out caprese salad kabobs, and the guests talked about European politics. She came by with an empty tray to collect used toothpicks and napkins, and guests talked about a blown glass artist in Rio. Mo noticed on a later pass a local weather anchor in her purple silk jumpsuit, her helmet of hair sprayed curls perfectly in place, just like on TV. There were plenty of people who gave off the impression of importance without her knowing what that importance was. She was grateful, suddenly, that Wes had been unpretentious. At least most of the time.

Thoughts of Wes kept intruding in her thoughts, the way she used to worry loose teeth constantly when she was a kid. Distracting, achy. Suspicious, magical-thinking Mo considered that even thinking of him might radiate through the air to his mom and cause Ulla to look at Mo more carefully. She didn't want to be noticed.

After clearing the appetizer dishes, Amy and Mo reconvened in the kitchen to plan for dinner service. Noticing where Ulla would be seated, Mo asked to take the other half of the tables. Amy agreed.

Mo trayed the salad plates and carried them into the dining area. She served the first few tables without incident, but at a table near the center of her area, a man at the six-spot rubbed Mo's arm as she put the plate in front of him. He was in his midsixties, with thinning brown hair and too-confident hands. A horrified shiver ran through her. "Thanks, doll," he murmured.

As she turned toward the kitchen, she felt a tug on her apron strings, which she'd double-knotted behind her back. The man jerked the strings back toward him and said, "I need more butter over here."

Mo's face flamed. He let go of the apron, and she felt like a dog unleashed. She was not the kind of server to spit in someone's food, but she was almost willing to make an exception. Swallowing her anger, Mo put on her best impression of a Midwest-nice smile and brought him an extra two pats of butter. He didn't even thank her for it, his mouth still full of bread.

Asshole. Asshole.

When she turned to face the rest of the room, she nearly dropped the empty glass she carried. Wes was there, next to his mom at the table across the room. Mo ran back to the kitchen, not caring who noticed her lack of cool. None of these people would remember her anyway—not her face, not her name, and not even her ass, which six-spot jerk had palmed after she dropped off his prime rib.

If Wes didn't see Mo, it would be okay.

If Wes didn't see Mo, she could get on the plane tonight and distract herself with everything that wasn't her book, wasn't his body, wasn't this mess of a city that she suddenly felt trapped in. The swinging kitchen door closed behind her, and she leaned against the wall of the walk-in freezer, breathing hard. Mo hated this.

Amy came in behind, running a hand through her curls. By the middle of service, both of them were usually sweaty, and today was no exception. Amy ran her thumbs under her eyes to clean up smudges of mascara gone askew. She looked at Mo's expression. "Oh no, what happened?"

"I'm okay. Just heartburn. Worse."

Amy grimaced. "Listen, you need to tell me what's up. Is it that guy at table four?"

"I can handle that asshole. It's okay. But I recently ended something with someone, and he's out there."

She wheeled around as if Wes were standing at the door. "Out there? Tonight?" Mo nodded, and Amy went to the peek-through window of the chef's door. "Which one?"

Mo wished she hadn't memorized every detail about him even in the short glance she'd had. "The one with the blue shirt and wavy hair. He's at table eight—"

Amy whistled and turned back. "He's kind of thick! And his cute little facial hair. Nice! I didn't know you were into that. Aaron was such a bald-face string bean. No ass at all."

"Yeah, well." Mo didn't want to talk about Wes's ass, which was prefect and could fill out a pair of pants. His weight as he pushed into her, the strength of his thighs and hips . . .

if she started thinking about this now, she would have to leave or risk doing something dumb like pulling him into the supply room for some hate sex. "We're not talking right now. It's really complicated, but his mom is Ulla. That woman with him?"

Amy glanced again through the window. "Really? She looks different without her apron and the cameras. I love that cooking show she did for PBS."

"I'm sure there are reporters here, even if we don't see them." Maybe even the man at six-spot. Mo turned to the cooler she had been leaning on, opening it. Inside were the tall metal racks that kept the salads cool in one zone and, farther back, the plated chocolate mousses even colder. She willed the cold air to make her feel better, more in control. "Is the coffee fresh?"

Amy knew without even checking. "Turned the percolators on about ten minutes ago. We should be good to go for the end-of-dinner service."

Mo sighed. It wasn't impossible to get out of this night unscathed. They could do it, and they would. She would stay on her side of the room and in what felt like her secret disguise: service worker. You could go undetected unless someone had something to complain about.

Until she went out to check on her tables and Wes was standing on the other side of the door.

CHAPTER TWENTY-EIGHT
Wes

Wes was 98 percent sure he didn't have magical powers. He had tried to conjure things into being as a kid. It was a regular thing in boarding school to sit around reading whatever wizard books were of the moment and then try to do magic in the community bathrooms. They collected all kinds of branches and leaves and ivy that grew on the ancient stone walls, because if any place was going to be a place where you could do magic, it felt like boarding school was. But since it never worked (examples: The rules were never changed to allow dogs, Wes failed a French final in eighth grade, and James Erickson didn't like Wes back in ninth), he had given up all hope.

But there was Mo, suddenly in front of him. He'd been looking for the bathroom, but instead he'd found the woman he had royally pissed off. If this was a kind of magic, it was a backward and twisted kind, that was for sure. He'd only come to Doug Buhman's retirement because Ulla had begged him to be her plus-one. Wes's dad was in Tahoe, and he'd always been on her arm for this kind of party. Wes had arrived late as it was, already feeling off-balance. Beforehand, he had been fielding calls from his boss, who'd asked for his assistance in the estate transition, and from Gary regarding Estelle's death. The lawyers had prepared for this moment since she was rehospitalized, but it didn't soften how awful it was to talk business in the aftermath of someone's death. Gary excused himself from the multiline call, his voice thick with emotion, leaving the lawyers to talk about the timeline for reading the will. Wes had barely known Estelle outside their client relationship and that one strange weekend. And now, after rushing to get to this party for someone he'd only met a few times, of course he would run into Mo.

Mo's face was set. With her hair back in a severe bun at the top of her head, her bangs shaded her eyes. They had gotten longer, long enough to need a trim, and he had the impulse to brush them aside to investigate her face more clearly. The room fell away, the low chatter as inconsequential as cicadas in a forest. "Mo, hi," Wes said dumbly. "Can we talk?" He hadn't planned what to say, and he did really have to pee but could hold off to sort things out. Nothing, not even a full bladder, was as uncomfortable as the air between them.

"I'm working," Mo said after a shocked pause.

Wes glanced at her black apron, which covered a button-down white dress shirt and modest black pants. "I didn't mean to give you the impression that—"

"I said I'm working, Wes." She shouldered past, toward the tables of other guests. He remembered her ex suddenly. The at-work proposal she'd turned down. He wasn't here to ask her that question. He wasn't here for her at all, but if he could find a way to talk to her, he could at least apologize. She was asking for her space, though, and she would be here at least until the end of her shift. Wes could regroup and find a different way to approach her. He didn't want to get her fired or get in her way, but he wouldn't be able to forgive himself if they didn't get a chance to talk.

The restrooms were down the hall opposite the kitchen, so at least it looked like an honest mistake. After washing his hands, he splashed water on his face. *Wake up,* he told his reflection. *Figure out something smooth to say.* Maybe smoothness wasn't the issue here, but honesty. He had closed so many deals, shaken so many hands, charmed so many people with his words, but he couldn't figure out how to explain that he hadn't screwed her over. He didn't know if she believed how much he loved her book, how often he thought about her—both her talent and her personality. Her body too, but he didn't think it was appropriate to mention that.

Wes was walking back to his table when he caught Mo's outline across the room. It wasn't that he couldn't *not* look at her but that her body language was basically screaming. She held a silver carafe of coffee, and the guest she was about to serve was holding his cup out of reach, moving it up, down, sideways. The movements were jerky—intoxicated, Wes thought as he started walking that way. The man's right hand was doing the cup game, while his left hand was cupping something else.

Wes couldn't stop himself. He moved across the dark space, maneuvering around other tables and chairs, and landed in front of Mo. As he got closer, he realized the man was a photographer, a big-deal one, but he certainly wasn't getting the picture here. Wes tried to remember the man's name, but it was hard, as his vision was going red. Might be Tim. Tom? He'd done some freelance work for Ulla, but Wes had never liked him.

The urge to do something he would regret was almost overwhelming, but Wes couldn't do that again. He could control himself, and the situation. He had to. Wes moved alongside the table and grabbed the cup from Tim's reach. He held it steady. Since he'd interposed, Tim's other hand broke contact with Mo's backside. Her cheeks were flush, expression pained.

"Tim," Wes said, voice full of false cheer and fist still tight around the cuff of his shirt. "Good to see you. Want some coffee? Might help you sober up."

Tim tried to take the cup back, but Wes held it steady directly over Tim's lap. Wes glanced at Mo, who looked away, but she still handed him the coffee carafe and moved back a few steps. "Hold still or I might spill this all over your lap, and we don't want that," Wes said. He didn't spill it, but he filled it all the way to the brim. After a second, Wes lowered the cup to the table as he maintained eye contact with Tim.

"Enjoy," Wes said. "Sorry if you wanted room for cream."

Wes turned away from the table and took a breath. He'd been well behaved enough. He didn't want to cause a scene for Ulla to have to clean up, like she'd had to with the NDA after he'd punched a guy. More than anything else, Wes didn't want to further embarrass Mo, but it certainly wasn't for Tim's sake that the man didn't get a scrotum-burning dose of half-caf. Wes handed her the carafe back. As he was walking back to Ulla's side, past the long tables covered with pictures and memorabilia from Doug's early journalism days, he felt a hand on his back and turned.

Mo stood in the corner of the room. This was as private a time as they would get, Wes realized. A few other people stood at a table six feet or so from them, paging through old newspapers and picking up framed photographs.

"You didn't need to do that," Mo said.

"I wanted to, though. I have really bad impulse control."

Seemingly despite herself, a smile tugged at the corner of her lips. He was so relieved to see it that he would have talked about anything with her in public. She could ask him anything and he would give her the truth. He owed her that much.

"It's so good to see you," Wes said.

She didn't respond for a moment, then said, "I really don't have anything to say to you except congrats, I think."

"Mo—"

"No, it's fine. Are you going to Estelle's funeral?"

"The wake, maybe." Wes didn't want to talk about Estelle. He didn't want to talk about anything except how he could get Mo back into his place to make sandwiches again. "Listen, I think it's kismet that you're here. My mom never invites me to these things."

Her expression dimmed. "I don't believe in fate. Unless your parents getting a divorce is all part of some grand plan."

"Maybe it is," Wes said. "My parents were going to divorce anyway. I see that. They weren't happy, but the timing worked out so that—"

"I think relationships end for all kinds of reasons, in their own time. Ours had an expiration date. You knew that. I knew that. You knew once one of our books was chosen it was going to be over."

It was the first time she'd acknowledged that they'd been something. Wes's heart clenched. He should have told her earlier just how much he wanted to be with her. He had never dated someone who hadn't asked a single thing from him before and whose interest in him seemed so genuinely based on who he was, not on what he could give her. And now, he would give her anything, make any number of promises, to find a way to make it up to her. "Nothing is official yet," Wes said.

"Our relationship never was either."

That stung. "I would buy a million fancy cheeses and watch ten million hours of bad television that you chose if you would come over again. I will watch *Lord of the Rings* with you high on edibles. I will carve you a whole-ass butter sculpture if you have dinner with me again."

She glanced over her shoulder, and Wes followed her gaze. More people were starting to mingle, leaving plates and silverware behind. "I have to clean up and get on a plane," she said. "And you need to go save your mother from whatever is happening over there." A jerk of her head directed Wes's attention to Tim pointing a finger at and animatedly talking to Ulla.

When Wes turned back, Mo was gone, and he couldn't find her again the rest of the night.

* * *

Wes woke up the next morning with what felt like a hangover, even though he hadn't drunk anything. His sheets rumpled around his body, and he wished they smelled like Mo. He wished they had Mo in them too. He had dreamt of her on an airplane flying away from him—farther and farther—and he was hanging on to the wheels of the jet that had never retracted.

Once he'd blinked the sleep from his eyes, he snatched the phone from the nightstand. He had a dozen missed calls. Four from Ulla, six from unidentified numbers, and two from Loris. Loris worked at the *New York Post*. Wes sometimes fed him publishing gossip, and he filled Wes in when his newsroom was sniffing around something that pertained to Wes's family. He hadn't had a call from Loris in two blissful years—blissful not because Loris was a bad guy but usually because this meant there wasn't drama to discuss, as Ajay took care of the social plans. Since the story of Wes punching the guy at the agency had gotten bought out, buried under an NDA, and stayed out of the papers, thanks partially to Loris's connections, Wes hadn't had a call.

But Loris had texted too. *Sorry, Wes. I tried to warn about the story getting out. Let me know how I can help. We love you.*

Wes was wide awake now. Not even seven thirty, and his brain whirred. *Story?* His brain first went to Estelle and the adaptations. He shouldn't have emailed anything to Elena. He Googled his name and checked the news section. It wasn't about the books at all. The first entry, published four hours ago: "DIVA DIVORCE? Ulla Unhooks From Hubby."

Wes skimmed the first paragraph of the article, heart turning to ice under his rib cage. "At a gala event last night, Ulla stepped out sans ring and sans husband. Her son, Wesley Spencer, confirmed at the event that Ulla is now a single woman. Her car-collecting ex-hubby has fled the city for parts unknown. Fortune hunters: start your engines!"

Oh fuck.

CHAPTER TWENTY-NINE

Mo

Seven puppies tumbled around Mo, three of them deciding to make her legs their wrestling mat. If puppies didn't cure her bad mood, Mo was pretty sure nothing could.

Mo, her father, and Anna were sitting in the dog barn, hiding from various family members. Or rather, Mo's mother had corralled most of the family members together for mandated fun that the rest of them had been allowed to skip. There were a few hours before the rehearsal dinner, and Mo was happy to help Anna with dog chores rather than think about the hours ahead. Her sister was getting married. In her head, Anna was still six years old, pigtailed and scabbed kneed, chasing the chickens and naming each of them (and each of their eggs). So much had happened since Mo graduated college, and it didn't feel like her trips home allowed her enough time to really take in all those transformations. Finally, being truly with her sister in this place Anna had built for herself, Mo understood the kind of woman Anna was: passionate, caring, and yes, still chasing around small animals and naming them.

Speaking of—unlike Maureen, Anna couldn't exactly take a day off. She had a pregnant mother dog, as well as this litter of puppies to train and socialize before their families took them home in a few weeks. This was the definition of a true farm-raised puppy—sheep to chase, lots of people to cuddle, and individualized love. The intense nature of her sister's business also meant that Anna and Kyle would have to take a delayed honeymoon. Their cousin, a small-animal vet, had volunteered to step in for a week over Christmas. It wasn't easy to find someone with the skill set to take care of so many dogs at one time.

For now, Mo got to enjoy the furry little bundles. One of the wrestling puppies, a multicolored brown-and-black Bernedoodle, fell asleep on Mo's lap while the puppy's brothers continued flip-flopping around her dad's legs. Anna returned a minute later, the mother dog at the end of a leash. Anna gave the dog an affectionate rub between the ears, then unlatched the harness. The dog's nails clipped against the floor as she walked over to her puppies. Every puppy except the one in Mo's lap ambled over to their mother, magnetized, and snuggled in to nurse.

"I think you and Mom had enough trouble with just the two of us. Can you imagine having seven at once?" Mo asked.

Her father gave her a level look. "Seven of you? Absolutely not. Seven Annas, well . . ."

Anna snorted, brushing her long blonde hair out of her face. "Dad," she chided, stretching the word out long. She was sweaty from the early heat of the day, and Mo tried to picture her in twenty-four hours, clean and pristine and bridal.

"Do you and Kyle want kids?" Mo asked.

Anna smiled. "Maybe in a year or two."

In a year or two, she would be the age Mo was now. Mo had such a different life than Anna did, but neither life was better or worse. Anna's heart had found its purpose: in work, in love, in family. Mo longed for that kind of certainty. She didn't need to get married or have children, but she admired how Anna knew what she wanted. How had they gone from two girls who made fart sounds in public and tried to catch turtles at Lake Rathbun to this—two women, responsible for much more than themselves and ready to take on more? "I want to be around more to see them," Mo said, realizing it was true.

Her dad paused in petting the dogs on his legs to look at Mo carefully. "Really." He didn't say it with judgment, with the calm air of someone used to working with stubborn, unpredictable animals.

"You're a natural with the dogs," Anna said, glancing at Mo. "If you ever moved back, I think you'd be a good partner here. I'd love to have the help."

"Oh. Thanks."

"Paid help. I'm not asking for favors. And not that I don't believe in what you're doing. I read your short stories, by the way."

"How do you know about my short stories?"

Anna snorted and raised her eyebrows. "Mo, we do have the internet out here too. I check your website for updates. I even"—here she paused and wiggled her hands like spirit fingers—"subscribe to your *newsletter*."

Mo laughed. "Sorry, didn't mean to suggest otherwise."

"I'm saying you could write here too. If you wanted."

"I wish I knew what I wanted," Mo said, realizing as soon as she'd spoken she hadn't meant to be that honest. She was used to pretending to know what she was doing. This instinct had served her well when she moved to the city. Eyes up, calm expression. People with confidence got what they wanted more than those without. But if you didn't know what that was? What use was confidence?

Anna and her father were giving Mo identical, careful looks. Mo had gotten in late and taken a rental car to Anna's place, snuck in the front door, and fallen dead asleep on the couch. With dog chores and frantic phone calls from the pastor and Mom and the family this morning, no one had had a chance to talk. Anna scooped the puppy from Mo's lap and gave her a quick snuggle, then nestled her among the others. Mo's father offered her a hand, raising her from the floor. "I think we need something stronger to add to our coffee," he said, and he led his daughters out of the barn and toward the kitchen.

* * *

Irish cream swirled in Mo's cup, and she traced her spoon in it, clanking it off the sides of the mug. It was easier to tell them everything with the warm cup in her hands. After she did so, Anna insisted on Googling Wes to see what he looked like. That was when Mo found out what had happened: The news had broken about the divorce. "An unnamed source had ascertained" it at a party, the tabloids reported. Mo's heart fell. Someone had overheard them last night. An immense pang of guilt overwhelmed her, even as Anna scrolled through the article to find a picture of Wes. There he was, some photo from a stock vault of them, in a well-cut blue suit with a crisp white shirt underneath.

Mo bit her lip. The divorce was the one part of the story she had left out with Anna and her dad for the sake of confidentiality for Wes's family, but now it didn't matter. "It's my fault the story is out there. You know how I said he was at the event last night? We talked about it, and—"

Anna touched Mo's arm. "Secrets want to be out," she said reassuringly. "I'm sure it sucks, but with celebrities, these things never stay hidden forever."

Mo supposed that was true. It was the news' job to break. It was everyone else's job to pick up the pieces. At least now Wes wouldn't feel the pressure to keep the secret.

Just the pressure to speak on it. The bottom of the article—all ten of them they had scrolled through—said that no one in the family could be reached for comment. Mo hadn't checked her phone, but she did now. Mo stiffened when she realized she hadn't gotten a text from Wes—still in her phone as King Sex God—and remembered she had blocked his number. Regret pooled in her stomach. Sometimes she forgot other people had feelings as big as hers. In the aftermath of the other night, she'd shut the door, but that wasn't the right move. She unblocked him and texted *I am so sorry that things blew up. I feel responsible.*

She held the phone in her hand for a few minutes, waiting to see the bubbles of his response, but then realized it was as likely he had blocked her too. Even in the best case, if he hadn't, his phone was probably a mess of notifications right now.

"I really might move back home," she told her dad, staring out Anna's kitchen window. The tent rental had arrived, and several beefy men were driving stakes into the middle of Anna's huge front lawn. There were handsome men here and there were social events. There were dogs and family and cities, even though they weren't *the* city. She could make a life here, and maybe she should.

"I think you're trying to run away from your problems," her dad said, gently patting her on the arm. "Not that I don't want you closer. I know you could write here. I know you could have a life here, a full and rich life, like your mother and I have had. We travel to other places, but we're always happy to land back home. I'm not sure you would be at this point, Mo-bear."

She looked at him, wishing he had all the answers like he'd seemed to when she was little. "But what should I do?"

He took a sip of his coffee and gave her a level look. "You should do whatever you think is good. You've got the right head on your shoulders and the right brain in that head. You'll find a way to make things right. And if this book isn't the book that makes you an author? Well, then we'll get everyone to order the one that is. We're so proud of you, Mo. I'm so proud of you, just for being you."

"Even though you couldn't handle seven of me?"

"The world only has room for one, and it only deserves that many too." He rubbed a hand across her cheek.

She realized she had teared up. There would be enough tears in the next twenty-four hours, and there had been enough in the twenty-four hours before. She wished she were a puppy right about now: happy to chill and tumble around, and where the worst mistake she could make was stepping on someone's tail or peeing on the floor, and the biggest decision she could make was where to nap.

CHAPTER THIRTY

Wes

Ulla was surprisingly steady for having her divorce revealed to the entire world. "It's not the first time my secrets have been spilled to the press," she said, and laughed. Wes was glad she'd handled the media so well and envied his mother's unflappable nature. Years in the public eye had taught her lessons about what things to not take to heart, and he saw that this was one of them.

Wes had picked her up at her estate before driving to the Episcopalian church for Estelle's wake. Wes's hands shook as he drove, probably from too much caffeine. He also hadn't been to anything death adjacent in years, since his grandparents had died when he was in high school.

They passed by the lines of flowering pear trees, sweeping white petals behind them as they drove. It was pretty here, though Wes couldn't imagine living here full-time as an adult. His mother liked it, saying that if you were going to live in a town designed for tourism, you might as well live in

Greenwich as Manhattan. "How's Dad handling everything?" Wes asked.

"Oh, fine, fine. You know they don't bug him as much. Plus, being in Tahoe makes him a bit harder to reach. If it weren't a mutual decision to divorce, this would all be terrible, but honestly, Wes, it's fine that things are out now. This wake will be intolerable, however."

Wes agreed, for a lot of reasons.

The actual part in the church was peaceful and serene—mostly because it was nearly silent, save for a string quartet from the Greenwich Symphony Orchestra, of which Estelle had been a benefactor, of course. Ulla was also in that category and nodded at the viola player, a longtime bridge circle friend. The reception in the church hall was another story, enough to make Wes wish he were a praying man. He would have happily taken a knee and taken religion for a few hours to keep those eyes off himself. Something about the heady smell of the peony flower arrangements mixed with the perfume and cologne from a hundred local blue-hairs was enough to make him wish for one pair of giant eyes in the sky to pass judgment instead.

He grabbed a glass of wine and a corner and played rude millennial, glancing at his phone mindlessly. He'd seen a text come in from Mo but hadn't trusted himself to open it until now. At least he wasn't blocked anymore, but he worried about what she'd written. He swallowed a steadying gulp of cab sauv and opened it.

I am so sorry that things blew up. I feel responsible.

She'd apologized, which felt all wrong. It had been both of them talking, not just her. Wes couldn't remember who had mentioned the divorce first, but he should have scanned the situation better. He couldn't text her back. A text was inadequate. He didn't know what to say, had nothing witty or smart, had nothing but mess to offer her. Maybe that was all he'd ever had to offer.

He glanced up from the phone, surprised to see Gary in front of him. Gary's eyes were red, but he held out his hand to shake. Wes took him in for a hug instead. "I'm so sorry for your loss," Wes said as he rubbed Gary's back.

Gary nodded as he stepped out of the embrace. "She lived a good life. One to admire."

"Where are Flor and Talia?"

"Still upstairs, mingling in the back of the church. I wanted to catch you before you left."

Wes swallowed more wine and a wry laugh at the same time. "How could you tell I was going to leave?"

"Ulla's being barraged with questions. I know she's strong enough to take them, but I can tell you're only so strong at letting her take them."

This was too apt. Wes hated to see his mother pecked at. "Tonight is not about us."

Gary nodded, then glanced around. "Things will be very weird for a while at the estate, and I wanted to warn you of that."

The out-of-place word *weird* hit home. On one hand, of course they would be. On the other, something in Gary's face made Wes pause. His expression told Wes he wanted to say something more, so he nudged with an "Oh?"

"When the will is revealed next week, communication might be dicey for a while with Estelle's children."

Oh, the old headache of inheritances. Such a mess, and something that had driven children and parents apart from even before *King Lear*. "I'm sure Talia will find a way to make good TV about it, whatever it is. Inheritance always gets messy once both parents are dead."

That response made Gary look almost sick. "Well, the thing is that Estelle had remarried," Gary said carefully. "A few years ago. And revised her will accordingly."

Wes spilled the rest of his wine on the floor in shock, lucky to miss splashing either Gary or himself in the mess. The implication was only too clear, the look on Gary's face—wary, sad, and still proud.

"What?" Wes whispered, not going to make the mistake of speaking too loudly at a party again.

"Again, it will all come out, but it . . . hadn't yet. I didn't mind not making it public knowledge. After all, it was unlikely that Estelle's children would ever really accept me as their family. And Estelle didn't want it to be part of the TV show, at least not while she was alive. Now, I suppose, I don't really have much choice."

The thought of it seemed to be an insult added to injury, a new loss on top of the loss of Gary's wife. "How—how long were your together?"

"About ten years. We just had our third wedding anniversary while she was hospitalized. Toasting with cups of Jell- wasn't as romantic as an anniversary cruise, but I'm grateful for the time we had."

Wes saw him, fully, now: the deep line between his eyebrows and the way his shoulders visibly seemed to carry a heavy weight. "You loved each other very much. I think I could tell that, but I wasn't looking closely enough."

"I was lucky to love her. Now I have to learn how to deal with everyone else learning that I did."

Wes glanced at Ulla, who was deftly flicking back the media that weaved around the room's notable figures. "I think I have someone who could help you do media training."

Wes hugged Gary again before leaving, tightly. As they broke apart, Gary held Wes by the shoulders. "I'm going to follow Estelle's wishes for the estate. She chose Maureen's book. I hope you know this doesn't mean that I didn't love your novel."

Wes's gut twisted, the ground wavering, but something else solidified under him too. At least here was an answer for the future of the Morgan estate, and an answer Wes found he was glad to hear. If his true passion in life was making sure the best books made it to market, here was another book that would soon find its audience.

It just wasn't his book.

"I understand," Wes said.

"It doesn't mean never," Gary added quickly. "Estelle was clear on that too. It's only for now."

So many things were just for now. So few things were promised, but here was a glimmer of something good on the horizon. Something that would change Maureen's life for the better. Wes knew the will wasn't open and that even Estelle's daughters had yet to be told, but he couldn't stop himself from wanting to tell her.

"Now is what counts," Wes said. He patted Gary on the shoulder and promised to talk soon. He had to get out of here, with a better excuse than escaping journalists. He rescued his mother—who seemed more than capable of frustrating the press for at least another hour—and started planning.

He'd made the mistake with Mo that he never wanted to make with his writing. He had let the idea of the perfect get in the way of the good. He had elevated the idea of what their relationship could be, this final finished product, and hadn't trusted the mess that it took to get there. He had written a book by typing every morning until he had something he could work with. Maybe a good relationship was a shitty first draft that you agreed to write together.

He just needed to find a way to ask her to work with him.

* * *

It was late that night before Wes pulled up in front of Mo's building. He found a meter a block away and parked, the sound of ambulances from the hospital chasing after him. The last time he had been here was to pick up the person he didn't know would change his life. He didn't know anyone else in town who would have the answers he sought, but he prayed that the roommates who had so eagerly sent eggplant emojis and made him lose his bet might let Wes up to talk for a few minutes.

He buzzed at the front door of the apartment building, waiting on the steps in the warm night. Wes didn't know which apartment number was hers of the hundred buzzers in front of him. Suddenly from behind came a tall, dark-haired woman who exuded suspicion. She eyed Wes warily as she reached for the door, then paused to look him up and down. "Do I know you?"

Wes didn't know how to answer this except, "Maybe? Do you know Maureen Denton?"

Her eyes narrowed further, and she reappraised him. "Oh, you're the literary fuckboi."

"Hi," Wes said, uncomfortable but trying not to sound guilty. "Uh, maybe?" He was going to offer his hand, but he didn't think she would take it.

"Come up. Mackenzie and I have been dying to probe you."

The words might have sounded like a double entendre from anyone else, but this woman's firm expression made him feel like he was about to be waterboarded. Still, he followed her up in the elevator and walked into Mo's apartment for the first time. Probably, he mourned, for the last time. He should have come here when she invited him, but Wes had been too comfortable in his own sphere and space. This shouldn't have been the first time he'd met her friends, her roommates that she had told him about on more than one occasion. The woman who let him up introduced herself as Sloan, making the other woman Mackenzie, a curvy, pretty blonde who must have tacked up the musical theater posters that lined the walls.

Sloan sat next to Mackenzie, unlacing her black sneakers and undoing her long black hair from its braid. It coiled around her shoulder, making her look a little bit Medusa, a little bit model. Mackenzie looked friendlier, smiling as she pointed to a spot on the pink chair opposite to sit on. Wes moved a fluffy yellow robe to make room.

"What are your intentions with our friend?" Sloan asked without further introduction.

Wes stammered, and before he could manage a response, Mackenzie added, "Take your time." He realized that she was holding something small on her lap—a hedgehog.

"Oh, that must be Perkins," Wes said, gesturing at the hedgehog.

Mackenzie gazed down at the little animal. "You can feed him a mealworm if you want."

"No, I'm okay."

She raised her eyebrows like this was obviously the wrong answer. Wes was failing this interrogation, even with the good cop of the pair.

"I really like Maureen," Wes said. Understatement wasn't usually his forte, and true to form, the phrase felt heavy and unexplored in his mouth. He wanted to unpack his adjectives like in that old *Schoolhouse Rock!* song. Mo was incredible, electric, brilliant, hot, inventive, and hilarious. He had never felt so much like himself as he did with her, as if the Wes he was with her was the Wes he wanted to be all the time. Except the lying parts. Those parts he would change. "But this is about more than my feelings toward her. It's about her book."

"Is it good?" Sloan asked. "She hasn't let us read it."

"She hasn't even let *me* read it," Mackenzie said, then she added, "I'm a librarian," in the same proud tone of ownership that people used when saying they were from the Bronx originally, not transplants.

"It's really good," he said. Again, the weight of the understatement shook him. He was dying to say more—about how they would get to read it, soon, but he didn't want to share that news with them first. "But more than that, she's good. She's amazing. I'm obsessed with her—her brains and her talent and her ridiculous sense of humor and her love of Ents."

"She is such a secret *Lord of the Rings* dork, and she does not show that side to everyone," Sloan agreed.

Mackenzie snapped her fingers like she had solved something. She looked sideways at Sloan. "Sam Gamgee. He has a total Sam Gamgee thing going on. With a beard, though."

"Oh, a hundred percent."

"Pretty sure that's why she likes you," Mackenzie said with an air of finality.

He knew he was blushing at the sideways compliment. "Thanks?" But that Mo liked him—that she had told her roommates that she did—was confirmation enough that Wes wasn't completely on the wrong path. "I don't want to wait to tell her, because I think waiting would ruin her weekend, but I don't know where she is."

Mackenzie smiled and turned to her roommate. "Oh, this boy wants to romantic-gesture our friend, Sloan."

"But should we let him?" Sloan looked thoughtful. She reached over and pulled the hedgehog into her lap. Finally, after a long second, she gave Wes a serious look. "Did she ever tell you about our ratports?"

He had thought Sloan's looks before were serious, but they were nothing compared to the death stare directed at him. The small animal on her lap only added to the Bond villain air of the moment. "What?" Wes was sure his mouth gaped open, but he didn't know how else to arrange his face. "Your—"

"Ratports. Every week, the three of us talk about rats we've seen. Around the city."

"So many rats," Mackenzie agreed. "And we started to talk about it because, well, if we talked about it and made it part of our lives, it would at least make us laugh. Or acknowledge how gross but normal it is. Life is gross and weird and normal and funny. Rats are a part of that."

"Okay." Wes could not see where this was going.

"And we just want to make sure you're not one," Mackenzie concluded.

Wes choked.

"That's not to say that rats don't have their charm!" Sloan said. "I don't hold the bubonic plague against them. That was really fleas. They get a bad rap. But, honestly, our friend deserves a better class of rodent. At least a hedgehog." Perkins, as if knowing he was being mentioned, curled tighter.

"I'm not a rat," Wes said. "Or at least, if I am, I promise to be better."

A glance passed between Mackenzie and Sloan, then Sloan replied, "Okay, but if you hurt her—"

"You'll have to kill me?" he helpfully supplied.

Mackenzie smiled sweetly. "Slowly and painfully."

Unpacking the adverbs this time, Wes noted. He didn't tell them that the upcoming airplane ride would feel both slow and painful, not even mentioning the apologies he had to concoct, but it was a price he was willing to pay to begin to set things right again with Mo. He only hoped he could get there in time to see her.

CHAPTER THIRTY-ONE

Mo

Kyle and Anna couldn't stop beaming at one another, and even the photographer seemed to be having trouble finding ways to coax new expressions out of them because they couldn't stop the widest smiles Mo had ever seen. She'd snuck away once the group shots were finished and found this deserted hayloft, up a ladder and overlooking the fenced lawn where Anna's dogs usually played.

Mo wasn't exactly hiding, but she didn't want to be found. Haylofts were perfect for that. She had about fifteen minutes to come up with something brilliant. As much as she had been helping with the wedding preparation, she had ignored this one important task. She sat with a notepad in her lap and pencil between her teeth, but in her hands, she held the phone that had been maddeningly silent all weekend.

It wasn't that Mo had expected Wes to text her back, but him not texting her back felt like death by a thousand cuts. She was supposed to be writing a heartfelt speech to the bride and groom, and she had put the writing of this speech off until the minute after the last minute. Anna and Kyle were finishing their post-ceremony shots with the photographer. The wedding ceremony had gone off without a hitch—including the part that was most likely to be hitchy: They had used two of their dogs as the ring bearer and flower girl despite Mo's anxiety dreams. The dogs—Melon and Burt—did amazingly well. Melon had carried a small bouquet in her mouth. Kyle's brother had flown a drone overhead that released flower petals as she scampered. The pros of an outdoor wedding, Mo guessed. Burt had been the perfect gentleman—gentledog?—and walked with no issues with the ring, which was the actual ring. She knew dogs rescued people from snowdrifts and fires, but those dogs weren't bred mainly for their fluff and goofiness.

From her spot, she could see the huge white tent and dozens of carefully laid tables ready for a feast soon. Too soon for Mo to come up with something good. Being a writer meant people expected you to write well all the time, when in her opinion, a toast should come to you in three minutes: brief and heartfelt and true. Like toast, she guessed. She could not think of a more honest food.

Kyle was growing on Mo. At the rehearsal dinner last night, he had brought everyone outside to see a metal bench he had made for Anna in the welding shop. Their initials were mixed in the metalwork of the bench's back. The seat looked like intricate bent-metal ivy, but if you looked closely, he had hidden their anniversary date inside. "So we can always sit together in the garden," he had said. Attached to the bench was a packet of daisy seeds. Okay, he loved Mo's sister, and yes, she had sobbed with the adorableness of everything.

Hay jabbed into her sides as she shifted to get more comfortable, and Anna's only horse, Cash, neighed softly under her. Mo glanced through the ladder slats to stare at her soft brown head. She could go pet the horse as a distraction, but she didn't need any more of those.

"What do horses think of love, Cash?"

Cash tossed her head, maybe to remove a fly or maybe to do a hard agree with how Mo felt.

Maureen hated how people referred to their wedding as the biggest day of their life. It was a day, and it was a big one, but she remembered how they'd celebrated when her sister started her business and when she'd signed the papers to buy this property. Mo remembered when Anna had graduated from college and even back when she'd won the seventh-grade geography bee. There were so many things she loved about her sister, and she had no idea how to shove them all into a speech that made sense and yet still connected to this admittedly big-ass day.

But divorce! Her brain bugged her, even as she was trying to celebrate this day for Anna. Half the married world would get divorced. She'd blasted the news to the world about Wes's parents' divorce, and she felt the aftershocks of it distantly. At the epicenter, back in New York, were Wes and Ulla. Divorce was ultimately good, though. She believed that. Hell, if Clive and Eliza could have divorced, maybe both would have had a happy ending. She needed to stop thinking of fictional people as real.

She'd kept a count: eight asks of "Do you have a boyfriend?" If only she could write a toast as good as the comebacks she didn't share to that question. Sometime between helping Anna put on her veil and watching her sister's hand shake as she put the ring on Kyle's finger, Maureen realized she would have been married to Aaron by now if she'd said yes. Aaron hadn't been perfect. Aaron never turned his socks the right way out when he threw them in the wash, plus the small issue of not respecting her life's passion. Knowing how things had turned out with her adaptation of *P&L*, Aaron was right. Maybe Mo did work too hard on something that wouldn't ever bring her success. Maybe it was too much to ask for a partner who believed in you and challenged you and loved you for who you were, just like it was too much to believe that hard work and time were enough to help you write something that could touch someone.

"You want too much," Aaron had said. Mo was too much for some people, but who got to set the parameters for what too much was, and why couldn't she ever be enough for someone? Or for something?

She tapped her pencil on the pad to focus herself back on the present moment. *Think about love. Think about happiness. Think about a couple that's meant to be together, despite all odds, and do not think about Wes's body against yours. Do not think about laughing with him or making grilled cheese. Do not remember throwing cheese at him. Do not think those cheesy thoughts about how his eyes make you feel. Don't think about his kindness, his uncertainty that he could be good enough.* Too much and not enough. What a pair they could have been. *Do not think of his name when you think of the word* love, *because that would be ridiculous.*

Wouldn't it?

Cash whinnied softly, like she was answering Mo's question.

Mo started to write. At least it would be something, and hopefully it would be enough to begin to tell her sister how much she was grateful for her, even if not for the whole general concept of love.

And just in time. After she looked up from her notepad, a few okay paragraphs written, she saw the stream of bodies of all shapes and sizes, wearing all colors and textures of clothing, massing toward the tent.

One thing was certain—Maureen was grateful there was an open bar and a loud DJ. Maybe no one would listen to the speeches at all.

CHAPTER THIRTY-TWO

Wes

Wes didn't drug himself too heavily on the plane because of the rental car waiting on the other side. A car would be the only way he could get from Omaha, Nebraska, to Walnut, Iowa, where the wedding was being held. The flight left at seven from JFK, and the only possible itinerary left had two layovers—one in Chicago and one in the Twin Cities. "Are you sure?" Wes asked on the phone to the airline while he waited standby for something direct. "There is nothing else available?"

With the World Series happening, Omaha was an unexpectedly popular travel destination. Wes was lucky—the airline's not-so-helpful attendant implied—to get this seat on such short notice. He tried to use "luck" as his sedative, but it surprisingly didn't work well. Wes had taken a Xanax and his Kindle full of client manuscripts to read, so he tried to make the best of it.

Thankful for no delays and no bad weather, he landed in Omaha at four and was out of the well-arranged airport with a car and luggage by four thirty. By that time, he'd already been smiled at by no fewer than twenty strangers in the airport. He checked his back pocket after the first few encounters, unused to the overly familiar friendliness. His wallet was still in place, but he wouldn't have been surprised if one of those strangers offered him five dollars if he needed it.

Wes left Omaha behind in the rearview, passing through fast but generally polite traffic on I-80 toward Iowa. Windmills waved from the endless farm fields outside Council Bluffs, tall and stiff as British beefeaters guarding the royal jewels. There was a flavor of beauty here that he wasn't generally used to—greenness, but not the green of forests or meadows. Green lines of corn in perfect rows so that the lines between them felt almost like a hidden image. It was pretty.

But maybe that was how *Children of the Corn* started.

Less than an hour after grabbing his suitcase, Wes took the exit for Walnut and cranked his phone's volume on high to catch the GPS directions as he hit the gravel road. He kept driving in a straight line so long that he wondered if he'd missed a turn. Finally, he turned into the long driveway that had a sign at its edge reading *Anna's Puppies*. A simple name—as an agent who always had ideas on titles, he could have given notes—but Wes knew today was Anna's wedding day, and he had a feeling she had other things to think about.

So did Wes. His heart sped up, faster than his humming engine, as he hit the line of parked cars along the edge of the driveway. He couldn't make it farther by car here, and so he got out and locked the door.

Also, he was wearing a tux.

The entire way from New York, he had been wearing that tux. Maybe that was why he'd been smiled at in the airport, he realized, straightening his lapels. How often did someone walk around an airport in a tuxedo? Not often enough, probably. He hadn't worn his tie in transit, and he removed it from the back seat, adjusting it in the side mirror. If he was crashing someone's wedding, he would look wedding appropriate, damn it. If there was one thing Wes knew from being raised by Ulla, it was that you could go anywhere if you knew how to dress. And if, he supposed, you could afford that kind of dress.

What he hadn't figured on was that no one else would be wearing tuxes. After all, it was a wedding, and he'd pictured something slightly different than the summery sundresses that greeted him. The men wore pressed shirts, but some of them had short sleeves. Wes hadn't understood exactly the situation he was walking into. Most "barn" weddings he had attended were set on fake agricultural properties, but this one seemed like a working farm. *Oh fuck,* he realized. He had missed the most obvious rule of wedding guest etiquette: Dress code changes based on the situation. Ulla would have laughed at him, but he had an excuse. Maureen scrambled his senses, all of them except his sense of humor, luckily.

Still smiling despite the half-mile walk up the driveway, Wes approached the wedding. The yard was huge, flat, and green, bordered by utility fencing that had been strung with green garlands mixed with electric lights for the occasion. Something like tiki torches but less rustic lined this part of the driveway as well as the sidewalk that led into the inner part of the property. This was nothing like the Morgan estate, but it had its own regal-hugeness. The oversize white tent at the center of the yard had the same torches near its corners. The sun hadn't set yet, but Wes could picture what this scene would look like in a few hours—and it would be gorgeous. If he didn't get kicked out, he would get to see it.

After a steadying breath, Wes realized that between his flight anxiety and the nervousness of getting here, he hadn't eaten all day. He prayed his endorphins could carry him through the next half an hour. He power walked to the edge of the tent. Now, more than during the past ten hours, it dawned on Wes that he really was about to crash someone's wedding. Or at least their reception.

A big man, balding and broad, stood smoking outside the tent. He eyed Wes up and down. "You here to sing or something?"

Wes shook his head. "Uh, no. Here to talk to—" And then he saw Mo on the raised dais inside the tent, her hair swept up into a curled mass on top of her head, tendrils of it escaping to frame her face. From this distance, he saw the pale pink of her cheeks, the way the daffodil color set off the red of her lips. It reminded him of the first night at Estelle's house, and a shiver passed through his spine. "I think I love her."

Wes hadn't meant to say it aloud, and the man ground his cigarette under his foot and looked sideways at him. "I'm assuming you don't mean the bride."

"No," he said. "This isn't a *The Graduate* situation."

"Which one is the one you're here for?" The man nodded his head toward the dais. The bridal party was all seated there, eating and laughing. Two other women wore the pale-yellow dresses, but he hadn't even noticed them. Wes barely even registered the tables spread below them on the ground level, packed with people. Maybe because he couldn't hear them over the pounding of his heart. He would step inside the tent in a minute, but this man was almost a test for his pitch.

You'd think he'd be used to pitching by now in his career, but it was different when what you were selling was yourself for a second chance.

"The maid of honor. She's the most brilliant person I've ever met."

"That woman is my daughter, and yes, she's one of a kind."

Wes swallowed—both his shock and almost his tongue. He looked over at the man with different eyes. He wasn't tall, but neither was Wes. He was sturdy, with broad shoulders and narrowed eyes, hazel like his daughter's. They appraised Wes under white-blonde eyebrows. Mo's dad looked Wes up and down. "You can't be Aaron."

"No—I'm Wes."

Mo's dad humphed, then stepped on the butt of his cigarette. "I've heard of you. Did she invite you all the way out to Iowa?"

"No, sir, she did not."

"Do you have useful skills?"

The question came out of nowhere, and Wes had to think that one through for a full minute. He didn't know what Mo's dad would consider useful or what Wes even considered useful. He didn't think her father would care as much about Wes's ability to do a lot of work on little sleep or remember most people's names after seeing them once. Instead, he focused on the tangibles. "I'm a decent boxer, can do an oil change, and can cook."

Mo's dad nodded. "And you do them all dressed like James Bond, I assume?" He laughed. "This isn't me getting in your way, by the way—I just want to know what skills my future grandkids might have." Wes's jaw must have dropped, because her father slapped him on the back, and he felt himself closing his mouth again. "I'm kidding, son. You think her bad sense of humor comes from anywhere but me?"

Wes laughed then, feeling better. If he could make it through this conversation, he could make it through the next. He hoped.

"She's been in a funk the past few days. Are you responsible for that?"

"Partially. Yes." Wes didn't tell him the kind of funk he'd been in too.

"Well then, you better go fix it," he said, giving Wes's back a shove into the tent. "But if you do marry into the family, you know that you're getting ribbed forever about this tux, right, son?"

Wes laughed under his breath, adjusted his sleeves, and stepped farther into the tent.

CHAPTER THIRTY-THREE

Mo

It was impossible to miss him. Well, Mo had been missing him in the heartsick way, but it was impossible to not see him come up through the center of the tent like a Men's Wearhouse ad but rumpled. His curls were slightly deflated in the humidity, and his cheeks blushed pink above his beard line from exertion. Mo knew what that kind of exertion looked like close up but was trying not to think about it. From her position at the head table, where she was half done with dinner, it felt like he was coming before her like a peasant petitioning a queen. She put down her fork.

They might as well have been invisible to everyone else in the tent, all of them too busy chewing and joking, toasting, and listening to the music. Invisible to everyone except Mo's sister. Seated beside Mo, wearing her floor-length, eyelet-lace-over-linen gown, Anna, the true queen at the table, saw him approach too. Her flower crown tilted slightly over one side of her face as she looked at Mo for confirmation. "Is that the sex god?"

Too nervous, too absurdly anxious and joyful to say anything, Mo nodded. She swallowed the bite of lamb chop in her mouth.

Anna nodded her chin at Wes as if to say *Go!* And Mo did.

He was closer now, just a few feet away from the table, and she caught his expression as she climbed down the stairs onto the tent's floor level. Mo didn't know how to arrange her face, or her thoughts, to greet him. He'd hurt her by going behind her back to the editor, and if she was being honest, she was hurt to have yet another book to put in the drawer, probably never to see the light of day. She had poured her heart and soul into the adaptation of *P&L*, and he'd played games behind her back with it. Mo was probably foolish to think they could have had a fair competition with all his connections, but she *had* thought that. After reading his book, Mo realized how much she was rooting for him anyway. How she was ambitious for him, wished him good things, and wanted to be part of his world not only when his book was published but also generally. She wanted to teach him how to make casseroles and ride the Ferris wheel at Coney Island with him and make fun of bad TV with him. She wanted to dance with him. She wanted to introduce him to her friends and family—and hedgehog. She wanted to get to know him well enough to know what the look on his face meant, because he looked a little like he might throw up.

She guessed it might mirror some of the nervous expectation she felt too. Unlike the horror when Aaron had surprised her at work, this felt different. They were around other people, way more people than before, but he wasn't here to be seen by them even though he'd dressed in a tux. He was here for Mo. The tux, which was ridiculously formal but adorable, was for her. When he offered Mo his hand, she took it. "Can we take a walk?"

Suddenly, once she got in front of him, all eyes turned toward the pair as if people were starting to piece the situation together. Older relatives couldn't possibly figure out how Mo, a verifiable old maid by their standards at thirty-one, was talking with this handsome stranger. "Yes, but I have to get back for the toast," she said.

They walked out of the tent near the DJ's table, passing a table of relatives. Two aunts gave Wes the full up-and-down. Mo knew they had to get farther from the tent to get any kind of privacy. She led him through the yard and to the training barn, hoping the yips of puppies would cover the conversation. The sun was nearly set, and she noticed some of the event staff walking around the perimeter of the yard, lighting the torches. Everything looked orange with the magic-hour light on them.

"You look ridiculous in that tuxedo," Mo said.

"Ridiculously handsome."

Privately she agreed, but she waited for him to go on, her heart thudding in her chest like a bass drum.

His expression was serious, and with one hand, he loosened his tie, looking away. "I am not perfect," he started.

She laughed. "Oh really? I hadn't noticed."

"I am, in fact, a disaster some of the time. Or maybe, more accurately, I am a construction zone and I'm not used to letting someone see the unfinished building."

"I'm not perfect either," she said. "I've been realizing that more and more these days. Nothing makes you come to your senses more than seeing your dream crash and burn."

He grabbed her hands. "I needed to come tell you in person that I talked to Gary."

"Oh." She couldn't think of anything else to say. Her brain had stopped processing words and left only that one letter in an entire dictionary's place.

"The adaptation is yours," Wes said, squeezing her hands in his. "I'm not going to draw this out or joke about it or pretend otherwise. I couldn't wait until the news could be official to tell you. And I know it's selfish that I wanted to tell you myself, be the one here to be with you when you knew. I know it's not a book deal yet, but—"

Her head was full of thunder, still trying to clear itself enough for her to take everything in. "It—Flor said that—"

"It's not her choice. It was Gary's, and he wanted to abide by Estelle's wishes. Before she died, she wrote down that she wanted you to be the adapter."

"Gary's?"

"It's a long story, and it's not mine to tell."

Everything she had expected from this conversation was turned upside down. He had given her the best possible news she could hear, hadn't he? It would change her life to have permission to go ahead with this book and have Yuri submit it to editors. She had wanted this since she was ten years old, but something in her still felt horrible about how she and Wes had left things. "I wanted to talk to you since I found out about the tabloids. I saw everything, and I'm sorry. I need to tell you how sorry I am for spilling the news of your parents' divorce. I didn't mean for that to happen."

"It takes two to have a conversation in public," he said, sighing. He didn't remove his hand. "It's going to be okay. Ulla and my dad are fine, and the media will get bored eventually."

Something loosened in her stomach at his confident tone, his easy acceptance of her apology, but his face was still serious. "I need to apologize too," he said. "About everything, probably. About not telling you about my connection with Yuri, about who I was when we met, about giving the book to that editor without your permission. I couldn't think straight. I wanted my book to be read—both our books to be read—by someone who would appreciate them, even if only one of them could be made. And I'm sorry that I didn't tell you about it as it was happening. I used my power and position in a way that was so unprofessional. Again, I'm sorry."

"Oh, the tux. I'll be honest, I thought . . ." She laughed ruefully, wiping tears away from her eyes that she hadn't known were there. "I thought this was a romantic-gesture thing."

He reached for her hand, and she let him hold it. He rubbed her knuckles softly with the tip of a finger. "And if it was? If I even asked your roommates for permission for that exact reason?"

She glanced at him. "You didn't."

"I didn't come out here for business and clearing the air. Mo, I need to know that what I'm feeling for you isn't in my head. I thought I was okay with being casual, with being friends, with being rivals with benefits or whatever we were, but Mo, I can't do that anymore. I want to be with you. I want it all, the mess and the fights and the bad television and the grilled cheese. I want to wake up and work with you, on our books but also on us. I thought if I flew out here to tell you you're going to be an author, it might put you in a good enough mood to consider it. To consider me." He took a step forward and ran his finger across her cheek to wipe away the tears. "You've gotten inside of my skin, Maureen. Your story, yourself, your jokes, your body. Yes, the news I came to give was about the best excuse I could have to shovel myself onto an airplane, but I didn't want to leave things how we left them. I thought if I could tell you—"

She couldn't wait for him to finish. "Wes, I can't stop thinking about you. I'm sitting here trying to write a toast about—" She swallowed, then steeled herself. "About love, and all I can think about is you."

"Maureen, if I can't kiss you right now, I'm going to die."

She smiled, leaning in to press her mouth against his. It took less than a second for her lips to soften, then open slightly. His arm wrapped around her, and she felt calmer, more present. She noticed everything about him at that moment. If someone had asked her to guess how many hairs were in his beard, like an old-fashioned jelly-beans-in-a-jar contest, she could have aced it. She took in his smell, the pressure of his hands on her back, and when they broke apart, he looked at her face like she was a miracle. "I don't think that's the kind of mouth-to-mouth that saves lives, Wes." She didn't know how to take that kind of admiration without softening it with a joke, but maybe she would learn to take the love from him, all of it, without protecting herself from the joy.

"Your dad approves of me, by the way," Wes said, face breaking out into a grin. "Or at least he didn't kick me out of the party."

"My friends and my dad in one day? We are getting cocky, aren't we." She could hear the distant tinkling of silverware against glass, like the chime of a thousand bells. "Okay, you need to fill me in on how embarrassed I should be right now, but we should get back to the party."

"We?"

"Oh, you think you could get out of being my date to this thing now? Fat chance, Wesley Spencer. I plan to dance with you all night and drag you back to the guest room to ravish you."

Wes grinned and took her arm. "That sounds amazing, but I need to eat something first."

"Pretty sure that they're serving ice cream with the cake, if you can put up with that."

"No gelato?" His grin widened.

She smacked his arm, then planted a kiss on his shoulder. "You have a lot to learn about loving the simple things, Wes."

CHAPTER THIRTY-FOUR

Wes

The day the Publishers Marketplace announcement appeared, Mo Denton gained four thousand Instagram followers. She was so overwhelmed that she had to hand her laptop to Wes, who promptly handled the comment responses of *Thank you!* with grace and a passable attempt at her social media diction. *Proud* by Mo Denton would come out in time for the hundredth anniversary of the original book. The winning editorial bid, it turned out, was Elena's. Wes hadn't been involved in the negotiation for the deal, but watching from the sidelines, he knew it was the kind of epic literary alignment of the stars that only happens every fifty years. At first, Yuri had been furious to hear that an editor had had an exclusive sneak peak of Mo's book, but when Elena was able to put in an offer during the first week the book was on submission, it set off a bidding war. Ultimately, Elena's offer had been the best. Not the highest—though it was close—but Elena had a vision for the book that Mo agreed with and Elena's imprint wanted two more books from Mo, including *At the Counter*.

"I just want to say that I always knew your first book was genius," Wes said when Mo finally stopped screaming and jumping up and down to tell him the full details of the deal.

"I just want to say that I love you," Mo said, pressing into him.

He believed in her—in everything she had made and in everything she could make.

She had been able to quit her job, something Wes always warned his clients against. Most authors couldn't make a living from their books, but with Mo's advance and the promise of more books to come, having the space and time to create meant more to her than continuing working for the catering company.

As a send-off, Amy and Rebekka had held a little celebration at their space. Everyone bussed their own plates and served themselves so that no one had to work. Ulla came, carrying appetizers made for a shoot at her magazine's test kitchen, and Mo's roommates brought boxes of wine. They had laughed and toasted late into the evening. When Mo and Wes took an Uber back to his brownstone, it was three AM before they stumbled into bed.

Most mornings, they were up together a few hours after that. Sunrise was Wes's new favorite hour. For the past few months, they'd agreed to wake up at five AM to write together before the day really began. Morning pages for two. This promise held true even on mornings when she woke up in her own apartment. *Good morning, babe*, he would text her.

Good morning, honey, she would text back. They were completely, disgustingly in love, and so happy to be that way.

Writing in the mornings had been the only way he'd finished his adaptation of *The Proud and The Lost*, and it would be how he finished this new romance novel. He'd found that after exploring Clive and Perkins's tragedy of a love story, he wanted to write the happy ending he wanted to see for queer characters. Logically, he knew that being in a heterosexual relationship didn't diminish his bisexuality, and the energy he had for this project had only confirmed that fact.

Mo was equally driven to work, mostly because the contract she was ironing out was a three-book deal. He liked mornings like this one, where they woke up in the same bed, bleary eyed and partially clothed, her hair rumpled from whatever they'd done the night before. She would slip on his robe, and he would turn on the fireplace in the living room, and they worked in the early stillness. He believed in her when the words weren't coming, like this morning. She stared at the computer, and he freshened her cup of coffee wordlessly, not wanting to break her concentration.

At six, they would make breakfast together, and by seven, he was checking emails and she was sitting down with her laptop again. In their coworking space, coffee breaks were sometimes forgone for quickies, and Wes had never been so grateful to be working from home.

On the day of her first editorial meeting after Elena's maternity leave ended, Jacob had invited Wes to sit in on the call as a former member of the estate's representation. Yuri would be there, and so would some other members of Elena's imprint. Mo wore the dress she had bought in Greenwich, the one that she had written a check to Ulla for to stubbornly reimburse her. This Mo, the one he deemed the meet-the-parents version of her, looked ready for her literary headshot. Still, despite the makeup, he noticed her hands shaking before the call began.

He snagged her fingers and kissed those hands—first the right, then the left—and looked at her. "You already know they love you. You already know they love the book. This is the day you get to start making it real for the world."

She took a deep breath and smiled at him. She seemed steadier. "Will it be weird if they notice we have the same Zoom background?"

"No, but we should probably save telling our love story until we get a film rights offer for it."

She smacked him with a pillow, laughing, then logged on to the meeting.

* * *

To Mo and Wes,

This letter was a difficult one to write, not only because I am not able to write it by hand, as is my wont, but because reading your books has been the ultimate lovely distraction for me these past few months—for me and for Gary both. As my health has suffered, he's taken to reading them aloud, continuing the tradition you began while you were here. He may say differently, but I think he's even come to appreciate the original book through reading your work.

By the time you get this letter, I will be unable to answer your questions anymore, and I'm sure you have many of them. I could say, "Add those to the long list that my children have." I have left them a much longer letter, that one written by my own hand last year when my health began to fail. I wouldn't make Gary write his own praises, like that letter is rife with.

What I've learned in my life is that love can drive our work, but it can change it, too. Many people asked me how it was to be born to a famous mother. I often responded, tongue in cheek, I didn't know what it was like to be born otherwise. What I knew they were really asking was, "Do you think your mother regretted having you, and did becoming your mother stifle her career?" In short, the answer to these questions is "no" and "I don't think so." My mother's love and care for me may have been the reason she didn't write a second full-length novel, but she might have said what she needed to say with *The Proud and the Lost*. More than motherhood, I think fame changed her. It made her feel watched, too observed. She told me once that she liked being my mother because children are the ones who watch their parents least carefully, forgiving them most faults and forgetting most errors.

When I started reading your projects, my heart wasn't set on selecting either one for publication. By the end of reading both, I knew both must see the world someday, and I hope that this comes to pass. Maureen, I ultimately went with your work because of your tender dedication to dismantling the power structures which have always divided society—now, as much as then, these barriers exist. I also think that my mother would have liked your spirit and sense of humor. She had a way of taking women writers under her wing. While I never inherited her talent, I did inherit her passion for mentorship, and I hope this is something that you, too, carry into your no-doubt long future career in writing.

To Wes, thank you for bringing me your book, your passion, and your perspective. Thank you for taking the trust I placed in you seriously during your work for the Estate. Know that I'm proud of you, whatever comes next.

Be gentle to one another. Gary told me you are friends now, and I'm glad. God only gives us few equals in this life, and rivals which we respect—even fewer.

Yours,
Estelle Morgan

EPILOGUE
The Adaptation

The Hill had sold out of tickets in less than twenty minutes. The event wasn't to raise money for the Hill's upkeep—the estate's 5 percent of profits from Mo's book did that work—but to go toward the charity for LGBTQIA+ youth that Estelle had supported in her later years. Even a year after the release of *Proud*, Mo found herself stunned by its success. Wes, on the other hand, was completely nonchalant. He sat in the front row of the audience as she took questions, arms crossed in the folding chair and glancing up at her with a devilish grin.

"What's something that surprised you about the release of *Proud*?" a young woman in the crowd asked.

Mo paused, considering the wide range of answers. "I'm always amazed at the hunger that we have to reimagine familiar stories. Look at how many books and movies we have every year that are remakes, or even retellings of folktales. We have an endless need to know again and again that happy endings are possible or that we really shouldn't trust wolves we meet in the woods. But I am most happy that my ending, my open-ended version, has been accepted so much by the public. I think having a happy ending doesn't mean that a book doesn't have literary merit. If fiction is meant to explore the human condition, which I think is its purpose, it's okay to tell a story that ends with joy. We experience joy too. We experience freedom from bad relationships and the hope for better ones."

There was some applause in the audience, and Mo smiled, then continued. "And I can't promise that every book I'll write will be joyful. Or a retelling. But I believe readers latch on to books they love and make them a success. I am so grateful to all of you for helping to do that for *Proud*."

More applause, then another hand in the audience. She pointed at the man, who cleared his throat and asked. "And what do you say about the rumors that the estate is allowing another adaptation to move forward?"

"Oh, well, I cannot comment on news that hasn't yet been made official, but if there were to be another adaptation, I would fully welcome it. Morgan's work is resilient, and I can't see it being dimmed by more retellings."

The same man spoke again, adjusting his glasses. "And your work? You're not worried about the direct competition of your book against another adaptation?"

"A little competition never hurt anyone," she said, eyes twinkling.

After the event, Wes took Mo's hand and they walked through the outer gardens of the Hill. It was their first time returning to the estate since their weekend together. In the meantime, the peonies had been manicured into a more formal garden and the fenced-in hot tub had been removed from the property. They walked past the place where it formerly had been, hand in hand.

"Too bad," Wes said, "I would have liked a second shot at it now that I always carry condoms on me."

Mo laughed and shushed him, looking around to make sure no one had overheard. They'd been living together for two years in his brownstone. Perkins's cage had a window view of the park, and when they let him loose in the evenings, he snuffled around and cozied up on the couch next to them as if he had had the long day of work, not them. Perkins didn't mind their new housemate either. After spending a year looking at local shelters, they had adopted a rescue chocolate Labrador retriever named Cookie, who ran with Wes in the mornings and cuddled with Mo all afternoon as she wrote.

It was surreal to be back here where everything had started. This time, Mo hadn't brought any edibles with her, and her outfit wasn't from Target. When she read her book now, it was to crowds at bookstores and auditoriums, not to just Wes or Estelle. And soon they could share the news of Wes's novel. The break of a few years between their release dates, plus the demonstration of market interest, had given Elena enough leverage to purchase Wes's project, but this wouldn't technically be his debut. He'd self-published his romance novel under a pen name last year, his passion project, and found a healthy demand for his work. Romance agreed with him, and writing stories with happy endings seemed to make him happy too. Still, Mo knew he was nervous and excited to have the clout of literary fiction behind *The Lost*.

And she felt a little lost, this far back in the formal gardens. The other meandering visitors had disappeared from around them as they wandered deeper into the roses. The smell of them draped around them, floral and heady under the bright June sunshine. A stone fountain jutted out in front of them from the middle of a paved circle, and Mo took a seat on its ledge to get her bearings and her breath back.

The next moment, Wes was kneeling in front of her.

"Oh," she said, all other words gone.

He smiled at her. "Maureen Denton, I am lucky to know you and love you. These past three years have been the most wonderful of my life. I will root for you until the end of the known universe, no matter what you aim for and who you want to be. I am so lucky to have you as my partner in love, literature, and life."

She felt a flush creep up her breastbone, heart thrumming madly.

Wes cleared his throat. "And knowing that, all that, Mo, I have to ask . . ."

Could she even hear him over the blood rushing in her ears? "Yes?"

"Would you do me the honor of blurbing my book?"

She laughed so hard she coughed, and he sat on the fountain next to her. When he did, she couldn't resist shoving him backward to splash into it. The movement made her lose her own balance too, and she ended up sopping wet next to him. They were both laughing now. Wes wiped his face with his soaked shirt, realizing it was making no impact at all.

"You absolute asshole," she said, splashing him.

"Does that mean you wouldn't marry me either?" He reached into the damp back pocket of his slacks and brought out a small square box. "I didn't want to romantic-gesture you at a work event or anything, but I thought it would be nice to do it here."

It took a lot of faith to believe in love that lasts, but Mo Denton was starting to have that faith. It was the same kind of daily effort that writing took—that attention to the small things, that push to move forward, even when it was hard. It was knowing what you had was good and working to make it better. "I will," she said, kissing him.

And she knew they were ready for the adaptations they would make together for the rest of their lives.

ACKNOWLEDGMENTS

This novel is a love letter to the weirdness of the book world. I'm lucky to have found my team after much searching. The initial idea for this book came from a single conversation with Laura Blake Peterson, and I've been growing the seed for a decade. Thank you to Veronica Park, who encouraged me to write the kind of romance I wanted to read, and a huge thanks to superagent Michelle Richter for taking the baton and finding the perfect home with Alcove.

Melissa Rechter, thank you for your thoughtful guidance and unending patience. I'm grateful for the editorial feedback, which tightened up the book and snapped everything into place. I'm forever humbled by copyeditors and am grateful to Rachel Keith for the notes and fact-checking, especially on businesses that no longer exist. Thanks to Stephanie Manova and Megan Matti for your acumen and to Rebecca Nelson and Thai Perez for your expertise. I'm lucky to work with the whole team at Alcove.

Acknowledgments

Thanks to Edith Wharton, who inspired some aspects of this book. This book is for people who wanted to throw *Ethan Frome* against a wall (and maybe did). This book is also for anyone who wanted better for every character in *The Great Gatsby*, and maybe who head-shipped Nick and Jay. Thanks to the English teachers, particularly Debra Welch, Maria Tucci, and David Ferranti.

Romance authors are the best community in the world (inarguable fact). I'm forever grateful for Denise Williams and Chloe Angyal for being my favorite group chat, and for Jen DeLuca, Jesse Sutanto, and all the 2020 debut romance folks for inspiring me to take the plunge. Thank you to all my blurb providers for reading and shouting out my work. I'm so lucky to have you in my corner. Thanks to the lit mags who've published me, especially *Split Lip*, who made me feel like an author. There are a zillion other writing folks to thank, but generally, to the writing community: Thank you for existing on the internet. It can get awful lonely out there with just a blank page for company. You show me good work every day, and good memes too. Thanks for taking me the right amount of seriously.

Personal thanks to my friends. Tiffany, thanks for carrying a million awkward things back and forth between our houses and for the best patio conversations of all time. Alysa, thanks for being my longest friend, and now family member. A special shout-out to my college friends, some of whom might see their names (or their hometowns) in this book. I miss you and want you to know that our late-night conversations and laughter taught me the kind of friendships I wanted to write in my books.

Acknowledgments

This book began as a pandemic depression project, and writing it helped me dig my way out. Huge shout-out to Zoloft, my therapist, and my doctor for helping me survive a dark time.

To my family: Thanks for putting up with me when I'm on deadline or feeling less than myself. I'm lucky to be related to all of you, or to have tricked my way into your family when I married your kid. I'm grateful especially to my siblings, who support me through thick and thin. Janine, you throw much better bachelorette parties than the one in this book. To my mom: Thank you for your joy and support, even if this isn't your favorite genre. Thank you to my dog Luna, and to the Animal Rescue League of Iowa who took care of her before we got to. To my littles: Don't read this book! It's very boring and about taxes of something. I adore you to pieces, though. To my dude: Thanks for all of it. So much.